I0831240

Redefining the Fringes in Celtic Studies

TRANSATLANTIC STUDIES
IN BRITISH AND
NORTH AMERICAN CULTURE

Edited by Marek Wilczyński

VOLUME 26

Aleksander Bednarski / Robert Looby (eds.)

Redefining the Fringes in Celtic Studies

Essays in Literature and Culture

PETER LANG

Bibliographic Information published by the Deutsche Nationalbibliothek
The Deutsche Nationalbibliothek lists this publication in the Deutsche Nationalbibliografie; detailed bibliographic data is available in the internet at http://dnb.d-nb.de.

Library of Congress Cataloging-in-Publication Data
A CIP catalog record for this book has been applied for at the Library of Congress.

Published with the support of the Department of Foreign Affairs and Trade of Ireland Cultural Grant-in-Aid.

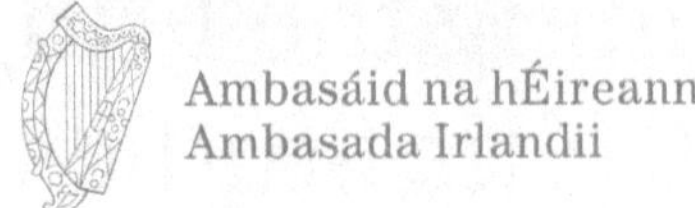

Reviewed by Professor David Malcolm, University of Gdańsk.

ISSN 2364-2882
ISBN 978-3-631-77530-1 (Print)
E-ISBN 978-3-631-77699-5 (E-Book)
E-ISBN 978-3-631-77700-8 (EPUB)
E-ISBN 978-3-631-77701-5 (MOBI)
DOI 10.3726/b15034

Peter Lang – Berlin · Bern · Bruxelles · New York · Oxford · Warszawa · Wien

This publication has been peer reviewed.

www.peterlang.com

Contents

Introduction 7

Anna Cisło
Three Blasket Autobiographies and the Editorial Design of Their First Editions 9

Elis Dafydd
The *Ienctid yw 'Mhechod* Saga 23

Marlena Gawlik
Irish Language and Identity in Contemporary Irish Poetry 35

Katarzyna Jaworska-Biskup
Some Remarks on the Periodisation of Welsh Medieval Law 51

Aleksandra Kędzierska
The Great Wars of Francis Ledwidge (1887–1917) 67

Brian Ó Conchubhair
The Polish Origins of Irish-Language Modernist Fiction? Joseph Conrad & Pádraig Ó Conaire 83

Breandán Ó Cróinín
A Portrait of the Artist in Late Modern Munster Irish 101

Mark Ó Fionnáin
Rats, Wraiths and Railways – The Irish Language in Science-Fiction and Fantasy 117

Pádraig de Paor
Aspects of Seán Ó Ríordáin's Poetic Idiom 133

Alyce von Rothkirch
Dragon Red in Tooth and Claw: Darwin, Nature and Morality in Niall Griffiths's *Sheepshagger* 145

Contents

Introduction

The selection of articles collected in this volume is based on an assumption that the fringes of Celtic Studies still represent a challenge and that established areas are worth revisiting. Peripheries and borderlands are always an exciting object of study: with their blank spots and unexplored territories they capture the attention of researchers. The chapters in this collection, by both established and young scholars, deal with a wide range of phenomena connected with the language, literature and history of the broadly speaking Celtic world, ranging widely over time, space and subject matter. One thing that the analyses share, however, is their focus on uncharted or little explored waters, which confirms that Celtic Studies, especially in their literary and cultural aspect, are an exciting and expanding discipline. The contributors' expeditions to remote or undiscovered areas include the design of autobiographies in the early years of the Irish republic, an overview of the controversy over a sex scene in a Welsh-language novel by John Rowlands, the poetry of the somewhat neglected Irish poet Francis Ledwidge, Irish-language science-fiction and comics, a cognitive ethological perspective on Niall Griffiths's novel *Sheepshagger*, and possible Polish origins of Irish-language modernist fiction. Other chapters offer a periodisation of medieval Welsh law, insightful analyses of Pádraig Ó Cíobháin's landmark novel *The Brightness Out There* and the work of Seán Ó Ríordáin – a poet little known outside the Irish-language world – as well as contemporary Irish-language poetry in the context of language loss.

By bringing together such heterogeneous but at the same time fresh insights into diverse areas of Celtic scholarship, this volume aims to invite further research in the fields probed by the contributors in their chapters.

We would like to thank Professor David Malcolm for his valuable insights and acknowledge the support received from the Department of Foreign Affairs and Trade via a Cultural Grant-in-Aid and thank his Excellency, the Irish Ambassador in Poland, Gerard McKeown.

Aleksander Bednarski
Robert Looby

Anna Cisło

Three Blasket Autobiographies and the Editorial Design of Their First Editions

Abstract: In the early years of the Irish Free State the physical book in Irish became a rich collection of signs offering assistance to political separatism, while typography evidenced the national parallelism approach and graphic design supported the process of national identity formation. This chapter discusses the context for the emergence of autobiographies by Tomás Ó Criomhthain (1855/6–1937), Muiris Ó Súilleabháin (1904–1950) and Peig Sayers (1873–1958) and the design of their first editions. It interprets the signs contained therein and discusses the extent to which they were symptoms of the era in which they were created.

Keywords: Great Blasket Island, An Gúm, autobiography, editorial design, Irish literature, book

1 Introduction

By the end of the 19th century, due to the politically controlled process of Anglicisation, the social upheaval following the Great Famine and the mass emigration of the native Irish from Ireland, which decimated their communities and necessitated their learning English, English in Ireland had become for most people the primary medium of spoken and written communication. It was the language of status, whose use was widespread, whereas Irish, then favoured by less than 30 % of the population, was used mostly by older, often illiterate people from disadvantaged classes in peripheral areas (Ó Murchú 1999: 10). Hardly anything was published in Irish and so, when the Irish language revival movement sought, among other goals, to restore the Irish book, not only did creative writers have to be found but also the lack of standards and norms in printed Irish had to be addressed. When the revivalists' attempts did bear fruit, the physical book in Irish became a rich collection of signs providing support for political separatism and the process of national identity formation. This article discusses the context for the emergence of the autobiographies by Tomás Ó Criomhthain (1855/6–1937), Muiris Ó Súilleabháin (1904–1950) and Peig Sayers (1873–1958), three inhabitants of the Irish speaking Great Blasket Island, and the editorial design of their first editions, which appeared in the Irish Free State, in the 1920s and 1930s: it will interpret the signs contained therein and will address the questions as to what extent they were symptoms of the era in which they were created.

2 Irish Language Literature of the Irish Revival and the Free State

Although at the turn of the 20th century the precipitant shift to English in Ireland was clearly under way, there were at least two factors which helped Irish survive. First of all, as it is summed up in *The Oxford Companion to Irish Literature*, "the rate of language shift slowed as it encountered around the western seaboard the densely populated areas, officially at the time called 'congested districts' [later collectively referred to with the term Gaeltacht], in which communities were almost autonomous in their subsistence economies and had little access to competence in English." Secondly, "towards the end of the 19th cent., there emerged a vigorous Irish-language restoration movement. The latter contributed significantly to a renewal of the idea of political separatism, and the aims of achieving the political independence of Ireland and of restoring the Irish language became for a time indistinguishable" (Welch 1996: 266). Among the organisations that came to be active in promoting the use of Irish in the fields of everyday life, education and publishing the most influential was Conradh na Gaeilge, known in English as the Gaelic League, founded in 1893 under the presidency of Douglas Hyde (1860–1949), the man who was to become the first president of Ireland, 1938–1945. Its objective, as was stated in an early pamphlet in 1896, was twofold: (1) "the preservation of Irish as the National language of Ireland, and the extension of its use as a spoken tongue" and (2) "the study and publication of existing Irish literature, and the cultivation of modern literature in Irish" (Ó Fearaíl 1975: 6). Such goals were later adopted by politicians of the Free State established in 1922. There is no evidence that the Gaelic League attempted to build a purely monolingual Irish society. On the contrary, one of its prominent members, Patrick Pearse (1979: 35), wrote in 1915 that "an Irish nation [needed] no more be a purely Irish-speaking nation; but [...] be permeated through and through by Irish culture, the repository of which [was] the Irish language." This language was to be the medium employed in education and in literature and so debates took place about the form of written Irish to be used and its graphic representation in printed books.

As to the form of literary Irish, some argued that it "should base itself on the last national linguistic norm that had existed, that of educated and professional writing of the seventeenth and eighteenth centuries" whereas others were of the opinion that "it should adopt the contemporary spoken vernacular, referred to as '*caint na ndaoine*' ('the speech of the people')" (Ó Ciosáin 2004: 7). This issue is believed to have been settled in favour of the latter by the success of *Séadna*, Peadar Ó Laoghaire's novella, written and published in contemporary Munster

Irish. In typography, a choice was to be made between using Roman and Gaelic types. The Gaelic League advocated the use of the latter and, indeed, "[the] vast majority of books in the early twentieth century used Gaelic type, chosen probably as a sign of the distinctiveness of gaelic [*sic*] culture" (Ó Ciosáin 2004: 5).

However, in the officially bilingual Irish Free State, as Brian Ó Cuív (1969: 26) points out, "there was a tendency from the outset to use Roman type," which was connected with calculating the expected high costs of the use of two types of fonts both in printed and typewritten materials. Still, when, under the auspices of the Irish Government, An Gúm, the state's organ for the publication of texts in Irish, was established as a publishing arm of the Department of Education, so strong was the conservative opposition to the Roman type that most of the books printed in the first thirty years of An Gúm's activity employed Gaelic characters and in 1928 the Gaelic League passed a resolution that "it [was] better for Irish that no great change be made in the type or the spelling of Irish until the language [was] out of danger of death or destruction" (Ó Cuív 1969: 29). It is also possible that An Gúm cared more for the content of its books than for their editorial form. Nothing critical of the new state or the Catholic church, which influenced this state's image and policies, would be accepted. Thus, the agency soon came to favour either translations from foreign languages, on subjects unrelated to Ireland, or native literary works impeccable from a moral point of view, preferably ones that enhanced the image of a brave, hardworking and innocent native inhabitant of Ireland and at the same time, reversing negative connotations attached to the Irish Celt in an earlier English-language Victorian discourse, described, among others, by L. Perry Curtis (1968 & 1971; Cisło 2004).

For Gaelic Leaguers, God's chosen people of pure blood were the people of the west-coast Gaeltacht (Doyle 2015: 196). It was hoped that with some encouragement "native speakers [of Irish] would learn to read and write and begin producing stories, plays, and poetry of their own" (Doyle 2015: 252). Indeed, "[w]ith time," writes Aidan Doyle (2015: 252), "a small percentage of native speakers did begin to write. The work they produced was heavily influenced by folklore tradition which was still very strong in the Gaeltacht areas […] [and included] written versions of folktales, with unsophisticated story-lines and stereotypical characters." A good example of such literature is the aforementioned *Séadna*. Apart from this kind of writing, a new genre developed – the autobiography, in which Gaeltacht inhabitants gave recollections of their lives, encouraged to do so by scholars and language enthusiasts making trips to the Irish-speaking areas in the West of the country. Thus, the development of this genre, which flourished in the Free State, can be considered a result of the Irish language revival as well as of a more general interest in aspects of Celtic cultures. It generated a romanticised idea of Celtic identity, which had been waiting to be explored and exploited in literature and politics. Therefore, places inhabited by native Celtic people were given special attention and to those belonged the Blasket archipelago: "the Blaskets," as Robert Kanigel (2012: 12) puts it, "weren't just islands in the farthest western reaches of Ireland. They were The West, which had come to stand for the deepest, purest wells of Irish nationhood."

3 The Great Blasket Island and Its Library

An Blascaod Mór/the Great Blasket is part of an archipelago of seven islands and numerous islets and rocks lying off the south west coast of Corca Duibhne/the Dingle Peninsula in County Kerry. Locally it used to be called simply – an tOileán/the Island or an tOileán Tiar (or Mór)/the Western (or Great) Island. The etymology of the word *Blasket* is not known. In the 18th century Charles Smith (1774: 182), a typographer, wrote that it might have originated from the term *blaosc* – "scale" or "shell" – as it was "supposed to have been scaled off the continent of *Ireland*"; whereas in the 20th century Robin Flower, a linguist and writer, suggested it might have come from the Norse word *brasker* – "sharp reef", "a dangerous place" (Mac Conghail 2006: 27; Ua Maoileoin [1994]: 2) because of its location, tough climate and rough rocks. The coastline of the Great Blasket, which itself, when looked at from Dingle may resemble a huge shell, is rocky and although the crossing from Dún Chaoin/Dunquin in Dingle/Deangain to Caladh an Oileáin on the island is only a 5 km distance, the waves of the Atlantic Ocean often make it impossible and there is a danger that a boat moored at the rocky landing place will be destroyed. For the latter reason people living on the Great Blasket used tarred, canvass-covered light boats, *naomhóga*, which they pulled onto the slopes of their island instead of leaving them in the water.

From a distance the Great Blasket looks big but in reality it is only 5.2 km long and about 1 km at its widest. Most of the island, on which there are no trees, is covered with furze, whins and heather, with peat beneath much of it. There are no solid roads, which Blasket inhabitants did not need because they had no wheeled vehicles but used donkeys to bring turf to the village from the hills where it was cut with spades. This turf was later used to heat their cabins. The island is rocky at the bottom with a white strand below the cliffs on the eastern side. Not far from here are the remains of the village, called simply An Bhaile, "the village", which, built against the side of the hill for shelter, consisted of no more than 30 houses, divided into the bottom and the top of the village. Although the Great Blasket is not the only island of the archipelago where there are spring water sources, it was the only one inhabited in the 19th and 20th centuries by more than just one or two families, which was the case with such islands as Inis Mhic Uíbhleáin and Inis Tuaisceart. The available census figures show that at the turn of the 20th century, when fishing was sufficient to provide a living, the Blasket archipelago was inhabited by more than 150 people; by the beginning of World War II the population had dropped to just above 100; in 1947 the community numbered about 50 people; and in 1953 the last 20 or so inhabitants were evacuated to the mainland (Mac Conghail 2006: 34; Lysaght 2006: 199). This small community lived in relative isolation. Life was very simple, with no electricity and no running water. Blasket inhabitants had their own *Rí* ("King") and *Dáil* ("Assembly"), which gathered in the evening to discuss events, and were able to provide most of what they needed for everyday life but the community was not fully self-contained: there was no doctor to help the sick and no priest to bury the dead. There was not even a graveyard, as funerals took place on the mainland. Occasionally, a priest would come to hold stations either outdoors or in the school. The latter was opened in 1866 and the only language of instruction used in it until the last decade of the 19th century was English. Then, due to the activity of the Gaelic League, Irish was introduced to it, as had happened in congested districts. This meant that islanders, who normally used spoken Irish, could now learn how to read and write it. This was also the time when the life of their isolated community in its glory days came to be described in autobiographical novels, sketches and letters, which are now known collectively as the Blasket (or Kerry) Island Library. In Muiris Mac Conghail's (2006: 162) opinion, this collection is unique in the history of literature:

> It was written by the Islanders themselves from within their own culture, a collective portrait of their community just before its destruction. When the Island community sensed that their world was coming to an end they wrote it all down. Some did it well and their writings now form part of a universal literature and Tomás Ó Criomhthain, Muiris Ó Súilleabháin and Peig Sayers will live as long as books are read. The rest is a small footnote for Irish readers and those interested in island cultures.

4 The Origins and Characteristics of the Autobiographies by Tomás Ó Criomhthain, Muiris Ó Súilleabháin and Peig Sayers

The first to contribute to the Blasket Island Library was Tomás Ó Criomhthain. Born on the Island either in 1855 or 1856, the youngest of the eight children of Dónal Ó Criomhthain and Cáit Ní Shé, he was to live the hard life of a typical islander, for whom the basic skills were of fishing, seal hunting and turf cutting, enriched in Tomás's case with the craft of masonry (Mac Conghail 2006: 126).

Also, like most men from the Island, he married and started a family. What made him stand out from the rest of his community was his interest in literature, which only began when he was over forty with his acquiring the ability to read in Irish. This he recalls in his autobiography *An tOileánach*:

> [I]t often happened that I would be held prisoner now and again out on the mainland in the winter season. In the house where I used to stay the children were always going to school. The Irish language was being taught in the Dunquin school in those days – as soon as it was in any school in Ireland, I think. The children of this house used to read tales to me all the time whenever I happened to be in their company until I got a taste for the business and made them give me the book, getting one of them by turns to explain to me the difficulties that occur in the language – marks of aspiration, marks of length, and marks of eclipse. It didn't take me long to get so far that I hadn't to depend on them to read out my tale for me [...] Very soon I had a book or two, and people on this island were coming to listen to me reading the old tales to them, and, though they themselves had a good lot of them, they lost their taste for telling them to one another when they compared them with the style of books put on them. It would be long before I tired of reading them to them [...] From this time on an odd visitor was coming to the Island. One Sunday at the beginning of July a canoe from Dunquin brought a gentle man to the Blasket. He was a tall, lean, fair-complexioned, blue-eyed man. [...] He asked the King who was the best man to teach him Irish. The King explained to him that I was the man, for I was able to read it and had fine, correct Irish before ever I read it. He came to me at once and questioned me. He put a book before me, [Peadar Ó Laoghaire's] *Niamh*. (O'Crohan 1951: 223–224)

The "gentle man" was Carl Marstrander (1883–1965), a Norwegian linguistics scholar and one of many people who in the era of the Irish revival came to the Great Blasket to learn modern Irish. Soon a pupil–teacher relationship developed between him and Ó Criomhthain. Hence, later, when his student, Robin Flower (1881–1946), an Oxford graduate employed in the manuscript department of the British Museum, where he was cataloguing sources in the Irish language, was going to the Island, Marstrander recommended Tomás to him as a teacher. Twenty seven years later Flower became the translator of *An tOileánach* into English, though he was not the one who persuaded Ó Criomhthain to write. Pivotal to Ó Criomhthain's development as a writer were two other men – Brian Ó Ceallaigh (1889–1936) and Pádraig Ó Siochfhradha, an Irish writer known as An Seabhac (1883–1964), who in the second decade of the 20th century was teaching Irish in the Killarney area. Their story, outlined by Mac Conghail (2006: 139–144), may be summarised in the following way:

Ó Ceallaigh was well-off and already well-educated when his mother turned to Ó Siochfhradha to help her son learn Irish. Ó Siochfhradha advised him to go to one of the Irish speaking areas and gave him a letter of introduction to Ó Criomhthain in case he chose the Great Blasket Island. This is where he arrived in 1917, and although much younger than him, he made friends with Ó Criomhthain. Seeing the islander's interest in literature he showed him Pierre Loti's *An Iceland Fisherman* (translated from French *Pêcheur d'Islande*) and some of Maxim Gorky's works. He wanted him to believe that great literature can be written about a simple life, like Tomás's, in an ordinary, unsophisticated language, like the one he spoke. So, when Ó Ceallaigh left the Island, Ó Criomhthain, supplied by him with sheets of bifoliate foolscap pages and his Waterman fountain pen, began to write a journal, later to be edited as *Allagar na hInise* (1928), and a more serious autobiographical work, an account of his life. As in the case of his journal, he continuously sent the autobiographical material to Ó Ceallaigh and when this was complete, Ó Ceallaigh felt obliged to have it published. He first brought the manuscript to the Irish Text Society in London but on seeing how much work was required to prepare it for publishing, they were not interested in undertaking the task. Next Ó Ceallaigh turned to Eoin MacNéill, the Minister for Education in the already established Free State, but the department had no scheme within which Ó Criomhthain's work could be published. As Ó Ceallaigh had decided to leave Ireland, he asked Ó Siochfhradha to look after the manuscripts and the latter, recognising the value of the material, agreed.

In 1926 An Gúm was established, managed by Coiste na Leabhar, or the Book Committee. On January 20, 1927 Ó Siochfhradha received a letter from its secretary, Leon Ó Broin – they were interested in publishing Ó Criomhthain's work. With the permission of Ó Criomhthain, who only asked to have his texts printed in Gaelic characters, Ó Siochfhradha engaged in editing and preparing the texts for publication (Breathnach and Ní Mhurchú). Thus, under the auspices of An Gúm, *Allagar na hInise* appeared in 1928, followed a year later by Ó Criomhthain's autobiographical novel *An tOileánach* (with Muinntir C.S. Ó Fallamhain i gComhar le hOifig an tSoláthair given in both editions as their publisher, it being responsible for preparing the texts for print). As noted by Philip O'Leary (2004: 141), although "in the manuscript of *An tOileánach*, Ó Criomhthain made clear that it was his intention to provide an absolutely accurate picture of island life [...] the text as it first appeared in print after having been edited by Pádraig Ó Siochfhradha is quite different from the text Ó Criomhthain had produced." Among other differences, all references to Tomás's interests in the opposite sex, regarded as indecent and too frank, were carefully removed from it as *An tOileánach* was primarily to contribute to the ideological construct of the pure noble Gaeltacht native speaker supported by the state's agency, An Gúm.

An tOileánach, as it was issued in 1929, appeared in hardback in a small format (approx. 12.5x19.5 cm), typical of early An Gúm publications. As requested by

Ó Criomhthain, it was printed in Gaelic characters. The credibility of the author of this 266 page long narrative in 25 chapters is enhanced by the book's frontispiece, which features a photograph of him taken by the Swedish folklorist Carl Wilhelm von Sydow (1878–1952). The photograph represents an elderly fisherman – a real islander and the believable narrator of the story of his life as presented in *An tOileánach*. The edition is also enriched with another photograph by the same author – of Tomás's house in the lower village, the sea in the background, as well as with a map which sketches the Blasket archipelago and the most westerly part of the Dingle Peninsula with Dunquin. Both the picture of the house and the map position the narrative in the geography of the western Irish coast. The most interesting and elaborate part of this book's design is its dust jacket. Its author is not known but the style, colours (blue, black, grey, orange and white) and content of the illustration resemble the graphic design of the dust jacket of *Allagar na hInise* signed by AóM, identified as the Dublin artist Austin Ó Maolaoid/Austin Molloy (1886–1961) (Ó Conchubhair 2011: 105–106). The dust jacket of *An tOileánach* represents a man, most likely an inhabitant of the Great Blasket Island, sitting on a hill above the village and smoking a pipe. Five houses of the village are represented below the hill and there is another man walking in the distance and two other figures in a *naomhóg* on the sea in the background. The sun is setting on the horizon behind two other Blasket islands, whose characteristic shapes also serve to position *An tOileánach* in the geography of the Blasket archipelago.

It is interesting to compare the face and posture of the man in *An tOileánach*'s jacket with those of an Irish Celt as represented in John Tenniel's drawing of "Two Forces," which appeared in the London comic magazine *Punch* in 1881 [Il. 1]. As noted by Edward Hirsch (1999: 34), "[t]he overwhelming squalor and poverty in the West during the horrible years of the famine [1845–1851] [...] led English writers to conclude that the Irish existed on a lower rung of the Darwinian ladder." This opinion, expressed also in various ways in private letters, public speeches, magazines and scholarly journals in Victorian England, contributed to the political discussion on the so-called Irish Question, in which it supported the view that giving the Irish any kind of autonomy was unreasonable. Tenniel represented the Irish Celt as aggressive and unpredictable, his hand raised with a stone, while the man on *An tOileánach*'s jacket is envisaged as contemplative and peaceful after a whole day of work. The face of Tenniel's Irish anarchist, simianised in nature, is in clear contrast with the noble face of the Blasket man. This face of a natural aristocrat not only enhances the image of an Irish citizen as promoted in the Free State but also contributes to the creation of a counter-stereotype which refutes the Victorian prejudice.

Il. 1: A detail from "Two Forces" by John Tenniel (left) published in *Punch*, London, October 29, 1881, image courtesy of Victor H. Yngve; and a detail from the dust jacket of *An tOileánach* (1929) (right), image courtesy of Máirín Daly, photograph by Anna Cisło.

In comparison to the cover design of *An tOileánach*, the dust jackets of two other Blasket autobiographies, Peig Sayer's *Peig .i. A scéal féin* (1936) and Muiris Ó Súilleabháin's *Fiche blian ag fás* (1933), issued by Clólucht an Talbóidigh/Talbot Press, are less elaborate with regard to the message contained therein. The green dust jacket of *Peig* has on its front a black and white photograph of the author sitting on a stonewall, an element so typical of the West of Ireland, and *Fiche blian ag fás* is covered with a reproduction of a Dingle landscape painting, part of which is the Great Blasket. In both cases, the titles and the names of the authors are written in Gaelic characters, in which the two books are printed. Like *An tOileánach*, the two Talbot Press books have photographs on their frontispieces. *Peig* has a photograph by Tomás Ó Muircheartaigh (1907–1967) of the author sitting in her kitchen and *Fiche blian ag fás* has a photograph (unsigned) of the Great Blasket. As with *An tOileánach*, these autobiographies are divided into chapters but these texts begin with decorated initials with characteristic Irish knot design, which enhance the Irishness of the books.

There were at least two reasons why Ó Súilleabháin's book did not appear under the auspices of An Gúm (Mac Conghail 2006: 151). First of all, the publisher wanted to remove from it one episode – the story of young Muiris going with his friend, Tomás, to a *naomhóg* race meeting in Ventry. The two boys try alcohol in a Ventry pub and get drunk and sick afterwards. As Gaeltacht inhabitants were to serve as examples of good behaviour, having two drunk Gaeltacht boys described in new national literature was unacceptable. The other reason stemmed from the condition of An Gúm that the text not be translated and published in the English language. To this neither Ó Súilleabháin nor George Derwent Thomson (1903–1987), a classic scholar from Cambridge, who helped Ó Súilleabháin have his autobiography published and was responsible for the author's contacts with publishers, consented. In the end, the novel, including the "alcohol episode," was published in Irish by Talbot Press and, in the same year, its English translation prepared by Thomson and the nationalist activist Moya Llewelyn Davies (1881–1943) was issued by Chatto & Windus in London.

To a certain extent, the influence of Thomson on Ó Súilleabháin's writing can be compared to the role Ó Ceallaigh and Ó Siochfhradha played in the case of Ó Criomhthain's work. As related by Mac Conghail (2006: 150):

> Muiris Ó Súilleabháin was interested in writing and wanted to become a writer. George Thomson encouraged him in this venture […] Muiris was a good storyteller, a facility which he had acquired from his grandfather […] but he could not, at that stage, re-create that talent in writing. It was the publication of Tomás Ó Criomhthain's *An tOileánach*, in 1929, which both acted as an incentive and provided an exemplar to Muiris.
>
> George Thomson persuaded Muiris to take Tomás's book as a model and to write the events of his life up to the time he joined the *gardaí* ["police"]. Muiris began to write *Fiche Blian ag Fás* in 1929 and to send it in sections as they were written to George Thomson.

The result, however, is a book very different from the old man's memoir. Ó Súilleabháin, born in 1904 and, after the death of his mother, until the age of seven, raised in an English-speaking orphanage in Dingle, from where he returned to the Island in 1911 (Welch 1996: 459–460), belongs to a younger generation of islanders. He wrote his autobiography when he was less than thirty, and so he describes only his joyful childhood and youth. Also, because the narrative was not modified as much as Ó Criomhthain's, the image of Blasket people is somehow less idealised and, as Liam Ó Rinn commented in 1936, "there are people who still have not recovered from the fit of anger that seized them because Muiris Ó Súilleabháin, out of sheer innocence, told the truth about the people of the Gaeltacht, that is, that they are not little clay and plaster saints, nor pseudo-aristocrats, but ordinary people…" (O'Leary 2004: 141).

More similar to *An tOileánach* is the overtone of the autobiography by Peig Sayers, who, being unable to write Irish herself, dictated it to her son, Mícheál Ó Guithín, when persuaded to do so by the visiting language activist Máire Ní Chinnéide (1879–1967), this autobiography's later editor (Mac Conghail

2006: 159). Sayers was born in 1873 into an Irish-speaking story-telling family, not on the Island but in Baile Bhiocáire/Vicarstown, Dunquin (Welch 1996: 509). There she attended the local school, where she learnt English, and, like many others from her generation, planned to emigrate to America, which she never did. When she was nineteen her marriage with Pádraig Ó Guithín from the Great Blasket was arranged and thereafter she lived with him on the Island. Peig is believed to have been a natural Irish storyteller (Almqvist 2004: 33), a female *seanchaí*. On the Island she was the queen of storytellers, "Queen Peig," as Eibhlís Ní Shúilleabháin (2009: 36–37) calls her in her letters from The Great Blasket Island. She knew and related hundreds of folk stories, Irish legends, and social stories of her unfortunate life. She opened her house for *céilí* dancing, which made her even more popular with community people. Her American dream never came to pass but she encouraged her sons to emigrate. A well-known part of her autobiography is one in which she turns to one of them saying:

> "My dear son", I said, "'Twould be a bad place that wouldn't be better for you than this dreadful rock. Whatever way things go you'll be among your own equals. All around me here I see nothing on which a man can earn a living for here there's neither land nor property. I wouldn't like to make a cormorant of you, my son, and already too many suffering misfortune." (Sayers 1991: 186)

Here Peig is not less elegiac that Ó Criomhthain when he talks about his misfortunate children dying of illnesses or losing their lives in various accidents (O'Crohan 1951: 147), and very far from the light-hearted approach to the life on the Island expressed in Ó Súilleabháin's work when, for example, one of his characters joyfully praises World War I and the narrator goes on to describe all the wonderful things it brought to their village each time a ship was sunk near the Island:

> "By God," one man would say, "war is good."
> "Arra, man," said another, "if it continues, this Island will be the Land of the Young."
> [...] There was good living in the Island now. Money was piled up. There was no spending. Nothing was bought. There was no need. It was to be had on the top of the water – flour, meat, lard, petrol, wax, margarine, wine in plenty, even shoes, stockings, and clothes. (O'Sullivan 1998: 131)

5 Conclusion

Although there are differences between old and young islanders' reflections upon the Blasket life, there is a lot the described Blasket autobiographies share. The accounts are unique as they all concern the community of a no longer inhabited Island and describe a world which ended well over half of a century ago. In compliance with the expectations of the Free State's authorities they contributed to creating new literature in Irish and to a large extent promoted the image of a noble Gaeltacht inhabitant, locating the core of the Irish culture in the West of the country. Such editorial features of the books' design as the Gaelic type in which they are printed and knot-decorated initials, enhance their Irishness, whereas such elements as maps, photographs of the authors and the images of the described place locate them on the border of literature and ethnographic documents and allow their readers to treat the authors not only as creative writers but also as trustworthy informants. Last but not least, the three books can be regarded as symptomatic of the time in which they appeared: they must have satisfied the 19th- and 20th-century nationalists' need for what Seán de Fréine (1978: 52–53) calls "national parallelism" – the need to enhance all elements which countered or stood in opposition to what was found in English culture. Hence, the Irish language was to replace English; Gaelic script was to replace Roman; and the image of a natural nobleman from the Gaeltacht was to replace the pejorative Victorian stereotype of an Irish Celt.

Bibliography

Almqvist, Bo. "The Scholar and the Storyteller: Heinrich Wagner's Collections from Peig Sayers." *Béaloideas*, Vol. 72, 2004, pp. 31–59.

Breathnach, Diarmuid, and Máire NíMhurchú. "Ó Criomhthain, Tomás (1855–1937)." Ainm.ie. https://www.ainm.ie/Bio.aspx?ID=713/ (25 Jan. 2018).

Cisło, Anna. "The Victorian Stereotype of an Irishman." In: *Hard-Science Linguistics*, eds. Victor H. Yngve and Zdzisław Wąsik. London and New York: Continuum, 2004, pp. 259–268.

Curtis, Lewis Perry, Jr. *Anglo-Saxons and Celts: A Study of Anti-Irish Prejudice in Victoria England*. New York: New York University Press, 1968.

Curtis, Lewis Perry. *Apes and Angels: The Irishman in Victorian Caricature*. Washington: Smithsonian Institution Press, 1971.

De Fréine, Seán. *The Great Silence: The Study of a Relationship between Language and Nationality*. Dublin and Cork: Mercier Press, 1978.

Doyle, Aidan. *A History of the Irish Language: From the Norman Invasion to Independence*. Oxford: Oxford University Press, 2015.

Hirsch, Edward. *Responsive Reading*. Ann Arbor: University of Michigan Press, 1999.

Kanigel, Robert. *On an Irish Island*. New York: Alfred A. Knopf, 2012.

Lysaght, Patricia. "Paradise Lost? Leaving the Great Blasket." *Béaloideas*, Vol. 74, 2006, pp. 155–206.

Mac Conghail, Muiris. *The Blaskets: People and Literature. A Kerry Island Library*. Dublin: Country House, 2006.

Ní Shúilleabháin, Eibhlís. *Letters from the Great Blasket*. Boulder: Mercier Press, 2009.

Ó Ciosáin, Niall. "Creating an Audience: Innovation and Reception in Irish Language Publishing, 1880–1920." In: *The Irish Book in the Twentieth Century*, ed. Clare Hutton. Dublin and Portland: Irish Academic Press, 2004, pp. 5–15.

Ó Conchubhair, Brian. "An Gúm, the Free State and the Politics of the Irish Language." In: *Ireland, Design and Visual Culture: Negotiating Modernity, 1922–1992*, eds. Linda King and Elaine Sisson. Cork: Cork University Press, 2011, pp. 93–113.

Ó Criomhthain, Tomás. *An tOileánach*. Baile Átha Cliath: Muinntir C.S. Ó Fallamhain i gComhar le hOifig an tSoláthair, 1929.

O'Crohan, Thomás. *The Islandman*, Trans. Robin Flower. Oxford: Oxford University Press, 1951.

Ó Cuív, Brian. "The Changing Form of the Irish Language." In: *A View of the Irish Language*, ed. Brian Ó Cuív. Dublin: Stationery Office, 1969, pp. 22–34.

Ó Fearaíl, Pádraig. *The Story of Conradh na Gaeilge: A History of the Gaelic League*. Baile Átha Cliath: Conradh na Gaeilge, 1975.

O'Leary, Philip. *Gaelic Prose in the Irish Free State, 1922–1939*. University Park: The Pennsylvania State University Press, 2004.

Ó Murchú, Helen, and Máirtín ÓMurchú. *Irish: Facing the Future*. Dublin: Irish Committee of the European Bureau for Lesser Used Languages, 1999.

Ó Súilleabháin, Muiris. *Fiche blian ag fás*. Baile Átha Cliath: Clólucht an Talbóidigh, 1933.

O'Sullivan, Maurice. *Twenty Years A-Growing*, Trans. Moya Llewelyn Davies and George Thomson. Nashville: J. S. Sanders & Company, 1998.

Pearse, Patrick Henry. *Quotations from P. H. Pearse*, ed. Proinsias Mac Aonghusa. Dublin: Mercier Press, 1979.

Sayers, Peig. *Peig .i. A scéal féin*. Baile Átha Cliath: Clólucht an Talbóidigh, 1936.

Sayers, Peig. *Peig: The Autobiography of Peig Sayers of the Great Blasket Island*, Trans. Bryan MacMahon. Syracuse: Syracuse University Press, 1991.

Smith, Charles. *The Ancient and Present State of County of Kerry: Containing a Natural, Civil, Ecclesiastical, Historical and Topographical Description of Thereof.* Dublin: Messrs. Ewing, Faulkner, Wilson, and Exshaw, 1774.

Ua Maoileoin, Pádraig. *Na Blascaodaí/The Blaskets.* Dublin: Stationery Office, 1994.

Welch, Robert, ed. *The Oxford Companion to Irish Literature.* Oxford: Oxford University Press, 1996.

Elis Dafydd

The *Ienctid yw 'Mhechod* Saga

Abstract: This chapter offers an analysis of one of the liveliest controversies in 20th century Welsh literature, concerning the novel *Ienctid yw 'Mhechod* [*Youth is my sin*] by John Rowlands. The novel, submitted for the prose medal competition at the National Eisteddfod in 1964, told the story of a Nonconformist minister and his extra-marital sexual affair and aroused controversy over its graphic description of a sexual act. The chapter traces the history of academic and journalistic discussion that the novel provoked, thus providing a valuable insight into the evolution of Welsh-language criticism and the development of the Welsh-language novel.

Keywords: Welsh literature, controversy, sex, John Rowlands, the National Eisteddfod

The annual highlight of Welsh cultural life in Wales is the National Eisteddfod, Europe's largest travelling cultural festival, which is a week-long event dedicated to literature, poetry, music, dancing, performance, crafts, and everything Welsh. The first recorded Eisteddfod was held under the patronage of the Lord Rhys in Aberteifi in 1176, and the Eisteddfod in its present form has been held continuously since 1861. Because of its longevity and significance, the Eisteddfod has been, over the years, the backdrop of many important and notable events and chapters in Welsh cultural and literary history. One such chapter started playing out at the 1964 Eisteddfod in Swansea.

In this period, the literary highlights of the festival were three ceremonies to honour the winners of the three most prestigious literary prizes, namely the Crown, awarded for free metre poetry, the Chair, awarded for an ode in the traditional Welsh strict-metres, and the Prose Medal, awarded in 1964 for a novel. The medal in that year was awarded by the three adjudicators, Glyn Ashton, John Gwilym Jones and Caradog Prichard, to Rhiannon Davies-Jones for *Lleian Llan-llŷr* [*The nun of Llan-llŷr*], a historical novel about a thirteenth-century nun.

However, it was the novel that was adjudged to be second best by Glyn Ashton and John Gwilym Jones, and third best by Caradog Prichard, *Ienctid yw 'Mhechod* [*Youth is my sin*], submitted under the nom-de-plume Emrys, that attracted the most attention because of its seemingly sensationalist story of a minister of religion's extra-marital sexual affair with a member of his congregation. Glyn Ashton said the novel told the tale of a "weak, unfortunate and inadequate minister's lechery" (translation mine, as are all translations unless otherwise stated) (Ashton 1964: 119–20) and Caradog Prichard announced that as far as he knew there had never been, before this novel, a "similar, and definitely not a better" description in the Welsh language of the "sexual act" (Prichard 1964: 112).

This created quite a commotion; so much so that the novel was mentioned on the day following the ceremony in the *Daily Mail*, a London-based English middle-market tabloid newspaper which seldom mentioned the Eisteddfod at all. It said that

> A novel which may remain unpublished and unread, was runner-up in the prose medal competition at the Royal National Eisteddfod [...] The book is a story of passion and illicit love between a middle-aged Nonconformist minister and a young girl in a village "somewhere in Wales." [...] Judges were shocked by the contents but they considered the literary standard extremely high. Only one person knows who wrote the book: the author [...] The writer's name is in a sealed envelope and if he does not ask for his work to be returned to him the sealed envelope and the book will be kept [...] in the University of Wales Library at Aberystwyth. (Daily Mail Reporter 1964: 3)

This quote suggests that the Welsh people in the 1960s were still considered by English journalists to be a nation of chapel-attending, hymn-singing, respectful Nonconformists, and that a Welsh novel dealing with sexual themes would come so close to winning one of the Eisteddfod's main literary prizes is really more of a shock to the *Daily Mail's* reporter than to the judges. The reporter's suggestion between the lines of this account is that the novel's author would never come forward; that he or she would be too afraid to admit that they were the one responsible for this scandalous, obscene novel.

However, he was wrong. The author of *Ienctid yw 'Mhechod* was one John Rowlands. A native of Trawsfynydd in the county of Meirionnydd, he had been a student at the University College of North Wales, Bangor (Bangor University, today) where he was instrumental in the establishing of a Welsh student newspaper and a literary magazine before going on to complete his doctorate at Oxford. He had already published two novels which were quite daring at the time, portraying disillusioned, directionless, frustrated male protagonists experiencing varying degrees of existential crises. John Rowlands's early novels are perhaps the closest Welsh literature came to having its own Angry Young Men movement.

It must be remembered that *Ienctid yw 'Mhechod* was notable for more than just its controversial theme and its daring sex scene. Caradog Prichard said that the author was a true novelist who could earn a comfortable living as a full-time writer if there were enough readers of Welsh novels. Considering the glowing adjudication his novel had received, Rowlands sent the manuscript of *Ienctid yw 'Mhechod* to Llyfrau'r Dryw [Wren Books] publishing house at Llandybïe, Carmarthenshire, the publishers of his previous two novels. Llyfrau'r Dryw's managing director, and the editor of its current affairs magazine *Barn* [*Opinion*] was Emlyn Evans, a socially and aesthetically conservative man. In the editorial of September 1964's edition of *Barn,* for instance, he lamented that "the deterioration in morals, behaviour and self-discipline" over the last quarter of a century had been "disastrous," that there were signs that the "foundations of civilised life were disintegrating," which would surely lead to social anarchy. He also complained that young authors, in the absence of anything important to say, had "developed an obsession with sex" (Evans 1964: 307).

Even though he himself had presided over the publishing of Rowlands's first two novels – which also dealt with adultery and contained sexual references – Emlyn Evans felt that *Ienctid yw 'Mhechod* went too far. He disapproved of obscene descriptions in literature, and also believed that the novel was insulting to the ministry; therefore he decided not to publish the novel, and informed Alun Talfan Davies, the press's owner, of his decision. He left the manuscript on his desk in his office and went on a family holiday for a few days.

When he came back to work the following week, he was stunned to discover that Alun Talfan Davies had sent the manuscript to the printers, having disregarded his initial decision. Evans came to the conclusion that there was only one honourable and conscientious thing to do, which was to resign, and that he did. On September 27, 1964 he drafted a letter of resignation to his employers saying that his term as managing director of Llyfrau'r Dryw and editor of *Barn* would come to an end on the last day of October. The news of his resignation spread quickly and it came as quite a shock to Emlyn Evans that it was the main story on TWW's television news the following night. After the broadcast, his telephone began ringing and rarely stopped doing so for several days.

One of the phone calls he received was from John Rowlands himself, asking him if there was anything he could do to help Emlyn Evans and get him to reconsider. Evans thanked him for his concern and assured him that there was nothing that would make him change his mind (Evans 1991: 284–86).

As can be expected, this was also a difficult and awkward time for John Rowlands. He had not expected, predicted or asked for this attention and he did not know how to defuse the situation. Immediately after the Eisteddfod, English journalists and publishers were telephoning his parents' home in Trawsfynydd asking for a translation of the novel, and after Emlyn Evans's resignation things got steadily worse. After the summer, Rowlands started working as a lecturer at Trinity College, Carmarthen, and according to Rowlands himself, the college's switchboard was having difficulties dealing with all the activity, though he himself was protected from most of the commotion by a senior colleague, Norah Isaac. He was in a quandary. Looking back at the saga in 2012 he explained that he did not know what to do: "What was my duty? Was I going to be responsible for letting a solid man like Emlyn Evans lose his job, or should I rescind my novel from the press and ensure that he could return to work?" He was advised by Norah Isaac to say nothing to the press, and to ride out the storm (Rowlands 2012: 28).

In the aftermath of the resignation, public opinion, or at least the opinions expressed in the press, sympathised a great deal with Emlyn Evans. John Ellis Williams, one of Wales's foremost journalists, in his column in *Yr Herald Cymraeg* [*The Welsh Herald*] steered clear of condemning the novel and its author but strongly commended Emlyn Evans for being brave enough to risk his own future as well as his family's comfort on a point of principle (Williams 1964: 8).

Apart from that column in the *Herald*, the discussion appeared mostly on the pages of denominational papers. *Y Llan* [*The Church*], the Church in Wales's newspaper, reported that a meeting of St David's Diocese's Temperance and Social Responsibility Committee had voted to send Emlyn Evans a letter commending his stand (St. David's Diocese 1964: 8). *Y Cylchgrawn Efengylaidd* [*The Evangelical Magazine*] went further, and was more militant in its attitude, by publishing a form of a public letter to Emlyn Evans, commending him on his stance in resigning rather than agreeing to publish a novel that was, in their view, notable mostly for its sexual descriptions. They also attacked Llyfrau'r Dryw by saying that they had once thought that some of the press's owners were "prominent people in ecclesiastical and religious circles" and said that it was not "a gift to Wales to add, in Welsh, to the enormous sum of English and American sexual literature which is so popular in this time of moral decay" ("Mr Emlyn Evans" 1964: 36).

The attitude of an association of the Congregationalist Union of Welsh Independents churches in Llŷn and Eifionydd was quite similar. A newspaper report in October disclosed that they had opted to send two letters: one to Emlyn Evans to applaud him for his stand, and one to Llyfrau'r Dryw, voicing their opposition to their decision to publish *Ienctid yw 'Mhechod* ("Yn Erbyn Cyhoeddi Nofel" 1964: 1). *Y Tyst* [*The Witness*] is the weekly newspaper of the Union of Welsh Independents, but the paper's official response to the resignation was less condemning than that of their ordinary members in Llŷn and Eifionydd. They refrained from condemning the novel and said that John Rowlands had the right to choose any theme he liked for his book. They also predicted that the novel, when published, would not leave a ripple in the water because the days of shock were over. They did not congratulate or commend Emlyn Evans's resignation either, but merely stated that they hoped that he would not be lost from publishing altogether because he was a talented and conscientious man ("Ieuenctid yw 'Mhechod" 1964: 1).

So, what do these responses tell us about Welsh society at the time? Firstly, they tell us that Welsh society was still a religious, Christian one. It was for religious reasons, after arriving at the conclusion that it contained obscene descriptions and insulted the ministry, that Emlyn Evans decided that he would not publish it, and all except for one of the other responses to the resignation or the novel come from religious periodicals or from a secular paper reporting on the response of a religious organisation. If *Ienctid yw 'Mhechod* was engulfed in a scandal at all, it was a moral and religious one.

Welsh society at the time was not only religious and Christian, but it was also still very denominational, with different Christian factions responding in different ways. The Congregationalist *Y Tyst*'s response is notably less condemning and more liberal than the publications of the more authoritarian Church in Wales and Evangelist Movement, for example.

But also, the wider, international context is quite significant. Across the world in the 1960s, young people were raising their voices and were rebelling against conventions and establishment. It was the decade of the Beatles, hippies, flower power, Woodstock and protests against the war in Vietnam and for civil rights. In Wales it was the decade which saw widespread protests against the drowning of Capel Celyn, a village in Meirionnydd, in order to supply water to the English city of Liverpool. It was also the decade in which young people, mostly students, established Cymdeithas yr Iaith Gymraeg [The Welsh Language Society], a pressure group to fight for the preservation of the Welsh language. The notable scholar of Welsh history, John Davies, referred to the decade as a period of youth rebelliousness, and John Rowlands's novels, and this novel in particular, were part of this rebellion. What is seen is not just John Rowlands the secular novelist on one side being met with suspicion and scorn from Christian denominations – he was also a young novelist on one side of what John Davies referred to as a "gulf between the proponents of popular culture and the older generation" (Davies 1987: 83).

It is a sad fact that no articles, letters or statements in support of John Rowlands were published. That may mean that Puritanism was alive and well in Wales in the 1960s and that Puritans were much more vocal than those who held more progressive ideas. But Wales was not the only country suffering from Puritanism during this period. In 1960, Penguin Books had been prosecuted under the Obscene Publications Act 1959 for publishing *Lady Chatterley's Lover*. Also, people who did support Rowlands might not have been eager to do so publicly until the novel had been published and they could read it for themselves. And of course, the novel had not yet been published. And it would not be published for nearly another year. This storm of opposition had erupted due to a novel that only a handful of people – its author, the three adjudicators at the Eisteddfod, Emlyn Evans and maybe Alun Talfan Davies – had actually read.

In the meantime, a few opinion pieces arguing the cases for and against literary censorship would be published in *Barn*. Censorship was a hot topic in Britain anyway during this period, and it was still enforced in the theatre. Every play had to obtain a licence from the Lord Chamberlain before it could be performed: censorship in the theatre was abolished only in 1968. Because of this context, it is unlikely that it was *Ienctid yw 'Mhechod* that had sparked the debate, and only one opinion piece, authored by Dewi W. Thomas, a clergyman in the Church in Wales, mentioned the novel by name, saying he hoped that it would never be published in its original guise (Thomas 1965: 189). There was a religious aspect to the arguments against censorship as well. R. Gerallt Jones published an article doing so but his reasons were wholly Christian: he believed that man did not possess the right to decide in which ways God would choose to reveal the truth (Jones 1965: 166).

The controversy surrounding the novel was like manna from Heaven to Llyfrau'r Dryw because it guaranteed a wide readership, though it seems they attempted to play down the controversial aspects. An advertisement in *Llais Llyfrau* [*The Voice of Books*] in the summer of 1965 said that everyone could "read it and decide for himself the value of this novel rather than depending on others" ("Rhestr Llyfrau Newydd" 1965: 26) and an advertisement in *Barn* said that "describing this novel as a story about sex would be a very superficial description" ("Llyfrau Newydd Llyfrau'r Dryw" 1965: 295).

Once it was published the controversial sex scene greeted readers on the sixth page. The novel opens with Emrys, the minister and the protagonist in the pulpit on a Sunday night. At the end of the service, rather than going home with his wife, he excuses himself and says he has to go to Elsa Richards' house because her mother is unwell. Elsa's mother is unwell, but he has another motive for wanting to visit her. He arrives at the house and Elsa tells him that her mother's condition has deteriorated and that she speaks of dying. He goes up to her and prays with her until she falls asleep. Emrys then descends the stairs and so begins the scene which made the novel so controversial:

> He opened the sitting-room door silently. The light had been switched off, but he could see Elsa lying naked in front of the fire, with the flames playing yellow and warm over her body. He lay down by her side and let his hand and lips wander over every bit of her.

> She trembled quietly like a lightly rippling streamlet, lay back passively inert, letting him explore her gently all over with fingers and lips.
>
> He kissed her lips and her trembling increased; the rippling brook was now a raging torrent. She was passive no longer. Their kissing was a joint effort, a striving to possess each other more fully. Her body shook convulsively. He unfastened his clerical collar and tore off his shirt. She peeled off the rest of the clothing. Their two naked bodies were like two magnets with an electric current flowing from the one to the other.
>
> She moaned as he probed her body. A skirmish had evolved into a conflict between them. She now surged round him like a sea, engulfing him. Her contact thrilled him, set him on fire. Her body overwhelmed him like a waterfall. His hands slithered through her hair and down her back. Experience intensified, widening out and closing in like a vast, illimitable sea. Their two bodies scaled each other's heights, moaning in the ecstatic torment of their lovemaking, maturing unbearably in the upsurging sea of experience. Wave succeeded wave ever more quickly. Her arms clutched him in alarm as she mounted to her climax. The current of her electricity shot through him with a convulsive shock, bringing culmination. (Rowlands 1966: 15)

That is the scene which created the furore. There is nothing pornographic about it, and in terms of style there is nothing obscene about it either; there is no individual word which would cause shock. What was condemned was that a sexual act was being described but there is nothing explicit about the description; everything is suggested quite tamely and if it were published today it would not draw much attention.

After they finish making love, Emrys and Elsa engage in a solemn discussion. Elsa does not believe she has a right to this kind of happiness but Emrys assures her that God would not have made them like that unless He liked seeing them enjoying pleasure. Elsa sits up and raises Emrys's clerical collar and puts it around her neck, "the collar white like ermine against her tanned skin, her full breasts rising and falling naked below it" (Rowlands 1966: 17). Emlyn Evans felt that the novel insulted the ministry and Elsa, naked, wearing nothing except a clerical collar with both of them discussing God could be more offensive to a Christian than the sex scene. After this, Elsa tries to break up the relationship when the doctor arrives. The three of them go upstairs to Elsa's mother who, sometime during the time when both of them were making love downstairs, has died.

This first chapter is the climax of the novel and the rest explores its aftershocks. The beginning of Emrys's complexities is portrayed, showing him as an isolated and bullied schoolboy who is shy and awkward around girls. He is shown in his present neurosis, fearing old age and trying to stay young, and his relationship with Elsa is an integral part of those efforts. The beginning of that relationship is described as Elsa endeavours to bring it to an end. Emrys and Gwen try, and fail, to save their marriage, and the relationship between Gwen and Elsa develop from their being strangers to being enemies to being some sort of allies. Elsa leaves Trearfon, the fictional town in which the novel is set, for another fictional town called Pengogarth, and Emrys and Gwen decide to divorce when Emrys suffers a heart attack. Elsa comes back to visit him one last time, and as she speaks with Gwen in the kitchen afterwards, she says that she has met a new man at Pengogarth. Gwen's response is that she also should pack her bags and move there. What is suggested is that Emrys, after recovering, will be left on his own with his neurosis, his insecurities, his complexities and problems and that the people who have suffered because of those things will be allowed to start anew.

So once the novel was out there in the public domain, what was the reaction to it? Although some reviewers referred to the controversial aspects of the novel, none of them did so in a moralising way. They all judged the contents on purely literary standards. The most positive review was penned by Harri Gwynn, who said that it was a "genuinely good novel" and that it had a "unity of form that is not better met very often" (Gwynn 1965: 2). But the other reviewers were not as kind. Harri Pritchard Jones said that although there were some excellent things in it, that there were too many inconsistencies and that "Mr. Rowlands can do much better than this" (H.P. Jones 1965: 55). Moreen Evans said that there had been an obvious deterioration in the standard of John Rowlands's novels and that *Ienctid yw 'Mhechod* had a "Woman's Own-like, superficial, rather childish story" (Evans 1965: 7). Lewis Valentine, a Baptist minister, and the only reviewer who came close to judging the novel based on its more controversial aspects, limited his comments to barely a hundred words, and abruptly finished by saying that he did not like the book and that the author's talent deserved a better theme (Valentine 1965: 82). Kate Roberts, before the publication of her review, said of John Rowlands in a letter to Saunders Lewis that "the boy hasn't the slightest idea" (Roberts 1992: 217) about the technique of writing a novel, and in the review itself said that the novel was much too short to do justice with the enormity of the themes. She went as far as to advise Rowlands not to write for a few years, and to dedicate his time to reading novels which are considered good ones before venturing to publish one of his own again (Roberts 1966: 2). Saunders Lewis also reviewed the novel and said that the novel's protagonist's sin, as well as the sin of the novel, is that he acted and thought as a fifteen-year-old adolescent (Lewis 1965: 8).

It was Kate Roberts who came closest to encapsulating the novel. She was right that it is much too short to do justice with the theme. Rather than portraying the story developing naturally it jumps into its climax straight away, meaning that the rest of the novel is mostly quasi-philosophical dialogue between characters or entire scenes played out in the characters' minds, which can come across as being quite abstract.

So what happened after these five reviews were published? What was the reaction from lay readers to this novel that had created such a stir before its publication? Nothing. The whole saga ends with these reviews. When research into this novel began it was expected, and indeed hoped, that the debate and the condemnation would continue in letter columns in newspapers and magazines for several months, with the debate becoming more and more intellectual and constructive as it progressed, but no. The affair ended as suddenly as it began. The discussion may have continued orally for a lot longer but none of that discussion has survived in print.

It is quite a mystery why this novel a topic of such lively discussion and condemnation before anyone – except for a handful of people – had even read it. And why did it stir up so much controversy in the first place? Emlyn Evans's resignation, of course, was an all-important element. The memory of the saga would not be still alive if he had stayed in his job, and maybe there would not have been a saga at all. But it must be remembered that he resigned, not because of the novel per se, but because his authority had been undermined. That was the reason; he did not resign from the publishing world in anger or disillusion because this novel had been written in the first place. *Ienctid yw 'Mhechod* wasn't the first novel to deal with such themes either, but it was the only one to face such a strong backlash, possibly because it was a minister of religion committing the adultery, rather than someone in another line of work. John Rowlands admitted in a 2007 interview that he made Emrys a minister in order to be daring and to shock people (Williams 2007: 18).

As previously noted, John Rowlands was a young man as well. He was only 25 years old at the 1964 Eisteddfod and realising that these were the sort of thing that younger authors were going to write about probably saddened and angered a lot of the older, more traditional generation. Youth was, indeed, his sin. But youth was also his virtue. It was a revolutionary and rebellious novel, published at the same time as other similar works in other languages across the world. Its publishing meant that the Welsh language was in sync with the rest of the world. It emerged also in a context of plentiful literary activity by young people in Welsh. John Rowlands, along with Jane Edwards and Eigra Lewis Roberts, were among the first young people to publish novels in Welsh, and that tradition is still going strong. Rowlands had established a student newspaper and a student literary magazine at Bangor and those in turn lead to the establishment of *Lol*, a satirical magazine which would become a source of many, many controversies over the years. *Lol* needed a publisher and y Lolfa was established specifically for that purpose. The press gradually started publishing books as well and by now it is by far the most productive and exciting publishing house in Wales. That means that the novel's quality is neither here nor there; its importance lies in its context and its effects, rather than its contents. If any lesson is to be learned from this saga, it is that the future of literature in any living language relies a great deal on young people's activity, productivity and rebelliousness.

This story has a rather interesting epilogue. Nearly half a century after the saga and his resignation in 1964, Emlyn Evans published an article in *Barn*, the magazine for which he acted as its first editor, under the title "Llenyddiaeth Gymraeg yn taro'r gwaelod" ["Welsh literature hitting rock bottom"] (Evans 2013: 76–7) where he argued that many books published during recent years brought shame on the nation. He said that swearing, particularly by women, was something he really hated, and he went on to list many volumes authored by women which contained swearwords, and complained that many of those books had received funding from the Welsh Books Council. He then went on to condemn a male novelist, Dewi Prysor, and said that his novels contained disgraceful and corrupt language and swearwords, as well as blasphemy.

He concluded the article by saying that the abolishment of censorship in the arts had been detrimental to social life in Britain and that it had led to a catastrophic collapse in moral standards. He suggested that this was the reason why the sales figures of Welsh books had decreased since the 1960s, and that Welsh readers had disappeared as the moral standards had deteriorated.

In the following issue of *Barn*, there was an article rebuffing Emlyn Evans's article, authored by none other than John Rowlands. He responded carefully, saying that he respected Emlyn Evans and he made it clear that he would respond only to Evans's views, rather than Evans as a person. He drew attention to the fact that Emlyn Evans had not noticed that most literary critics had dubbed this period a golden age of Welsh fiction and that Evans had declared his chauvinism completely openly by saying that he hated swearing by women in particular and that it was "obvious that we have not moved on from the pre-deluge age if a lot of people agree with him" (Rowlands 2013: 54–5). Rowlands insisted that Evans's reactionary views must be challenged no matter how much respect one had for him, and that the funeral of the Welsh language and its literature would be held if Evans and those who agreed with him had their way. He concludes his rebuttal by saying that Welsh literature in this period did not hit rock bottom but rather reached new heights, and he said that he thanked heavens for all the authors condemned by Emlyn Evans, as well as a number of other good novelists which were not named.

The discussion did not continue after that. In 2013, as in 1964/1965, the last word belonged to John Rowlands.

Bibliography

Ashton, Glyn M. "Beirniadaeth G. M. Ashton." In: *Cyfansoddiadau a Beirniadaethau Eisteddfod Genedlaethol Frenhinol Cymru Abertawe a'r Cylch 1964*, ed. E. Lewis Evans. Llandysul: Gwasg Gomer, 1964, pp. 113–22.

Daily Mail Reporter. "Eisteddfod novel shocks the judges." *The Daily Mail*, August 6, 1964, p. 3.

Davies, John. "Wales in the Nineteen-sixties." *Llafur*, Vol. 4, 1987, pp. 78–88.

Evans, Emlyn. "Yr anghydffurfiaeth newydd." *Barn*, September, 1964, p. 307.

Evans, Emlyn. *O'r Niwl a'r Anialwch*. Dinbych: Gwasg Gee, 1991.

Evans, Emlyn. "Llenyddiaeth Gymraeg yn taro'r gwaelod." *Barn*, July/August, 2013, pp. 76–77.

Evans, Moreen. "Dirywiad." Review of *Ienctid yw 'Mhechod*, by John Rowlands. *Y Dyfodol*, November 11, 1965, p. 7.

Gwynn, Harri. "Cymysgedd o gydymdeimlad a dirmyg yw agwedd yr awdur tuag at ei brif gymeriad." Review of *Ienctid yw 'Mhechod*, by John Rowlands. *Y Cymro*, September 9, 1965, p. 2.

"Ieuenctid yw 'Mhechod." *Y Tyst*, October 22, 1964, p. 1.

Jones, Harri Pritchard. "Un a lysg, – nid canol oed!" Review of *Ienctid yw 'Mhechod*, by John Rowlands. *Barn*, December, 1965, p. 55.

Jones, R. Gerallt. "Ar Ymyl y Ddalen." *Barn*, April, 1965, pp. 166, 171.

Lewis, Saunders. "Dwy Nofel." *The Western Mail*, September 11, 1965, p. 8.

"Llyfrau Newydd Llyfrau'r Dryw." *Barn*, August, 1965, p. 295.

"Mr Emlyn Evans." *Y Cylchgrawn Efengylaidd*, Vol. 6, No. 2, October–November, 1964, p. 36.

Prichard, Caradog. "Beirniadaeth Caradog Prichard." In: *Cyfansoddiadau a Beirniadaethau Eisteddfod Genedlaethol Frenhinol Cymru Abertawe a'r Cylch 1964*, ed. E. Lewis Evans. Llandysul: Gwasg Gomer, 1964, pp. 109–12.

Roberts, Kate. "Nofelydd a gymerodd ormod o gowlaid." Review of *Ienctid yw 'Mhechod*, by John Rowlands. *Baner ac Amserau Cymru*, January 27, 1966.

Roberts, Kate. "Letter no. 195." In: *Annwyl Kate, Annwyl Saunders*, ed. D. Ifans. Aberystwyth: Llyfrgell Genedlaethol Cymru, 1992, pp. 216–17.

Rowlands, John. *Ienctid yw 'Mhechod*. Llandybïe: Llyfrau'r Dryw, 1965.

Rowlands, John. *A Taste of Apples*. Trans. R. Ruck. London: Tandem Books, 1966.

Rowlands, John. "Sgandal *Ienctid yw 'Mhechod*." *Barn*, November, 2012, p. 28.

Rowlands, John. "Culni siofinistaidd." *Barn*, September, 2013, pp. 54–55.

St David's Diocese. "Pwyllgor Dirwest." *Y Llan*, October 16, 1964, p. 8.

Thomas, Dewi W. "Hawliau'r Artist." *Barn*, May, 1965, p. 189.

Valentine, Lewis. "Blas ar Lyfrau." Review of *Ienctid yw 'Mhechod*, by John Rowlands. *Seren Gomer*, October, 1965, p. 82.

Williams, Elen Mererid. "Holi John Rowlands." An interview with John Rowlands in *Ysgrifau Beirniadol*, Vol. 27, 2007, pp. 13–24.

Williams, John Ellis. "Y golygydd a giliodd." *Yr Herald Cymraeg*, October 26, 1964, p. 8.

"Yn Erbyn Cyhoeddi Nofel." *Y Cymro*, October 8, 1964, p. 1.

Marlena Gawlik

Irish Language and Identity in Contemporary Irish Poetry

Abstract: This chapter presents a close reading and analysis of a single poem, "ScnØd: míniú," by Gabriel Rosenstock. The poem is read against the background of the decline of the Irish language, even as it remains an important marker of national identity with a substantial symbolic and culture-forming role. The efficacy and the ambiguity of the Irish language in playing this role, Gawlik argues, is the subject matter of this poem, which also explores issues of untranslatability.

Keywords: Gabriel Rosenstock, ethnic identity, language loss, Irish literature, Gaeltacht

1 Introduction

The results of the latest census conducted in Ireland show that the total number of Irish speakers plummeted from 40.6 % to 30.3 % over the preceding five years, and the Gaeltacht areas, i.e. primarily Irish-speaking regions in Ireland, underwent an 11 % decline in the number of the Irish-language population (Central Statistics Office 2012 & 2017). This state of affairs is no longer merely a continuation of the trend of language decline observed over the last few decades (cf. Ó Riagáin 1997; Central Statistics Office 2007); rather, the decline is gaining momentum. At the same time, the Irish language is the first official language in Ireland and a working language of the European Union. While these facts may seem contradictory or at least inconsistent at first glance, they become less striking when one considers the role language plays in establishing the sense of national selfhood. It seems that the Irish language is part and parcel of everyday Irish life, whether actively spoken or not. Simultaneously, the omnipresence of English makes the two tongues clash and collide at all times. The conflict surfaces in the lives of Irish individuals, but it also manifests itself in Irish contemporary poetry. For centuries, the Irish language has been protected and celebrated by the *literati*, who have made it a recurring theme both in poetry composed in Irish and in the medium of English. Today, they both have their say on the intricate language-identity interface on the Isle of Ireland.

2 Identity

The notion of identity can be viewed from a number of perspectives: various studies distinguish between personal, relational and collective identities. Some perceive it as relatively stable, others as fluid and subject to change. Finally, there are those who claim that identity is discovered, and those who assert that it is constructed (Schwartz et al. 2011: 8). The present study focuses on certain general phenomena or tendencies regarding identity that can be observed in the context of minority languages. Therefore, the question of whether identity is stable or fluid is of little relevance here. By the same token, it is not of particular importance whether identity is a matter of realisation or whether it constitutes a conscious expression of self. Talking about a language, however, involves speakers of that particular language, and they can be treated as a collective body or as individuals. The very notion of minority languages implies power relations – if one language is considered a minority language, it is normally classified as such in relation to a majority language or languages. Yet even the personal identity of speakers of any given language can be influenced and defined by collective cultural processes which, in turn, are usually relative by nature. In this chapter the language-identity interface is examined in contemporary Irish poetry, both in Irish and in English. Poetry itself can be said to represent a personal experience that embodies problems important to a given community, which is an indication that individual and collective identities remain interrelated.

2.1 Ethnic Identity

According to Fredrik Barth, the emergence of an ethnic identity is dependent on the existence and maintenance of a boundary, be it a conventional one, such as a territorial boundary, or a social one, i.e. one that manifests itself, for example, in dress, language, or lifestyle, but also in a value system. In other words, the ethnic identity of a given group is set up in a relation to some other group or groups with which it wishes to contrast itself. Therefore, the construction of ethnic identity does not merely consist in developing a sense of belonging to a given group – it also involves demonstrating a lack of belonging to any other group (Barth 1969: 9–15; Tovey et al. 1989: 7; cf. also Heinz 2003: 267–88).

If exercising ethnic identity entails contrasting oneself with others, then any such identity exists within a broader cultural context: a polyethnic system. As much as such a polysystem remains heterogeneous, it is also stratified; i.e. some cultures occupy the centre of the system, while others are confined to the peripheries. In other words, cultures enjoy different statuses in terms of their relevant power and prestige (Tovey et al. 1989: 7; Even-Zohar 1990: 88). Such disparities are a result of former historical relations, availability of economic resources, media control, etc. Central or dominant cultures aim at maintaining the existing power relations, which they often do by means of perpetuating the belief that ethnicity is not something that defines them: ethnicity is an attribute that distinguishes members of lower-status groups, and in such a context, it is commonly equated with backwardness, parochialism and barbarism, while dominant cultures are the progressive, the forward-looking, the "civilised" ones (Tovey et al. 1989: 7).

Today's United Kingdom of Great Britain and Northern Ireland as well as the Republic of Ireland can be said to constitute a polyethnic sub-system, a system that is marked by colonisation and conquest. As Jude Collins writes, "[…] to be truly successful as a conqueror you don't simply suppress resistance; you work on the natives so that they connive in their own subjugation. This is done in a number of ways, but one of the most effective is to teach the native to think of him/herself as inferior. Their dress is inferior, their hairstyles are inferior, above all their culture as embodied in their music and language is inferior" (Collins 2017). That was precisely how Irish-British relations were structured: the English have always been the cultured enlighteners, while the Irish have been depicted as primitive, uncivilised, ludicrous, etc. (cf. Tovey et al. 1989: 7–8; 12; Ó Ruairc 2001: 43). As a consequence, centuries of anti-Irish propaganda brought about the internalisation of the coloniser's view by the Irish people and instigated subsequent language shift:

> There are Irish people who still refer to Irish music as "diddly-dee" music, thus ranking it with top-of-the-mornins' and leprechauns, thatched cottages and old men with no teeth singing tuneless dirges. […] More successful, from the British point of view, was the suppression of the Irish language. School children who were heard speaking their own language were punished and forced to speak English; and soon there was an Irish population that had been taught to see the Irish language as tying them to a poverty-stricken past. Emigrants were warned that they'd never get anywhere if they didn't abandon their native tongue. (Collins 2017)

Even nowadays, in the collective Irish mind, the Irish language is associated mainly with folklore (or folk lore) as well as lack of technological advancement, and there is still a strong prejudice against Irish speakers, Hiberno English speakers or users of any other Irish variety of English (Tovey et al. 1989: 29). At the same time, Irish is valued for its symbolic function and culture-forming role, and, in collective terms, remains a chief marker of the Irish ethnic identity. Even those who claim to have no Irish at all, know and use pieces of Irish vocabulary on a daily basis. These include: words related to Irish administration, e.g. *Garda*

Síochána [Police Force], *Taoiseach* [Prime Minister], *Oireachtas* [Parliament];[1] names of political parties, e.g. Fianna Fáil [Warriors of Ireland], Fine Gael [Tribe of the Irish], Sinn Féin [We Ourselves]; words denoting phenomena typical of Irish culture, e.g. *céilí* (social gathering normally involving playing traditional music and dancing), and *Nollaig na mBan* (Women's Christmas, which takes place on January 6th and marks the twelfth day of Christmas). All the names and expressions in question are normally expressed in Irish and their English equivalents are not used; i.e. whenever any media, be it English- or Irish-medium ones, want to discuss any undertaking of the *Taoiseach*, they resort to this particular word. Similarly, Irish policemen are only and exclusively *gardaí* (or *garda* in the singular), and not anything else. On top of that, there are certain grammatical structures that derive from the Irish language and were transferred into (Irish) English, such as "I do be learning/working/etc." which denotes that the action in question is done habitually, and originates from the Irish habitual tense.

The ambiguous status of the Irish language in Ireland reveals itself more explicitly in the attitudes the Irish people have towards the language. According to the report "Attitudes towards the Irish Language on the Island of Ireland," only 1 % of the Irish population would like Irish to be the principal language of the country, 17 % would like Irish to be preserved as a spoken language, but only in the Gaeltacht areas, and 25 % are in favour of retaining Irish in the realms of music and arts for its cultural and historical value (Darmody & Daly 2015: 85). This shows that despite the falling number of Irish speakers, the Irish language remains, in one way or another, a key marker of Irish collective identity.

Having said that the common conscience of the Irish society is shaped by the Irish language, one may ask whether the bilingual (to various degrees) reality of Ireland has any influence on individuals. In order to answer this question, one needs to consider the potential language-related phenomena that occur in the mind of a user of more than one language. Alexander Guiora postulates that language is a means of self-representation and introduces the concept of a "language ego," modelled on the Freudian concept of "body ego" (Guiora 1972: 144). One of the essential functions of the ego in general is to "maintain one's identity separate from others" (Guiora 1972: 148). The "body ego" serves largely the purpose of setting a physical border between the self and the world of objects. The concept can then be extended to language, which provides a more subtle and less tangible way of delineating the boundaries of one's own unique identity, i.e. of marking the

1 *Oireachtas* can also refer to an annual festival of Irish culture, also known as *Oireachtas na Gaeilge*, which was invented in 1897 and modelled on its Welsh equivalent (cf. Asmus 2015: 24).

contrast between the self and the other (Guiora 1972: 144–8). Learning another language, however, requires taking on or incorporating at least some aspects of another identity, thus extending the language ego so as to "incorporate a new system of communication" (Guiora 1972: 145; Guiora et al. 1972: 112). In the light of the concepts stipulated above, it seems more than plausible that Irish individuals who are either to a varying degree bilingual or operate in a bilingual context of Ireland in a dyglossic way have two separate language-related identities.

Research shows that when asked whether there are any differences Irish speakers feel within themselves while speaking Irish and English, they point to a number of phenomena, such as having stronger identity when speaking Irish, behaving differently while speaking Irish or perceiving Irish as far more expressive than English. Furthermore, they suggest that there is some kind of spiritual or emotional reality that is not (as easily) accessible in English as it is in Irish, e.g. they tend to find Sunday Mass in the Gaeltacht more meaningful, seem to have better understanding in a relationship when the partner is an Irish speaker too, or feel a stronger connection between Irish speakers in general, etc. (cf. Ó Ruairc 2001: 37–45).

To sum up, in the context of obligatory Irish teaching since the 1920s, it seems that the personal identity of an Irish person is at least to some extent shaped by the two languages or even that two separate identities come into play. Also, if one of the ego functions is to keep one's identity distinct from others – in this case, particularly from the English – it seems plausible to state that Irish individuals can face tensions that may affect their psychological integrity. After all, how can one be clearly distinct from the coloniser while speaking the coloniser's language?

3 Poetry, Language and Identity

Even though poetry usually draws from personal experience, it also treats of problems that are important to a larger group of people. No wonder that one can find multiple references to Ireland's linguistic situation in the works of such contemporary poets as Eavan Boland (1941–present), Paul Muldoon (1951–present), Michael Hartnett (1941–1999), Gabriel Rosenstock (1949–present), Biddy Jenkinson (1949–present), Nuala Ní Dhomhnaill (1952–present) or Gearóid MacLochlainn (1966–present) to mention some major influential figures. Among these authors, there are those who write only and exclusively in Irish, those who work through the medium of English, and those who employ(ed) both languages in their literary craft. Some of these authors do not mind their works being translated into English, while others strongly oppose such a procedure. Despite all these differences, when it comes to the importance of the Irish language, the poets speak in unison: the language is essential for the survival and well-being of Irish society. It is considered precious and worth protecting, a unique feature of Irish identity and a link to Irish history. Yet it is also depicted as fragile, impaired, unworkable or disturbing. It is confined to the past, but also an entity one longs for.

I am of the opinion that studying poetry makes it possible to embrace both the personal and collective perspective on identity in Ireland and capture the ways in which it manifests itself through language. In order to illustrate the phenomena discussed above, in this paper, a poem by a contemporary Irish writer, Gabriel Rosenstock, is introduced and analysed. He is a predominantly Irish-language author and internationally recognised human rights campaigner as well as a master of the Japanese Haiku.

3.1 Gabriel Rosenstock's "ScnØd: míniú"

The poem "ScnØd: míniú" comes from the volume *Rogha Dánta/Selected Poems* from 2005, which is a bilingual edition of Gabriel Rosenstock's poetry, featuring translations done by Paddy Bushe. For the sake of the present analysis, the poem is presented here, with the kind permission of Gabriel Rosenstock, in extenso, along with my translation thereof. Even though the piece of work has been translated into English, poetic translation involves making compromises of different sorts in the struggle to reflect both the form and the content of the original in the target text so as to reproduce or recreate the effects the original text has on its audience. If one is to know what effects the original can possibly produce, it seems reasonable to focus on different meanings of words and possible interpretations. Literal translation can bring to the fore these aspects of meaning that are otherwise likely to be lost in the process; therefore, the English rendition presented below is my own literal translation of the poem. Since one's awareness of multiple senses may influence one's understanding of the text, additional translations are included in round brackets. All quotations that follow come from the aforementioned volume.

"ScnØd: míniú" – ScnØd: an explanation (interpretation) – begins with the speaker introducing him- or herself as Sklog, who is almost ninety years old:

> Sklog is ainm domsa.
> Táim ag tarraingt ar 90 bliain d'aois.[2]
>
> [My name is Sklog.
> I am nearly (approaching) 90 years old.]

2 Rosenstock 2005: 96. All quotations from the poem are to this edition.

Then the reader is told that Sklog can speak Trillish, which is a fictitious language made up by the author. For Sklog, this is the language that was passed down to him or her by his or her mother, possibly his or her mother tongue. Yet, somehow Sklog finds him- or herself talking to a machine, not another human being:

> Trillis an teanga a fuaireas ó mo mháthair.
> Táimse ag labhairt isteach i meaisín.
>
> [Trillish is the language I got (acquired) from my mother.
> I am speaking into a machine.]

At this point, the reader does not know why some kind of a device is Sklog's only listener – is he or she lonely? Is there nobody else who would like to listen to him or her? Or maybe there is nobody left who can understand Trillish? The answer comes in the subsequent lines:

> Níl scríobh na teanga agam.
> Ní raibh aibítir scríofa riamh againne.
> Nuair a chaillfear mise
> Caillfear an Trillis.
> Níl sí ag éinne eile a thuilleadh.
>
> [I cannot write the language.
> We never had a written alphabet.
> When I myself die,
> Trillish will die.
> Nobody knows (has) it anymore.]

The language has no written tradition, and Sklog is the only living speaker of Trillish left. We can see that "speaking into a machine" is the only possible way to keep a record of the language: first of all, the language has never been codified, so the speaker has no idea how to write it. Secondly, there is no one the speaker can talk to, because nobody knows the language anymore. Hence, the only way to stop the language from falling into complete oblivion is to record at least a small portion of it using the technology available. Sklog realises that the language is probably going to die anyway. Still, he or she wants to give future generations a chance to listen to Trillish:

> Ach cuirfear an píosa cainte seo
> Ar fáil do na glúine a thiocfaidh
> Más mian leo éisteacht leis.
>
> [But this fragment of talk (speech)
> Will be available for the future generations
> If they wish to listen to it.]

Here, as if to justify the very act of making the recording, the protagonist observes:

> Tá focail againn sa Trillis
> Agus cheapfainn nach mbeidís ag mórán eile.
>
> [We have words in Trillish
> That, I would think, not many others have.]

Sklog feels that the language is unique in its own way – there are cognitive concepts that are probably not present in any other language, or cannot really be expressed so powerfully via any other tongue. The speaker gives an example:

> ScnØd, cuiream i gcás.
> Sé is brí le ScnØd ná… bhuel, is scéal fada é…
>
> [Let's say, ScnØd.
> The meaning of ScnØd is… well, that's a long story…]

The word "ScnØd," given as a example, proves largely untranslatable, i.e. the meaning that is encapsulated within a single word in Trillish, can only be explained or described, it is "a long story," requiring resorting to a larger cultural context:

> Tá crann ann ar a dtugtar an ko-eewa.
> Ní bhláthaíonn sé ach uair amháin i dtréimhse 20 bliain –
> Blátha áille dearga.
> Bláthaíonn sé agus ansin titeann na blátha an tráthnóna céanna.
> Is féidir saghas tae a dhéanamh as na duilleoga
> Ar leigheas é ar scamaill chorcra san intinn.
>
> [There is a tree that is known as ko-eewa.
> It blossoms but once in a period of 20 years –
> Beautiful (lovely) red flowers.
> It blossoms and then drops the flowers down the same evening (afternoon).
> One can make a kind of tea from the leaves
> Which is a medicine (cure) for purple clouds in the mind.]

Clearly, in order to be able to grasp the meaning of the word "ScnØd," one needs to possess knowledge of extra-linguistic phenomena, such as the existence of the ko-eewa tree, its appearance, its properties, its life cycle. Getting an idea what "ScnØd" stands for involves empathising with the experience of a speaker of Trillish:

> Anois, is é is brí le ScnØd ná seo:
> Samhlaigh éirí na gréine ina laomluisne ar fhíor na spéire.
> Féachann tú amach agus tá an ko-eewa faoi bhláth!

Tosnaíonn tú ar dhamhsa beag a dhéanamh ansin.
Stop! Féach arís!
Níl ann ach solas na gréine ar ghéaga loma.
Seachmall. Féachann tú an treo eile ansin.
Níor mhaith leat bheith ag féachaint rófhada ar rud nach bhfuil ann.

[Now, this is the meaning of ScnØd:
Imagine the sunrise blazing up on the horizon,
You look away (out) and the ko-eewa is in bloom!
You begin to do a little dance, then.
Stop! Look again!
There is nothing but sunlight on bare branches.
An illusion (abstraction). You look the other way, then.
You would not like to be looking so (too) long on something that is not there.]

Only by relating to the Trillish cultural milieu can one comprehend the exact meaning of the word in question:

Míniú cruinn ar ScnØd:
An ko-eewa faoi bhláth, mar dhea,
Damhsa beag áthais, athfhéachant ar an gcrann
Agus iompú do radhairc uaidh.

[Exact (accurate) explanation (interpretation) of ScnØd:
The ko-eewa in bloom, forsooth,
Little dance of joy, second glance on the tree
And turning your eyes away.]

The protagonist of the poem is on the brink of turning ninety years old and well aware that his or her life will probably come to an end soon. It is known that Sklog is the last living speaker of Trillish. He or she says "[w]hen I myself die,/Trillish will die." Hence, the urge to leave a trace: if Sklog does not make a recording, and does not do that now, nobody will ever know that such a language with its specific concepts and features ever existed.

Sklog got the language from his or her mother, yet "[n]obody knows (has) it anymore," and he or she is "speaking into a machine" instead of talking to another human being – why is it so? The issue is not resolved in the poem. However, there are at least three possible explanations: the first and the most straightforward one would be that Sklog simply has no children. Therefore, he or she was not able to pass the language down – end of story. But what if Sklog actually has or had some offspring and was willing to bestow the language on them? What stopped him or her from doing so? One reason would be that speaking the language was simply not allowed. There were times in the 18th and 19th centuries when people were persecuted for using the Irish language in Ireland. Nonetheless, there were individuals who organised so-called hedge schools, i.e. illegal schools, typically located in places that were hard to find, to teach the Irish language and culture. Yet there were probably also those who switched to English in fear of their own lives or the lives of their loved ones. Perhaps Sklog, too, chose the safety of family over native language. Now the oppression is probably gone and the language could flourish again, but it does not. Are the children too old to learn it? Or do they not want to? It may well be that the new generations no longer perceive the tongue as something valuable or practical. Finally, is it possible that Sklog intentionally decided not to hand the language down? The history of the Irish language is full of examples of parents deciding to bring up their children through English to make it possible for them to advance socially and economically (cf. e.g. Ó Ruairc 2001: 43). Yet history also shows that instances of parents that later regretted such a decision are more than incidental. Perhaps Sklog thought "ní thagann ciall riomh aois" [sense does not come before age], as an Irish saying goes. What once might have seen as a good idea, in the twilight of his or her life, becomes rather a failure. Filled with remorse, Sklog then commits him- or herself to preserving the language in any form available in his or her final years.

The poem makes it clear that writing the language down is out of the question, because its speakers "never had a written alphabet," which suggests that Trillish comes from a rich oral tradition, just as Irish does. Apparently, there is no one who would even like to listen to him or her either; therefore, Sklog is "speaking into a machine."

Looking back at the history of different languages, and especially at the history of cultural conquest, one can see a common dichotomy in perception: the dominant language (and culture) is the advanced, the universal one, while the minority language (and culture) is the backward, parochial one. To some extent, the dichotomy can be observed in Ireland up to the present day. It is the English language that is associated with the city, and hence with modernity and technological development, while the Irish language is still seen as a part of the rural landscape, thus evoking connotations with obsolescence and folklore more than anything else. While the English established their cities in the east of Ireland in the 17th century, the Irish were pushed to the less fertile areas in the west. Therefore, if one wanted to escape poverty, one had to move to the urban areas, which meant one had to have English. Hence, in the popular mind, English became the language of technological development, and Irish the language of agriculture. We do not know whether this was also the story of Trillish, but it is not unlikely. Even in recent history there are plenty of examples that show how technological growth leads to the devastation of the natural environment, which, in the best case, causes deterioration of living conditions of remaining tribal societies along with their languages, and in the worst case, results in their demise. Ironically, the technological development that might have contributed to the loss of the language now seems to be the only "rescue" for Trillish. Sad as it is, more often than not, all that can be done for severely endangered languages is to preserve them in the form of an artefact or exhibit so that future generations will at least be aware that such a language ever existed, and this seems to be the case with Trillish. Still, the audience will probably only be passive onlookers, or in this case – listeners – unable to learn such a language and use it themselves: "[…] this fragment of talk (speech)/Will be available for the future generations/If they wish to listen to it." It seems that even with the use of modern technology, all a single person can do is preserve a fraction of the whole language system that can later be presented as a curiosity more than anything else.

The subsequent lines of the poem touch the very core of the issue of linguistic diversity, but also shed light on the question of identity: "We have words in Trillish/That, I would think, not many others have." Any language possesses certain words, expressions and concepts that are unique and are not to be found in any other tongue. A language is also a depository of cultural concepts and an encoded history of a given community. Bearing in mind that ethnic identity is established by means of differentiation from others, it becomes clear that language is a powerful tool for marking off such differences. As an example, the speaker of the poem recalls the word "ScnØd." However, it quickly turns out that there is no direct equivalent of the concept in the target language: the term is "a long story" and it proves largely untranslatable.

The speaker evokes the image of a tree called "ko-eewa." It is said that the tree "blossoms but once in a period of 20 years –/Beautiful (lovely) red flowers" and "[o]ne can make a kind of tea from the leaves/Which is a medicine (cure) for purple clouds in the mind." There are several aspects here that may suggest that the tree is, in fact, an Otherworldly tree. First of all, red is one of the colours associated with Celtic Otherworld(s), and trees, as such, very often constituted entrances to the Otherworld. Secondly, the tree apparently has healing properties, which is true of the leaves, flowers or fruit of various trees, but is also in line with Celtic belief that trees can offer protection. Providing help, shelter or recovery was also one of the main function of the pre-Christian Celtic Otherworld. The significance of trees is also encoded in the Irish language proper in the forms of such expressions as "crann do shláinte leat!" [lit. "tree of your health to you; the best of health to you, good yourself"[3]], "is díon an crann fad is díon dó féin é"

3 All literal translations are mine; English equivalents are given after the online version of Ó Dónaill's *Foclóir Gaeilge-Béarla*, https://www.teanglann.ie/en/fgb/.

[lit. "a tree is a shelter as long as it is a shelter for itself"; "a tree provides shelter, but only until it becomes saturated"], "dul as do chrann chumhachta" [lit. "to go [down] from your magical/supernatural/power tree"; "to lose control of oneself", "get into an uncontrollable rage"), "rud a tahbairt i gcrann" [lit. "to bring something in a tree; to develop something fully"], "bheith faoi chrann smola" [lit. "to be under a blighted/decayed tree"; "to be blighted cursed"], etc. Also, it does not seem coincidental that the tree in question blossoms every twenty years. According to Caesar (2004), twenty years was the period of time one needed to spend studying in order to become a druid, and druids are also known for their connections with trees (Heinz 1999: 139–145; 277–283). Still, there is also something very peculiar about the tree in question: "[i]t blossoms and then drops the flowers down the same evening (afternoon)." The appearance of flowers evokes joy, a festive feeling, and inspires one to "do a little dance"; yet in the blink of an eye, the tree loses its flowers, leaving nothing but "sunlight on bare branches." Hence, the tree that seems to enjoy an extraordinary status, proves dysfunctional and the Otherworld itself is no longer accessible: "ko-eewa" bears flowers, but a moment later they are gone; thus, their properties cannot be put to use or if they can be utilised, it is only to a limited extent. The tree is so transient that one cannot fully appreciate it, so one starts doubting if it is genuine or just "[a]n illusion," an abstraction, a figment of the imagination. Jubilation gives way to self-consciousness – after all, "[y]ou would not like to be looking so (too) long on something that is not there." That seems to be the predicament in which many Irish speakers, even the fluent ones, find themselves: on the one hand, they celebrate and cherish the language but on the other, the very same individuals will often say that Irish is a dead or useless language. By the same token, depending on the circumstances, fluent users of Irish will call themselves native speakers in order to express their pride in cultural heritage or learners in order not to be seen old-fashioned, dull, etc.

The poem closes with an "exact" or "accurate" meaning of the word "ScnØd" which is the following: "[t]he ko-eewa in bloom, forsooth,/Little dance of joy, second glance on the tree/And turning your eyes away." Ironically, the description could also serve to summarise the current language situation in Ireland: each year there are country-wide celebrations of *Seachtain na Gaeilge* [*Irish Week*], and 2018 was proclaimed *Bliain na Gaeilge* [*The Year of the Irish Language*], while what should actually be taking place, as Máire Ní Fhinneadha points out, is *Bliain na hÉigeandála* [*Year of Emergency*]. Ní Fhinneadha observes that "foilsíodh figiúirí Pobal ón bPríomhoifig Staidrimh, a léirigh gurb iad na ceantair is láidre Gaeilge sa tír na ceantair is mó atá faoi mhíbhuntáiste ó thaobh fostaíochta, deiseanna, acmhainní, oideachais agus ioncaim agus is in olcas a chuaigh a bhformhór ón anailís dheireanach" ["figures from Central Statistics Office revealed by Pobal[4] made it clear that the areas where Irish is the strongest in the country are the most disadvantaged ones in terms of employment, opportunities, resources, education and income, and most of them got worse since the last analysis" (translation mine)] (Ní Fhinneadha 2017; cf. Pringle 2017). The number of Irish speakers in the Gaeltacht areas, still the most vibrant Irish-speaking communities, is declining due to lack of job opportunities, basic facilities and services as well as poor infrastructure that leads to out-migration (cf. Ní Fhinneadha 2017; Pringle 2017; Brophy 2018). At the same time, Foras na Gaeilge, a body responsible for the promotion of the Irish language, will spend €450,000 during *Bliain na Geailge* to "an pobal a spreagadh chun ár dteanga dhúchais a labhairt agus í a chur i lár an aonaigh" ["encourage the community to speak our native tongue and put it in the heart of things" (translation mine)] (Department of Culture, Heritage and the Gaeltacht 2017), while local communities in the Gaeltachtaí that prepared language plans aiming to preserve the language and create new opportunities in these areas were told that they could get €25,000 instead of €100,000 that was needed (cf. Tuairisc.ie 2017). While there is nothing wrong with promoting the use of the Irish language throughout Ireland, it is debatable whether the amount of money spent will be proportionate to prospective effects. Will street festivals and school competitions really make the Irish more willing to speak their native tongue in everyday life? Or will it just be "a little dance of joy" and then "turning your eyes away" again?

To summarise, "ScnØd: míniú" pinpoints the role of language in the formation of ethnic identity. The poem shows that shared linguistic, and hence cultural, knowledge is one of the factors that makes a given community unique and unlike any other group of people. The poem also hints at the individual struggles and internal tensions of speakers of minority languages. Making use of specific Celtic elements, it seems to be a clear allegory of the present-day situation of the Irish language in Ireland: it portrays the ambiguous reality in which the Irish language is appreciated and valued on the one hand, and is so fragile and transient on the other that maybe there is no point in actually speaking it anymore.

4 Conclusions

The number of Irish speakers in Ireland has been falling for decades, and Gaeltacht areas, the last havens for Ireland's native tongue, are now threatened

4 Pobal is a non-profit company managing programmes on behalf of the Irish Government.

with depopulation. Having said that, the language still remains one of the major constituents of Irish identity, which is present in the everyday life of the whole of Irish society, irrespective of the language a given individual speaks. It constitutes an integral and recognised part of Irish culture. The resulting feelings of conflict and ambivalence that affect the lives of ordinary people have also made their way into contemporary Irish poetry, in both Irish and English. The shaky status of Ireland's native tongue proves a recurring theme in the works of numerous Irish authors, who may have contrasting approaches to writing or translation, but share a common cause of protecting Ireland's native tongue. What follows from their literary endeavours seems to confirm the fact that on the whole both the attempts to revive and to retain Irish have had little effect so far: the language is either lost altogether or it survives, but is so viable that it can be used only passively.

Bibliography

Asmus, Sabine. "Culture-defining trends and traditions in Irish and Welsh dictionaries." In: *Representations and Interpretations in Celtic Studies*, eds. T. Czerniak, M. Czerniakowski and K. Jaskuła, Lublin: Wydawnictwo KUL, 2015, pp. 13–48.

Barth, Fredrik, ed., *Ethnic Groups and Boundaries: The Social Organization of Culture Difference*. Boston: Little, Brown and Company, 1969.

Brophy, Daragh. "Families say they will leave Tory Island if 42-year-old ferry comes into service." *Thejournal.ie*, February 9, 2018, http://www.thejournal.ie/tory-island-ferry-ow-2-3841581-Feb2018/ (3 Mar. 2018).

Caesar, Julius. *"De Bello Gallico" & Other Commentaries*. Project Gutenberg, 2004, http://www.gutenberg.org/cache/epub/10657/pg10657-images.html (25 Apr. 2018).

Central Statistics Office. *Census 2006, Volume 9: Irish Language*. Dublin: Stationery Office, 2007.

Central Statistics Office. *Census 2011 Results, Profile 9: What We Know*. Dublin: Stationery Office, 2012.

Central Statistics Office. *Census 2016 Results, Chapter 7. The Irish Language*. Dublin: Stationery Office, 2017.

Collins, Jude. "Irish culture and lessons in self-loathing." Jude Collins – Writer & Broadcaster, October 15, 2017, http://www.judecollins.com/2017/10/irish-culture-lessons-self-loathing/ (25 Apr. 2018).

Darmody, Merike and Tania Daly. *Attitudes towards the Irish Language on the Island of Ireland*. Dublin: The Economic and Social Research Centre, 2015.

Department of Culture, Heritage and the Gaeltacht. “Pacáiste Maoinithe Ceadaithe do Bhliain na Gaeilge 2018.” Department of Culture, Heritage and the Gaeltacht, November 3, 2017, https://www.chg.gov.ie/ga/funding-package-approved-for-bliain-na-gaeilge-2018/ (25 Apr. 2018).

Even-Zohar, Itamar. “Polysystem Studies.” *Poetics Today*, Vol. 11, No. 1, 1990, pp. 85–94.

Guiora, Alexander Z. “Construct Validity and Transpositional Research: Toward an Empirical Study of Psychoanalytic Concepts.” *Comprehensive Psychiatry*, Vol. 13, No. 2, 1972, pp. 139–50.

Guiora, Alexander Z., Robert C. L. Brannon and Cecelia Y. Dull. “Empathy and Second Language Learning.” *Language Learning: A Journal of Research in Language Studies*, Vol. 22, No. 1, 1972, pp. 111–30.

Heinz, Sabine. *Symbols of the Celts*. New York: Sterling Publishing Co., Inc., 1999.

Heinz, Sabine. *Welsh Dictionaries in the 20th Century – A Critical Analysis*. München: LINCOM Europa, 2003.

Ní Fhinneadha, Máire. “Cén mhaith ‘Bliain na Gaeilge 2018’ don Ghaeltacht? Bíodh ‘Bliain na hÉigeandála’ againn…” Tuairisc.ie, November 15, 2017, https://tuairisc.ie/cen-mhaith-bliain-na-gaeilge-2018-don-ghaeltacht-biodh-bliain-na-heigeandala-againn/ (25 Apr. 2018).

Ó Riagáin, Pádraig. *Language Policy and Social Reproduction: Ireland 1893–1993*. Oxford: Clanderon Press, 1997.

Ó Ruairc, Micheál. *An Inquiry into the Experience of Language Shift in an Irish Context*. Unpublished MA Thesis in Transpersonal Counselling and Psychotherapy, England, De Montfort University, 2001.

Pringle, Thomas. “Pringle says Donegal deprivation levels due to retreat of rural services.” Thomas Pringle TD, November 9, 2017, http://www.thomaspringle.ie/2017/11/09/pringle-says-donegal-deprivation-levels-due-to-retreat-of-rural-services/ (25 Apr. 2018).

Rosenstock, Gabriel. *Rogha Dánta/Selected Poems*. Indreabhán: Clo Iar-Chonnachta, 2005.

Schwartz, Seth J., Koen Luyckx Vivian L. Vignoles, eds., *Handbook of Identity Theory and Research*. New York: Springer Science and Business Media, 2011.

Tovey, Hilary, Damian Hannan and Hal Abramson. *Why Irish? Language and Identity in Ireland Today*. Dublin: Bord na Gaeilge, 1989.

Tuairisc.ie. “Roinn na Gaeltachta chun tuilleadh machnaimh a dhéanamh ar chás phlean teanga Chois Fharraige.” November 10, 2017, https://tuairisc.ie/roinn-na-gaeltachta-chun-tuilleadh-machnaimh-a-dheanamh-ar-chas-phlean-teanga-chois-fharraige/ (25 Apr. 2018).

Katarzyna Jaworska-Biskup

Some Remarks on the Periodisation of Welsh Medieval Law

Abstract: This chapter presents an overview of current approaches to Welsh medieval law, a field that continues to generate dissenting views in the context of historical, legal and literary studies. It focuses on the problem of the periodisation of medieval Welsh law and traces its evolution from the pre-codification period to the Acts of Union of 1536 and 1543. By locating the Welsh legal system in the broader context of the legal history of Britain and Ireland, and considering relevant material found in pseudo-historical literature as well as Welsh vernacular literature, the paper presents Welsh law as a comprehensive and flexible system that was capable of absorbing new elements while retaining its efficiency.

Keywords: Welsh literature, Welsh medieval law, legal history

1 Introduction

Welsh medieval law has been the subject of many scholarly works, including those in the field of historical, legal and literary studies. Despite a rich literature surrounding this topic, however, there are still issues that generate dissenting views thereof, such as the origin of the Welsh legal codification supposedly produced by Hywel Dda in the tenth century or the correlation between Welsh codified law and Roman law, Anglo-Saxon law, Norman law and English common law. The present paper presents an overview of existent approaches to Welsh law, with a special emphasis being put on its periodisation. By referring to data obtained from various sources, including research publications treating of the legal history of the Isles, historical and pseudo-historical literature, as well as Welsh vernacular literature, an approximate timeline of the evolution of the Welsh legal system from the earliest recorded times until the first half of the sixteenth century is sketched and briefly commented on.

2 The Proposed Periodisation of Welsh Medieval Law

For the purpose of the study, the following periodisation of Welsh law may be proposed:[1] 1) the pre-codification period (from the earliest times until the

1 The periodisation of Welsh law presented here summarises the findings of the research on Welsh and Scottish medieval law and literature conducted in my book *Selected*

codification of Welsh law in the mid-tenth century). This period may be further subdivided into three phases, namely a) the pre-Roman period, b) the Roman period, and c) the Heroic Age; 2) the period since the codification of law in the mid-tenth century until the conquest of the Principality of Wales by Edward I in 1283 and the ensuing enactment of the Statute of Rhuddlan in 1284. In this time span, two major landmarks may be distinguished: a) the codification of law by Hywel Dda in the mid-tenth century, and b) the Anglo-Norman conquest of Wales during the eleventh and the thirteenth centuries, which ended with the Welsh Wars of Independence of 1276–1277 and 1282–1283; and 3) the post-conquest period encompassing the years after the conquest of the Welsh Principality in 1283 until the promulgation of the Acts of Union of 1536 and 1543.

2.1 The Pre-codification Period

The beginnings of Welsh law are traceable to the earliest, ancient period, when Wales did not exist as a separate political and legal unit but was a constituent of the ancient Britain. In this period of the history of the Isles, Britain was inhabited by various tribes (Davies 2000: 48). Scholars frequently call the corpus of law that governed ancient Britain and Ireland "Celtic Law," or, after F. Kelly, "Common Celtic Law" (Kelly 2016: 241). According to this line of reasoning, "Celtic Law" provided a core of legal codifications of Wales and Ireland, and was discernible in common legal terminology (Kelly 2016: 231–232; Stacey 1994: 19). A note of caution, however, should be attached to the postulated term "Celtic Law" in relation to the earliest law of Britain not least because, convenient as this name is, it was popularised much later than the timeframe under discussion herein, that is, in the eighteenth, nineteenth and early twentieth centuries. Since what is called "Celtic Law" was an unwritten collection of tribal customs and practices, a plethora of which were attributable to many tribal societies, particularly but not exclusively to ancient British society, it seems, therefore, more accurate to speak, rather, of "British Tribal Customary Law."

The pre-Roman period ended around AD 43, when the Roman Emperor Claudius invaded Britain, thus giving way to the infiltration of Roman culture into the British province (Davies 2000: 89–93). Britain suffered some impact of Romanisation; however, its exact scale is impossible to measure. Historians approach the issue of the Romanisation of Britain, especially the influence of Roman law on Britons' customary laws, from different angles. In general, the prevailing attitudes thereto can be classified into two groups: those who think Romanisation had an enduring effect on Britain's laws (e.g. Watkin 2006: 213–215; Watkin 2007: 16–25, 29–43; Korporowicz 2012: 133–150), and those who believe Romanisation insignificant or peripheral (e.g. Davies 2000: 119; Lloyd 1911: 87–89). Both categories of scholars give valuable arguments which, if interpreted in tandem, yield some clues on the legal and social landscape of Britain in the post-Roman period.

The pro-Romanisation standpoint can be corroborated by the following considerations: a) the adoption of some Latin legal terminology, which was used as an apparatus for drafting Roman legal texts, by Welsh legislators, b) parallels between specific legal institutions and practices of Roman and Welsh law, c) the establishment of Welsh kingdoms on the administrative foundations laid down by the Romans in Roman-dominated Britain (e.g. Watkin 2006: 213–215; Watkin 2007: 29–43; Korporowicz 2012: 133–150).

The preserved literary evidence, on the other hand, undermines the hypothesis that Romanisation endured in the post-Roman period in Britain. Such literary sources as Bede's *Historia ecclesiastica gentis Anglorum* from the eighth century, pseudo-Nennius's *Historia Brittonum* from the ninth century and Gildas's *De excidio Britanniae* from the sixth century, all being the accounts of the earliest history of Britain, document an abrupt and permanent cleavage between the Roman period and the post-Roman period in Britain. As these sources narrate, after the British province had collapsed, the Britons rejected Roman laws and administration, the symbols of their servitude to the Roman Empire, and adhered to their own customary laws. In the words of pseudo-Nennius, "[...] the Romans governed them [the Britons] four hundred and nine years. After this, the Britons despised the authority of the Romans, equally refusing to pay them tribute, or to receive their kings" (Giles 2007: 14). As Gildas wrote in his *De excidio Britanniae*, the Romans brought to the lands of the Britons "laws for obedience without opposition." The Britons, in return, "gave to the edicts merely a skin-deep obedience with resentment sunk deep into their hearts" (Williams 1899: 7). Gildas continued that Britain emerged from the post-Roman era as a land of chaos and lawlessness ruled by tyrants with no regard for law and order, a land which "retained the Roman name, but not the morals and law" (Williams 1899: 10). The post-Roman historical and pseudo-historical writing is not devoid of ideological overtones. The primary purpose of the authors who represented this genre of literature was to criticise British society for failing to observe the Christian faith and its indulgence in sin. Thus, the credibility of such narratives in portraying the condition of Britain in the post-Roman period may be challenged. For this reason, among the literary collections illustrative of the post-Roman state of the British society, it is worth considering Welsh vernacular prose.[2]

The first example is *Ystoria Drystan*, dated probably to the period between the fifth and ninth centuries, a story of two fugitive lovers who elope to the Caledonian forest to continue their secret affair. Contrary to what continental, distorted versions of the Welsh tale present, *Ystoria Drystan* is not the account of a tragic love of the titular characters. In fact, the nub of it is a legal dispute between Trystan and March, Esyllt's husband. March instigates a legal action against his adversary, Trystan, demanding from him *sarhaed* (a compensation due from the wrongdoer in insult cases) for the breach of his honour. The dispute is settled by Arthur, who adjudicates that both conflicting parties should have an equal right to Esyllt, a right which shall be exercised by both men by spending a specific amount of time with the woman. In relation to the present survey, it is apparent that *Ystoria Drystan* is a repository of old tribal laws. No vestiges of Roman legal practices can be found therein (Heinz 2008: 89–127).

Similar observations can be made about another collection of Welsh literature *Pedair Cainc y Mabinogi* which was probably written down in the eleventh or twelfth centuries (Breeze 2009; Johnston 1994: 18). Although the stories that form the corpus known in short as the *Mabinogi* were not compiled in the Post-Roman period, they reflect upon early tribal laws. The discrepancies between Roman and Welsh law, as enshrined in the *Mabinogi*, pertain, in particular, to marriage and family law. In the *Mabinogi*, marriage is not proceeded by *sponsalia* – as was common in Rome. Rather, the marital union is consummated by sexual intercourse between the bride and the bridegroom in a private chamber after the wedding feast. Furthermore, no institution of Roman *patria potestas*, giving a man ultimate power over life and death of his dependants, is recorded in the *Mabinogi* either. As far as the laws relating to children are concerned, it is foster parenthood, alien to Roman law, that provides a framework of the Welsh familial relations (Davies 2007).[3]

---

2 There is very little poetry that can clearly be dated to the Post-Roman period. Watkin claims that *Y Gododdin* reflects minor aspects of Roman law (Watkin 2007: 38); however, this poetry has not been retained from before the thirteenth century (see S. Heinz, *Celtic Literatures – Discoveries*, 2007 and S. Asmus, "A Sketch of Major Developments in Early Insular Celtic Literatures." https://www.academia.edu/31876984/A_sketch_of_major_developments_in_early_Insular_Celtic_literatures._Braslun_o_hanes_cynnar_llenyddiaethau_Celteg_eu_hiaith. Accessed 10 July 2018.) Any analysis thereof would therefore require a separate research project.

3 Compare A. Breeze's discussion on Welsh law as reflected in the *Mabinogi* (Breeze 2009: 34–53).

The degree of the Romanisation of Welsh law can also be assessed on the basis of Welsh legal sources proper, such the *Surexit Memorandum* from the eighth century and *Cyfraith Hywel* from the tenth century. First and foremost, these sources feature a unique Welsh legal language terminology. Furthermore, the law which is contained in these texts encodes many old tribal principles that were not preserved in the manuscripts of neighbouring Scotland and England (Jenkins and Owen 1984: 91–120; Jenkins 1990). It is hard to disagree entirely, then, with the prominent Welsh historian J.E. Lloyd who, in his seminal book on Wales' history, wrote that "[...] the main ideas reflected in these codes [Welsh legal codifications] are the primitive and tribal, and it is, in particular, difficult to imagine any race which had gone through the mill of Roman jurisprudence retaining the blood-feud and the composition for manslaughter" (Lloyd 1911: 88).

Taking the archaeological, legal and literary data together, it appears that Romanisation affected only certain areas of British law and administration, which is proved by the similarities between particular legal concepts and procedures contained in the Roman legal codifications and the law of Hywel Dda. Definitely, there was no direct incorporation of Roman law by the Britons, nor an entire replacement of local customary laws and practices by the laws of the Roman conquerors. The Romans did not impose their laws on the conquered inhabitants of Britain by one legal act either. Quite the opposite, they allowed the British tribes to observe their own laws. However, some form of interaction between both legal cultures must have existed, which prompted a transfer of certain legal concepts and institutions into the customary law of the British society. Secondly, Roman law penetrated predominantly the south and east of Britain, the so-called lowland zone. The territories in the north and west, by contrast, suffered little degree of Romanisation. Last, but not least, Romanisation reached the most privileged classes of British society, to which belonged, without doubt, the free citizens of the province dwelling in big *civitates* and *villas* (Davies 2000: 101, 118–119).

The customary laws of the early inhabitants of Britain were greatly influenced by Christianity, which is vividly documented by the conformity of specific legal provisions constituting a Welsh medieval codification with the laws found in the Bible, canon legal texts and the *Saints' Lives* (Watkin 2006: 213–215). Christian elements in Welsh Hywelian codification include the following: a) the prohibition of such behaviour as adultery, polygamy, pre-marital sex, b) regarding virginity as a pre-condition of marriage, c) evoking God in legal declarations and while taking oaths, d) the exclusion of liability under the law of sanctuary, and e) the privileged legal position of the church and the clergy, e.g. the involvement of the clergy in the affairs of the secular court and everyday courtly routine, such as singing mass, blessing food, offering legal advice to the king, alongside the engagement of the clergy in the legal actions of private individuals, such as, *inter alia*, deathbed donations and affiliating the child (Jenkins 1990).

Many similarities can be recognised between certain laws recorded in Welsh legal texts and literature to those in the Bible. The first example worth mentioning is the common symbolism represented by the concepts of a beard, blood and an owl. Both in the Bible and Welsh law and literature, a beard connotes wisdom, authority, respect, dignity, truthfulness and masculinity. The Biblical prohibition of cutting off beards (Leviticus 19:27), as well as the injunction imposed on priests to wear beards as a manifestation of their holiness (Leviticus 21:5), may easily be compared to the requirement of Welsh law ordering judges to grow beards as a token of their dignity and wisdom (Jenkins 1990: 141–142). The Biblical scene of shaming and insulting David's servants by cutting off their beards by Hanun, the king of the Ammonites (2 Samuel 10:4–5), relates to the Welsh act of "shaming one's beard" reflected in Welsh law and the *Mabinogi* (Jenkins 1990: 52–53; Davies 2007: 34). The Bible, like Welsh law and literature, makes frequent references to animals. An illustration of equivalent animal symbolism in the Bible and Welsh legal and literary sources is the owl. The Bible allocates this animal to the category of the so-called "unclean beasts," creatures which, due to their corrupted natures, are not suitable for consumption (Leviticus 11:16). Furthermore, the owl is depicted as a wild predator bringing suffering and calamity to human beings (Job 31:29; Isaiah 13:21, 34:11). The negative symbolism of this bird is sustained in the *Mabinogi*.[4] In the fourth branch of the *Mabinogi*, Blodeuwedd, one of the major characters, is punished by Gwydion for adultery and aiding and abetting in the homicide of her husband, Llew, by being transformed into an owl (Davies 2007: 63). One more instance of the Biblical symbolism alluded to in Welsh law is the symbol of blood, to be more precise, the polluting effect the blood has on the land onto which it is poured (Numbers 35:33). According to Welsh laws concerning the value of the human body, likewise, one of the so-called "three stays of blood" included blood which contaminated the earth (Jenkins 1990: 197). Also, land forfeited to redeem a relative found guilty of homicide from death was called "blood-land" (Jenkins 1990: 111).

The next example which might indicate that the redactors of Welsh law and literature used the Bible as an inspiration for formulating their legal

4 The development of the motif of the owl in Welsh literature has been fully explained by Heinz (2007) and by Asmus and Degórska (2013).

provisions is using God as a surety in contractual obligations, placing oaths and reaching agreements. The scene from the Bible in which Laban and Jacob make a covenant by referring to God as a witness (Genesis 31:44–55) corresponds to the scene from the *Mabinogi*, in which Manawydan promises Cigfa fealty and friendship, calling on God as a guarantor of his words (Davies 2007: 40). The regulations stipulating that the guilt of the individual constituted a major determinant of his or her liability overlap in the Bible and Welsh law as well. By way of illustration, the legal provision of the law of Hywel Dda placing the liability for the burning of a house on the man who laid the fire is equivalent to the analogous provision in the Bible (Exodus 22:6; Jenkins 1990: 169–171). There also exists a striking resemblance between the Biblical approach to a woman's servile position in marriage with certain laws stipulated in Hywel Dda's codification and the *Mabinogi*, e.g. examining a maiden's virginity (Deuteronomy 22:13–30; Jenkins 1990: 49) and the eviction of a woman from the marital house by her husband after he has repudiated her (Deuteronomy 24:1–4; Jenkins 1990: 47). Finally, under Biblical and Hywelian law, perpetrators were offered protection from liability if they found shelter in places designated as God's sanctuaries (Exodus 21:1–13; Jenkins 1990: 81–83).

Another carrier and conduit of legal influences in the post-Roman period was Ireland. The Welsh and Irish affinity pertained, in general, to the Irish settlement in Wales, political, economic and cultural cooperation, common proprietary interests and Welsh/Irish intermarriage (Jankulak and Wooding 2007). To start with, the Irish contributed to the formation and development of such kingdoms of Wales as Dyfed, Gwynedd and Brycheiniog. According to pseudo-Nennius, a certain Cunedda expelled the Irish from Gwynedd and established his own dynasty thereon around the fifth century (Giles 2007: 9). Reciprocal contacts were also fostered by British/Welsh and Irish trade and commerce, which flourished in the Roman period. Another form of Welsh and Irish cooperation was the exchange of missionaries, monks and poets. Many prominent Welsh rulers maintained strong connections with the Irish court, as was the case with Gruffudd ap Cynan, whose long and complicated road to power in Gwynedd is described in *Historia Gruffud vab Kenan* (c. 1160). It emerges from this piece of literature that Gruffudd ap Cynan was born in Dublin, where he received his early education learning Irish manners. In the moments of domestic strife when he was pursued by his enemies in Wales, he always found shelter in Ireland (Jones 1910). A conjunction between Ireland and Britain is highlighted in the *Mabinogi*. In the second branch, the king of Ireland travels to the court of Bendigeidfran, the ruler of Britain, to ask him for his sister's, Branwen's, hand.

Once the marriage is solemnised, the newly-wed couple sail back to Ireland where the rest of the action of the story takes place.

The period of the late eighth and ninth centuries saw the infiltration of Scandinavian culture into England, Ireland and Scotland because of the Viking raids on these lands. The presence of the Scandinavians in Wales was, nonetheless, less pronounced, marked solely by the pillaging of Welsh territories, murdering of people and the destruction of monasteries and churches, such as St David's and Llannbadarn Fawr. Scholars agree that these contacts did not leave a permanent trace on the culture, language and law of Wales (Davies 2000: 219).

2.2 The Period since the Codification of Law in the Mid-tenth Century until the Edwardian Conquest of Wales in 1283

The most important date in the legal history of Wales was the codification of law by the king of Deheubarth, Hywel Dda (c. 880–949/950), somewhere in the middle of the tenth century. The codification embraced revised British customary laws and practices and some Roman, Irish, Anglo-Saxon, Biblical and Canon laws. In historical and legal literature, the Welsh legal system is called a *Volksrecht* system of law, a law based on customs as opposed to the laws promulgated by the ruler and secured through penal sanctions. The law was a living instrument adaptable to the volatile social and political environment, not an amalgam of fossilised, impractical customs and legal archaisms. It was law intended for lawyers to be applied to cases which they handled in their everyday legal practice (Roberts 2008: 85–86). Some Welsh lawyers' opinions concerning the interpretation of specific legal provisions were inserted into the passages of the law, for example those of Goronwy ap Moriddig (Jenkins 1990: 48), and Iorwerth ap Madog ap Rhawd (Jenkins 1990: 190). The laws of Hywel Dda were amended in the subsequent years. The names of reformers are also mentioned in the legal manuscripts, for example Bleddyn ap Cynfyn, the ruler of Powys (Jenkins 1990: 98–99, 165), and Rhys ap Gruffudd of Deheubarth (Jenkins 1990: 164).

The supposed codification of law by Hywel Dda has been contested in some historical and legal literature. Among the most frequently raised questions relating to the law of Hywel Dda, the following seem to prevail: Was Hywel Dda the first codifier of Welsh law? Did the codification of laws at the gathering convened by Hywel Dda in Whitland in the tenth century really happen? And finally, what was the bearing, if any, of the laws of Wessex promulgated by Alfred the Great on the Hywelian codification? (e.g. Pryce 2000: 39–63; Roberts 2008: 85–86). When attempting to address all these queries, it is necessary to point to the relevant legal, historical and literary data.

As far as the first point is concerned, legal and literary texts mention the figure of Dyfnwal Moelmud, a ruler of Britain who reportedly established Britain's laws for the first time. Pursuant to one of the passages from the law of Hywel Dda, the laws of Dyfnwal Moelmud had been in force in Britain until Hywel Dda abolished them in favour of his own codification. The only regulation that allegedly survived from the period when the laws of Dyfnwal Moelmud were binding was the measurement of lands. No further information is given as to the content, origin or events surrounding the enactment of Dyfnwal Moelmud's laws (Jenkins 1990: 120). Dyfnwal Moelmud's legislation is also referred to by Geoffrey of Monmouth in *Historia Regum Britanniae* (1136). In *Historia Regum Britanniae*, Dyfnwal Moelmud figures as the king of Britain who enforced the laws of sanctuary rights (Thorpe 1966: 89–90). Against the background of the eleventh- and thirteenth-century Anglo-Norman and Welsh discord over the supremacy over the Isles, it also seems very likely that Dyfnwal Moelmud's codification was the product of Welsh lawyers created to resist the Anglo-Norman imperial claims. In this sense, Dyfnwal Moelmud resembles other pseudo-historical figures, such as Brutus, the supposed founder of Britain and its first lawgiver, and Kenneth MacAlpin, the reputed progenitor of the kingdom of the Scots and alleged codifier of Macalpine laws from which Scottish laws developed.

Moving on to the second issue, which is the precise dating of the Hywel Dda's law, many historians assume that it might have been formulated in the later period, approximately in the twelfth and thirteenth centuries, when the Welsh-Anglo-Norman conflict escalated (e.g. Pryce 2000: 39–63; Roberts 2008: 85–86). This supposition finds confirmation in the following textual features of the law: a) the highlighting of the special role of the Church and Papacy in the revision and legitimisation of Welsh customary laws to counter the Anglo-Normans' allegations of preserving pagan laws, b) the emphasis of the dominant position and special status of Gwynedd in Wales to secure the interests of the Principality of Wales, c) the allusions to mythology and the ancient past to forge the image of the Welsh people as the continuators of the British legal heritage.

Hywel Dda's codification is often compared to the laws of the king of Wessex, Alfred the Great, which were enacted somewhere between 880 and 890. The similarities between Welsh and Wessex laws are visible, in the first place, in the preambles to these laws. The preambles in both collections of law explain how customary laws were revised by a special commission comprising both distinguished lawyers and clergymen during a special gathering. More parallels concern a compensatory method of dispute resolution, which was represented by *wergild* in Wessex law and *sarhaed* and *galanas* in Welsh law, as well as equivalent provisions on sanctuary rights, liability for negligent conduct resulting in damage or harm, owner's liability for animals, and penalties for injuries to various body parts (Keynes and Lapidge 1983: 163–170; Jenkins 1990). Scholars have also identified specific legal concepts in Welsh legal manuscripts which, in their opinions, testify to the borrowing of some laws enacted by Alfred the Great and another king of Wessex, Athelstan, by Welsh lawyers. The most often mentioned instance of Anglo-Saxon borrowings is the legal concept of *edling* designating an heir apparent nominated from the king's sons or nephews in the Welsh legal language, which allegedly originated from the Anglo-Saxon *aetheling* (Jenkins 2005: 26–27; Roberts 2008: 89–90). The view holding that Hywel Dda emulated the kings wielding power in Wessex while drafting his own legal codification is anchored in the historical facts, particularly the frequent visits of the Welsh ruler to Wessex. Also, in many historical works, Alfred the Great is given as an example of an eminent jurist and governor, who was an inspiration for other rulers of his time, including Hywel Dda, the alleged admirer of his Wessex counterpart. Geoffrey of Monmouth, for instance, claimed that Alfred the Great launched a project of translating ancient laws promulgated by British rulers into the English language (Thorpe 1966: 93–94). However, the conjecture of a transfer of certain Welsh laws into Alfred the Great's codification cannot be eliminated. There seems to be no better argument substantiating the hypothesis of the Welsh impact on Alfred the Great's court than the presence of Asser, a Welsh monk of St David's, at Alfred the Great's court. Asser is believed to be the writer of Alfred the Great's biography, *Life of King Alfred*, written in approximately 893. If we trust this source, Asser, as Alfred the Great's adviser, contributed to shaping Wessex law (Keynes and Lapidge 1983: 65–110).

The development of the Welsh legal system was interrupted by the invasion of the Isles by the Normans in the eleventh century. Having accommodated themselves in England, the Normans embarked on the reformation of Germanic tribal laws. In the long term, the Anglo-Norman legal activity in the occupied England led to the formation of the common law, the creation of which was also significant for Wales. Firstly, it deepened the abyss between the tribal, pastoral Wales and the Anglo-Norman, feudal England. Secondly, it boosted the vehement anti-Welsh hate rhetoric which reached its climax during the Edwardian wars of 1276–1277 and 1282–1283. During the Welsh Wars of Independence fought with the English army commanded by Edward I, Welsh "primitive" law was incessantly juxtaposed with the English "sophisticated" common law (Williams 1991: 85).

The Norman expeditions into Wales led to the emergence of the legal and political entity along the border of Wales and England called the March (from

French *marche* denoting a border) controlled by the lords. Wales was divided into two opposing legal and cultural centres called *Pura Wallia* where Welsh law was binding and *Marchia Walliae* where the laws laid down by the Marcher lords prevailed (Roberts 2008: 92–93; Watkin 2006: 217; Watkin 2007: 81).

Strong as the Welsh resistance to the Norman invasion and intrusion was, it did not prevent certain Norman laws and practices from affecting Welsh laws. The legal reforms of the eleventh and twelfth centuries, such as the feudalisation of property law or attempts to circumscribe some institutions of native law, were often perceived of as methods of alleviating the position of a prince at the cost of individual freedoms and privileges. Social anti-Anglo-Norman sentiments were given voice in poetry, the best examples being *The Privileges of the Men of Powys* and *The Privileges of the Men of Arfon*. Both sources express the protest of the *uchelwyr* against newly imposed laws, such as women's rights to inherit property, the prince's entitlement to a third of plunder, the prohibition of fishing without the lord's permission, the obligation to quern in the lord's mill, the duty to offer hospitality to the lord and his companions when they were on the circuit, and vesting administration in the officers of *rhingyll* or the *serjeant* (Charles-Edwards and Jones 2000: 191–223; Owen 2000: 224–254).

The formal recognition of the Welsh Principality under the Treaty of Montgomery signed by Henry III in 1267 ushered in legal reforms in Gwynedd. The changes included the extension of the princely power, the replacement of *galanas* (blood-fine) by the criminal procedure of determining guilt by a jury, the introduction of new officers of *rhaglaw* (the equivalent of the English bailiff) and *rhingyll* (the equivalent of the English sheriff), and trial by inquisition (Jones-Pierce [1963] 1972: 376–379; Pryce 2000: 55–56; Williams 1991: 73–75). The legal reforms implemented by the princes of Gwynedd might be a telling sign of the development of Welsh criminal law and, by implication, the emerging differentiation between private and public law (Jones-Pierce [1963] 1972: 377).

The fall of the Welsh after the Second War of Independence in 1282–1283 gave Edward I carte blanche to impose some English laws in the occupied Principality of Wales under the Statute of Rhuddlan of 1284. This document envisaged the following legal vicissitudes in Wales: a) the introduction of English administration based on shires, b) placing the execution of justice in the offices of the sheriff, coroner and bailiff, c) the imposition of English criminal law, d) depriving illegitimate heirs of inheritance, e) the establishment of writs, such as the writ of novel disseisin and mort d'ancestor, as major instruments of instigating legal proceedings and enforcing one's rights, f) equipping women with dower rights (Davies 2000: 317; Watkin 2007: 106–113).

2.3 The Post-conquest Period since 1283/1284 until 1536 and 1543

The period after the conquest of the Principality of Wales in 1283 witnessed further legal repercussions against the Welsh people, among which there were the confiscation of lands and properties, the eviction of people from their homes, and the exploitation of Welsh laws. Although the Statute of Rhuddlan of 1284 was enforced only in the Principality of Wales, and, theoretically, Welsh law was still enforceable in the lands beyond this region, the native laws of Wales were slowly losing their premier status (Williams 1991: 91).

Owain Glyndŵr's uprising was yet another pretext for the English to introduce new laws that punished the Welsh for their acts of insubordination and used to prevent more resistance in the future. In 1402, the Penal Laws against Wales were enacted. The laws forbade the Welsh from bearing arms, purchasing properties in England, building and possessing castles, and sentencing Englishmen in Wales. They also restricted them from holding public offices such as justice, sheriff, coroner and steward. The Penal Laws concerned also the Welsh language by limiting the education of Welsh children through the medium of their native language (Watkin 2007: 116–119).

The final, culminating dates putting a formal end to the evolution of Welsh law were 1536 and 1543, when the Acts of Union were enacted by the English parliament under the reign of the English King Henry VIII. Pursuant to these acts, Wales was incorporated into the Kingdom of England and adopted English common law in its entirety. Welsh ceased to be the language of the law and the court. The document also abolished the Marcher law (Watkin 2006: 218; Watkin 2007: 124–134).

3 Final Comments

As has been demonstrated above, in the long course of its evolution Welsh law came into contact with various cultures that left some imprint on specific legal provisions. In the earliest phase of Welsh legal development, the customary laws of the British inhabitants were subject to some impact of Roman law. The period of the Roman occupation of Britain might thus have affected certain aspects of British customary law, which might be indicated by the similarities of some legal provisions codified in the law of Hywel Dda to Roman law. The evidence from literary sources, particularly prose tales, does not, however, explicitly testify to the considerable Romanisation of Welsh law. Welsh vernacular literature reflects tribal customary laws rather than the laws and practices of the Roman invaders. It might be concluded, then, that the Romanisation of Welsh law was subtle, limited only to certain areas of law. A much more substantial influence on Welsh laws was exerted by Christianity. Based on legal and literary texts it emerges that Christian ideas penetrated all fields of law and the primary source of the Christian faith, the Bible, was an influential source of law. Close political, economic and cultural connections between Wales and Ireland in the post-Roman period should be considered as well in the legal development of Wales. Although different in many respects, Irish and Welsh laws shared a great number of similarities which might result from the same Celtic legal background, as some scholars would assert, as well as the interaction of Irish and Welsh cultures. Some analogies between Welsh legal provisions and those in the codes of Alfred the Great might suggest some form of interrelationship between Welsh and Anglo-Saxon law as well. In contrast to Scotland and England, there was no importation of Scandinavian laws into Wales and, consequently, legal and administrative institutions of Scandinavian origin did not replace Welsh tribal structures. In the Anglo-Norman period of the twelfth and thirteenth centuries, Welsh law underwent politically induced reforms which were necessary to maintain the status quo of the Principality of Wales. The long-term development of Welsh law was interrupted by Edward I in the years of 1267–1284 after the military occupation of the Principality and the imposition of English law and administration on the dominated areas. The Edwardian policy of destroying Welsh law was finalised by the Acts of Union of 1536 and 1543.

The study undertaken in the present survey has also demonstrated that Welsh law was not an archaic, primitive bundle of tribal laws unsuitable to the social realia, but a comprehensive and flexible legal system constituting a fusion of various elements, receptive to outside influence. Welsh law evolved over the analysed period, absorbing new legal concepts, retaining, at the same time, those that were still practical, effective and commensurate to the needs of the society.

Bibliography

Primary Sources:

Biblia. *Pismo Święte Starego i Nowego Testamentu*. Nowy Przekład z Języków Hebrajskiego i Greckiego Opracowany przez Komisję Przekładu Pisma Świętego. Warszawa: Brytyjskie i Zagraniczne Towarzystwo Biblijne, 1990.

Davies, S. Trans. *The Mabinogion*. Oxford: Oxford University Press, 2007.

Jenkins, D. Ed. and trans. *The Law of Hywel Dda: Law Texts from Medieval Wales*. Llandysul: Gomer Press, 1990.

Jones, A. Ed. and trans. *The History of Gruffydd ap Cynan. The Welsh Text with Translation, Introduction, and Notes*. Manchester: University Press, 1910.

Keynes, S. and M. Lapidge. Eds. and trans. *Alfred the Great. Asser's Life of King Alfred and Other Contemporary Sources*. Harmondsworth: Penguin Books, 1983.

Giles, J. A. Trans. Nennius. *History of the Britons (Historia Brittonum)*. Dodo Press, s. n., 2007.

Thorpe, L. Trans. Geoffrey of Monmouth. *The History of the Kings of Britain*. Harmondsworth: Penguin, 1966.

Williams, H. Ed. and trans. Gildas. *De excidio Britanniae; or, The Ruin of Britain*. Edited for the Honourable Society of Cymmrodorion, 1899, reprinted by Dodo Press, s. n., 2010.

Secondary Sources:

Asmus, Sabine. "A Sketch of Major Developments in Early Insular Celtic Literatures." https://www.academia.edu/31876984/A_sketch_of_major_developments_in_early_Insular_Celtic_literatures._Braslun_o_hanes_cynnar_llenyddiaethau_Celteg_eu_hiaith. (10 July 2018).

Asmus, Sabine and Malwina Degórska. "Pozytywne i negatywne aspekty motywu sowy." In: *U źródeł fantasy: postaci i motywy z literatury niemieckiej w relacjach interkulturowych*, eds. E. Kamińska and E. Hendryk. Szczecin: Przedsiębiorstwo Produkcyjno-Handlowe Zapol, 2013, pp. 211–226.

Breeze, Andrew. *The Origins of the Four Branches of the Mabinogi*. Leominster: Gracewing, 2009.

Charles-Edwards, T.M. and Nerys Ann Jones. "Breintiau Gŵr Powys: The Liberties of the Men of Powys." In: *The Welsh King and His Court*, eds. T. M. Charles-Edwards, M. E. Owen and P. Russell. Cardiff: University of Wales Press, 2000, pp. 191–223.

Davies, Norman. *The Isles: A History*. London: Papermac, 2000.

Heinz, Sabine. *Celtic Literatures – Discoveries*. Frankfurt am Main: Peter Lang, 2007.

Heinz, Sabine. "Textual and Historical Evidence for an Early British Tristan Tradition." *Proceedings of the Harvard Celtic Colloquium*, Vol. 28, 2008, pp. 89–127.

Jankulak, Karen and Jonathan M. Wooding, eds. *Ireland and Wales in the Middle Ages*. Dublin: Four Courts Press, 2007.

Jenkins, Dafydd. "Borrowings in the Welsh Lawbooks." In: *Adventures of the Law. Proceeding of the Sixteenth British Legal History Conference, Dublin, 2003*, eds. P. Brand, K. Costello and W. N. Osborough. Dublin: Four Courts Press in Association with the Irish Legal History Society, 2005, pp. 19–39.

Jenkins, Dafydd and Morfydd E. Owen. "The Welsh Marginalia in the Lichfield Gospels Part II: The 'Surexit' Memorandum." *Cambridge Medieval Celtic Studies*, Vol. 7, 1984, pp. 91–120.

Johnston, Dafydd. *A Pocket Guide: The Literature of Wales*. Cardiff: University of Wales Press, 1994.

Jones-Pierce, Thomas. "The Law of Wales – The Last Phase." In: *Medieval Welsh Society: Selected Essays by T. Jones Pierce*, ed. J. Beverley Smith. Cardiff: University of Wales Press, 1972, pp. 369–389 [1963].

Kelly, Fergus. *A Guide to Early Irish Law*. Dublin: School of Celtic Studies, 2016.

Korporowicz, Łukasz Jan. "Roman Law in Roman Britain: An Introductory Survey." *The Journal of Legal History*, Vol. 33, 2012, pp. 133–150.

Lloyd, John Edward. *A History of Wales from the Earliest Times to the Edwardian Conquest*. 2 vols. London, New York: Longmans, Green, and Co., 1911.

Owen, Morfydd E. "Royal Propaganda: Stories from the Law-Texts." In: *The Welsh King and His Court*, eds. T. M. Charles-Edwards, M. E. Owen and P. Russell. Cardiff: University of Wales Press, 2000, pp. 224–254.

Pryce, Huw. "The Context and Purpose of the Earliest Welsh Lawbooks." *Cambrian Medieval Celtic Studies*, Vol. 39, 2000, pp. 39–63.

Roberts, Sara Elin. "By the Authority of the Devil: The Operation of Welsh and English Law in Medieval Wales." In: *Authority and Subjugation in Writing of Medieval Wales*, eds. R. Kennedy and S. Meecham-Jones. London: Palgrave Macmillan, 2008, pp. 85–97.

Stacey, Robin Chapman. *The Road to Judgment. From Custom to Court in Medieval Ireland and Wales*. Philadelphia: University of Pennsylvania Press, 1994.

Watkin, Thomas Glyn. "The Death and Later Life of Legal Symbols: Welsh Legal Symbols after the Union with England." In: *Symbolische Kommunikation vor Gericht in der Frühen Neuzeit*, ed. R. Schulze. Berlin: Duncker and Humblot, 2006, pp. 213–224.

Watkin, Thomas Glyn. *The Legal History of Wales*. Cardiff: University of Wales Press, 2007.

Williams, Gwyn. *When was Wales? A History of the Welsh*. London: Penguin Books, 1991.

Aleksandra Kędzierska

The Great Wars of Francis Ledwidge (1887–1917)

And a voice in the distance calls
"Come," and "Come..."
("The Song Time is Over")

Abstract: Irish war poet Francis Ledwidge (1887–1917) is a somewhat neglected figure. Despite being a supporter of the Irish Nationalist cause, Ledwidge fought under British Army command in Gallipoli and the Balkans and on the Western Front. He has been described as one of the most important Irish poets of the 20th century but at the same time remains virtually unknown to wider readership. By analysing a selection of poems representative of the three fronts on which Ledwidge fought, the paper demonstrates the universal dimension of his work, thereby confirming his position as one of the leading poets in modern Irish literature.

Keywords: Francis Ledwidge, war poetry, Irish literature, World War I

1 Introduction

The historical significance of the First World War is taken for granted in most European countries; however, as noted by Charles Townshend, in Ireland, "the memory of the war was for a long time marginalised. A kind of collective amnesia discarded it as a British experience, dwarfed by an event that was, in physical comparison with the titanic battles on the western and eastern fronts, tiny" (Townshend 1999: 68). "It was the Easter Rising, not the Great War," Victoria Crossman argues, "that was seen as the watershed in Irish history, responsible for rousing nationalist public opinion from its apparent torpor and revitalising separatist republicanism" (Crossman 2001). For most of the twentieth century, Ireland "effectively expunged from public memory" (Haughey 2002: 61) the soldiers whom she considered traitors for their having joined up with the British Forces to fight against the Germans.

One such forgotten hero, described by Seamus Heaney as "our dead enigma" in which all strains of Irishness "criss-cross in useless equilibrium" (Heaney

1979: 3) is Francis Ledwidge, who was missed by the literary canon-makers but who was one of the most tragic Irish soldier poets of the years 1915–1917. Although he was a supporter of the Irish Nationalist cause and the aspirations of those involved in the 1916 Easter Rising, he fought under British Army command and was involved in many campaigns in Gallipoli, the Balkans and, finally, the Western Front.

Although a century has passed since Ledwidge's demise, only one biography of the poet (Curtayne 1972), together with a handful of usually short critical, often biographical essays, either Introductions or Afterwards, written by, among others, Seamus Heaney (1979), Terence Brown (2010), Fran Brearton (2012), Liam O'Meara (1997, 2006, 2013), and Dermott Bolger (2007),[1] have mercifully saved Ledwidge from oblivion and have shed light on the extent of the academic under-appreciation his work has suffered. The situation has changed thanks to an acclaimed book by Miriam O'Gara-Kilmurry (*Éire's WWI War Poet*, 2013) which, responding to the canonical neglect of Ledwidge's poetry, did much to "start the campaign for Ledwidge to be reclaimed by modern Ireland as Éire's WWI War Poet."

Born in Slane, County Meath, Ledwidge came from a poor, rural background, which allowed only for a basic education, yet due to the patronage, literary and financial, of Lord Dunsany, who realised Frank's promise, Ledwidge was brought into contact with William Butler Yeats, Katharine Tynan and Thomas McDonagh (Curtayne 1972: 48), and would have some poems published during his lifetime. The first volume, *Songs of the Fields*, ready in 1914, postponed by the outbreak of the war, finally appeared in 1916, with *Songs of Peace* following that same year. *Last Songs*, also collected by Dunsany, was issued posthumously in 1918 and "the three books, bound in one volume, were published as *Collected Poems* in 1919" (O'Meara 1997: n.p.). Not well known in the 1980s, by 2017, the year marking the centenary of his death, he was nationally acknowledged and commemorated as Ireland's celebrity. Numerous concerts, poetry festivals, academic events popularising his works, TV and radio broadcasts, the unveiling of monuments and statues, and, perhaps, most importantly, the reissuing of his works – all of these have made Ireland's neglected son Ireland's very own.

1 Other important contributors to Ledwidge criticism include Keith Jeffery (2000), Nuala Johnson (2003), Jon Stallworthy (2005), Ian Kennedy (2007), Marguerite Helmers (2012), Thomas Barrett Ward (2012), and Arthur Russell (2013).

2 Francis Ledwidge and His Wars

Having enlisted in 1914, Ledwidge was both a soldier and a witness in the war to end all wars, its greatness measured by its political impact and territorial scope, yet, above all, by human losses and the devastation it caused the world over. In defending "our civilization," Ledwidge saw a way to dedicate himself to a struggle much closer to his heart, that for an independent Ireland, for which, his pre-war activism notwithstanding, he could otherwise fight mainly through his poetry. Last but not least, there was his battle to preserve – in poetry – the beauty of the world in the midst of infernal horrors, the sight of which "must have made the soul of Dante envious" (Curtayne 1972: 142). In its attempt to familiarise the reader with some of the most famous "war poems" by Francis Ledwidge, this essay, which demonstrates his "art of indirectness" (O'Connor 2015), will focus on his determination not to allow the plight of the trench world to master the poet in him, and on the effort to get the better of the war by fighting its destructive potential with love and hope.

3 The Specificity of Ledwidge's Treatment of War

Ledwidge's unwillingness to make the horrors of the Great War a dominant theme of his works reveals itself in his avoidance of the direct treatment of it. Out of one hundred and eighty poems he penned during the three years of his soldiering, merely thirty contain some clear, however scarce – sometimes just one word – reference to the conflict. Most often the clues are provided by the titles: "In the Mediterranean – Going to War", "The Irish in Gallipoli", "War", "Serbia", "The Cobbler of Sari Gueul", "In France", "The Dead Kings", "Ascension Thursday 1917", "A Soldier's Grave", "To a German Officer", or "Autumn Evening in Serbia." Yet even the poems they thus "advertise" hardly ever portray No Man's Land. A few works feature location-specific details, referring, for instance, to a war zone café ("In a Café"), "Allah", "oriental Spring" and "distant sands" ("Wander Song"), "the Turkish shores" and the Vardar river ("At Currabwee"), the lake of Doiran ("Serbia"), or some military situation, such as crossing the wide seas while going to war ("Una Bawn", "Jim West"). However, due to the specificity of the poet's persona, content to imaginatively "walk the old frequented ways" (Smyth), he recreates his beloved home wherever he turns, thus effectively erasing the war or pushing it aside.

> Whatever way I turn I find
> The path is old unto me still.

> The hills of home are in my mind,
> And there I wander as I will.[2]

Thus, quite frequently (and paradoxically), Gallipoli, Serbia, Belgium and France emerge as battlefields dominated by the Irish Front, the central theatre of Ledwidge's war, which is also reflected in his many poems that are primarily focused on Ireland, including, for instance, "The Dead Kings", "The Lanawn Shee", "The Blackbirds" and, most famously, "Thomas McDonagh." By exploring Irish history (the Battle of the Boyne, the Easter Rising 1916) and myths in these works, the "singer of Erin" (O'Connor 2017), determined to save its heritage and its people, chronicles "the beauty of his birthplace" (Smyth).

This interconnectedness of purpose was already evident behind the reasons for Ledwidge's controversial decision to enlist, which he divulged in his letter to Prof. Lewis Chase:

> Some of the people who know me least imagine that I joined the Army because I knew men were struggling for higher ideals and greater empires, and I could not sit idle to watch them make for me a more beautiful world. They are mistaken. I joined the British Army because she stood between Ireland and the enemy common to our civilization, and I would not have her say that she defended us while we did nothing at home but pass resolutions. I am sorry that Party politics should ever divide our own tents but am not without hope that a new Ireland will arise from her ashes in the ruins of Dublin, like the Phoenix, with one purpose, one aim and one ambition. I tell you this in order that you may know what it is to me to be called a British soldier, while my own country has no place amongst the nations but the place of Cinderella. (Curtayne 1972: 84)

4 Soldiering

One of the Inniskillin Fusiliers, he served in the 10th Division, "the first Irish Division that ever existed in the British Army" (Jeffery 2000: 41). Unable to ignore "the wail of [Ireland's] wild despair," if only because these desperate pleas had been falling on so many deaf ears, Ledwidge, "the slave of the calls" ("Morning in January"; CP 132), was doomed to go to war. Hence, when he heard the voice "come…come" ("Song-Time is Over") calling to him from the distance, he could only "arise and go" ("The Call" CP 134).

Having survived the Gallipoli and Dardanelles campaigns (July-October 1915), in the winter of 1915 Ledwidge served on the Greco-Serbian/Balkan front

---

2 *Francis Ledwidge. The Complete Poems*, ed. Liam O'Meara (1997: 232). Unless otherwise stated, all my citations refer to this edition, abbreviated as CP, with page number provided in brackets.

(winter 1915). Invalided out with a severe back injury, he was hospitalised first in Cairo and then in Manchester, where he finally learnt the tragic fate of the Easter Rising and the executions of its leaders. This drama, which was also a personal one, stimulated his talent to produce some of his best works, including the lament for his friend, Thomas McDonagh. After a short leave home, he found himself stationed at Ebrington Barracks in Derry from which his regiment left for the Western Front to take part in the Third Battle of Ypres. From January to June 26 1917 (Baxter) he served in France and later in Belgium, where he was killed by a stray shell while in reserve, building a road in Pilkem Boezinghe some days before his thirtieth birthday.

5 Harnessing the Horrors of the War

Three years in the "Gethsemane" of the war ("Ascension Thursday 1917") familiarised the poet with its many hells: literally suffering from homesickness,[3] living on starvation rations and quietly freezing in Serbia, almost drowning in rivers of Flanders' mud, being haunted by the scarred landscape, the screaming of the wounded and the moans of the dying. And yet, taking these horrors in his stride, Ledwidge was able to see through them, as it were, and drink in the unique beauty his soul could still sense was there to be discovered. One of his letters to Tynan reads:

> We have just returned from the line after an unusually long time. It was very exciting this time, as we had to contend with gas, lachrymatory shells, and other devices new and horrible. It will be worse soon. The camp we are in at present might be in Tir-na-n'Og, it is pitched amid such splendours. There is barley and rye just entering harvest days of gold, and meadow-sweet rippling, and where a little inn […] holds its gable up to the swallows, bluebells and goldilocks swing their splendid censers. There is a wood hard by where hips glisten like little sparks, and just at the edge of it mealey leaves sway like green fire. I will hunt for a secret place in that wood to read […] I anticipate beautiful moments. […] It is midnight now and the glow-worms are out. It is quiet in camp but the far night is loud with our guns bombarding the positions we must soon fight for. (Curtayne 1972: 185–6)

3 In one of his letters to Katharine Tynan, Ledwidge wrote: "You have no idea of how I suffer with this longing for the swish of the reeds at Slane and the voices I used to hear coming over the low hills of Currabwee" (qtd. in Russell). According to Terence Brown, the prevalence of homesickness as a theme in Ledwidge's poetry is symptomatic of the suffering within his psychological life (Brown 2010: 76).

Arranging to meet Edward Marsh, he encouraged the critic

> to come up the [front] line at night to watch the German rockets. They have white crests which throw a pale flame across no-man's-land and white bursting into green and green changing into blue and blue bursting and dropping down in purple torrents. It is like the end of a beautiful world! (Curtayne 1972: 184)

This strategy of suppressing the horrors of war proved even more effective in poetry, when, for instance, writing from France in 1917, instead of registering the plight of the soldiers Ledwidge creates what can be perceived as a trench-world paradise. In an almost Wordsworthian manner, the poem captures an epiphany: a perfect spot in time in which man can feel at one with the world. Offering delights of fragrance and colour, the glories of spring ("Spring") "surprise the valleys" with the energy of life enhanced by the voices of the river and the "rainbow" of the kingfishers in flight. Nevertheless, the poem's closing lines make clear that the picture of peace wrapping "all those hills of mine" is but a mental photograph of his homeland, imposed on the reality of the war. Briefly evoked by the "noisy brink," the war can be instantly stopped, shelved away to "my dearest memory" where peace rules unthreatened ("Spring" CP 241).

6 The Realism of War

A rare case of trench world realism can be found in Ledwidge's "Jim West" (first published in Cairo, 1915), which, with its catalogue of tropes, represents the most conventional of his Great War poems. The narrative of Thomas, a survivor with an ear for soldier's slang, concentrates on the experience of two rivals for the heart of Julia McKay – rivals who, driven by a sense of adventure and patriotic sentiment, find themselves "fighting the Turk" (CP 163).

The man describes the hardships of soldiering – it "isn't an easy job" – enumerating such trench routines as tiring drillings and fencing the ditches but also the thrill of the bayonet charge. He also speaks about the danger of getting entangled in barbed wire, a hazard eliminated by the heroic action of Jim West, who sacrifices his life to save his severely wounded rival.

7 The Greco-Serbian Front

Along with his insight into the brotherhood-in-arms – emphasising the positive side of the conflict – and a lesson on "how to die," (CP 165), Ledwidge demonstrates how best to live. This can be found in "The Cobbler in Sari Gueul," a quaint and beautiful Serbian town whose heart beats in the shoemaker's repair shop. Like a king ruling his kingdom from his three-legged stool, the old man, "hammering leather all the day," epitomises the joy and love for the children who noisily play around him. The poet would gladly trade his art for some of the cobbler's contentment and his gift to celebrate life despite its dramas of poverty and war, whose only reminders in the poem are the exotic strangeness of the place and the hammering, evocative of artillery thundering in No Man's Land.

Incidentally, the same respect for humanness and humanity permeates the only poem by Ledwidge about a German officer. Never resorting to scorn or invective (where many would call the enemy "Boche" or "Hun"), his epitaph, demonstrating "an awareness of the common brotherhood of the battlefield" (Phillips 2008: 398), stresses the nobility of the man who "died a true gentleman" (CP 255). He would surely find peace in the trench-world heaven, a "dug-out made of gold" (CP 255), where, regardless of nationality, the brave men of noble souls will rest, ultimately united in death.

8 Meditations on the War Itself

Apart from poems capturing different aspects of the human experience of the war, some offer meditations concerning its origin and character, and even uniquely allow war to speak for itself. In "War," the Ledwidge persona, a mouthpiece for war itself, and hence an expert in its ways, brings forth such of its attributes as darkness, wind, and thunder, all mothered by a storm. Classified thus as a phenomenon of nature, war is further neutralised by the humanising reference to family. Most importantly, however, it emerges as even more complex due to the feelings it is invested with: not only does it know pride, love and hate, with "the terrible mind/of vicious gods" (CP 209), but the war also acquires a divine status, while its epic potential constitutes additional guarantee of its indestructibility.

According to Ledwidge, war is caused by the disappearance of Love and Beauty. When these wander away "at the end of the world's untruth," the young are forced to prove their hearts in the ordeal of the trench world ("When Love and Beauty" CP 155). Interestingly, even as late as 1917, the poet still believed in the righteous cause of the war, a conviction articulated in "The Irish in Gallipoli," where the speaker argues his case as follows:

> [...]
> Neither for lust of glory nor new throne
> This thunder and this lightning of our wrath
> Waken these frantic echoes, not for these
> Our cross with England's mingle, to be blown
> On Mammon's threshold; we but war when war
> Serves Liberty and Justice, Love and Peace.

> Who said that such an emprise could be vain?
> Were they not one with Christ Who strove and died?
> Let Ireland weep but not for sorrow. Weep
> That by her sons a land is sanctified
> For Christ Arisen, and angels once again
> Come back like exile birds to guard their sleep. (CP 240)

9 The Interconnectedness of the Fronts (Turkish and Irish)

The poem above well exemplifies the interconnectedness of Ledwidge's fronts. The Irish involvement in Turkey, well documented by the title, refers to a specific topographical and historico-political moment in time, yet simultaneously to the situation of martyrdom in which, for once, Britain and Ireland share the cross. More significantly still, comparing them to angels, "Ledwidge placed the [fallen] soldiers within the ranks of the Easter Rising leaders to whom a sense of martyrdom can thus be ascribed" (Romp 26). The work's opening, stressing the epic dimension of the war, captures the wild "threatening splendour" of the cliffs of the Aegean, their bristling menace suggestive, perhaps, of the dangers awaiting the soldiers after the landing, the plight additionally highlighted by the allusions to *The Illiad* and the Passion of Christ. In Gallipoli "old Silences are burst," and taking his chance to remind the reader of the Irish stake in the war, the poet expresses his hope that since Ireland bears her suffering with Christ, her "emprise" will not be "vain" and she will have her share in His resurrection. In the meantime, facing the unknown, the soldier pleads with God to "Let Ireland weep …not for sorrow," but for pride in her rebellious sons who sanctified her land. No longer the "exile birds" they used to be, the Irish soldiers will find – indeed they have found – their home in Christ Arisen, with angels guarding them in their sleep.

10 The Interconnectedness of the Fronts (Irish and Western)

Interrelatedness, this time of the Irish and the Western fronts, is an organising principle of "The Dead Kings," a poem which, by introducing the legendary rulers of Rosnaree, confirms the centrality of the Irish question in Ledwidge's depiction of the Great War. In his dream, the poet is addressed by the Kings, who each tells his tale of "ancient glory" turning into sorrow: singing can no longer gladden their "heavy hearts," the poets have "perished," and the gold tinted starry dark has been replaced by "blue and grey." The sleeper then offers his own (war) story of the "fourth sorrow." Suddenly, the sound of men who have fought near the Boyne river down the ages is replaced by the sound of an exploding shell and

Ledwidge's persona, violently wrenched from his dream, wakes in Picardy (CP 231), realising it is daybreak in the battlefields of the Somme.

The soldier's awakening can be even ruder in England, on the home front which, one would imagine, should constitute an enclave of safety, unthreatened by shells exploding overhead. However, the soldiers' life in the barracks is far from peaceful. As demonstrated in "After Court Martial," an Irishman can never forget about, or stop, his war for independence. In the British Army, the Anglo-Irish alliance translates into exploitation and enslavement, robbing the soldier of his beliefs.

Allegedly, when frustrated by the news of the suppression of the Easter Rising and devastated by the destruction of Dublin, Ledwidge heard a comment his officer made about it, he retorted with something that was not taken very well by his superior (Baxter 21–2). As a soldier cannot win against the king, he must suffer ostracism and humiliation ("vile names"), and bear his loneliness and shame with dignity. This nightmare of "*horror* and loud sufferings," (CP 196, emphasis added) – he never uses an equally strong expression describing the frontline hardships in other poems – which permeates his stay in the barracks reinforces his belief that his loyalties lie with the kings of Rosnaree, and not Babylon.

11 The Irish Front

"The Blackbirds" further explores the Anglo-Irish conflict, focusing on the complaint of the Old Woman (an allegorical representation of Ireland) who was robbed by a fowler. The thief came at the break of day and "took my blackbirds from their songs." As the birds symbolise the executed martyrs of 1916, she can but "grieve the silent bills." The final quatrain provides the ultimate sense of loss by locating the Old Woman in Derry, the loyalist province of Ulster which, Ward avers, separates her from the Republican south. Simultaneously, it condemns "her to wander among foreign hills of English controlled Ireland, showing divisions as another nightmare of modern Éire" (2012: 34).

Sometimes, in the Irish theatre of the war, where indirectness no longer matters, the real names of real fighters introduced into a poem constitute yet another strategy of waging war against the English oppressors, and, as is the case with "At Currabwee," give Ledwidge a chance to pay his last respects to Joseph Plunkett and Patrick Pearse, the leaders of the Rising. Commemorating the sacrifice of the two heroes, Ledwidge perceives them as the teachers of the greatness of Irish culture. Woven into this lesson is the tale "about shoemakers who repair fairy boots at night, while they sing of free Ireland" (Romp 2017:19). Unlike in "Ireland," where the poet speaker reveals his disappointment at missing the rebellion,[4] here, perhaps inspired by the closeness of the leaders, and with his patriotism, for once reconciled with his wartime service, Ledwidge proudly introduces himself as their follower, yet also a soldier who "applaud[s] himself for maintaining patriotic fervour for his country while wearing the British uniform" (Ward 35):

> And I, myself, have often heard
> Their singing as the stars went by,
> For am I not of those who reared
> The banner of old Ireland high,
> From Dublin town to Turkey's shores,
> And where the Vardar loudly roars? (CP 220)

The most famous and most artistically accomplished amongst his "Irish war" elegies is "Lament for Thomas McDonagh."[5] McDonagh was Ledwidge's fellow poet, best friend and one of the seven signatories of the proclamation for the Republic, whose death, Stallworthy avers, "was to 'hurt [Ledwidge] into poetry' more than the Great War" (2005: 50). Apart from paying homage to McDonagh, the poem's opening lines, a rendition of an ancient Celtic poem "The Yellow Bittern" ("An Bonnán Buí" by Cathal Buí Mac Giolla Ghunna), show his mastery of the translator's art:

> He shall not hear the bittern cry
> In the wild sky where he is lain,
> Nor voices of the sweeter birds
> Above the wailing of the rain.
> Nor shall he know when loud March blows
> Thro' slanting snows her fanfare shrill,
> Blowing to flame the golden cup
> Of many an upset daffodil.
> And when the dark cow leaves the moor
> And pastures poor with greedy weeds
> Perhaps he'll hear her low at morn
> Lifting her horn in pleasant meads. (CP 175)

---

4 "And then I left you," he writes, "wandering the war / Armed with the will, from distant goal to goal, / To find you at the last free of yore, / Or die to save your soul / And then you called to us from far and near /To bring your crown from out of the deeps of time, / It is my grief your voice I couldn't hear / In such a distant clime" (CP 197).

5 For many years, this single poem brought Francis Ledwidge into Irish classrooms and, as Dermot Bolger says, "managed to link Ledwidge tangentially to the Easter Rising" (Thurbidy 2013).

Combining a Celtic structure with an Old Testament lamentation (O'Connor 2015), Ledwidge mourns his loss, his bitter cry against the cruelty of his friend's death amplified by the "wailing of the rain" and "the distinctive, booming sound of the bird" (Helmers, "Lament..."), a distant echo of the Rising. The cry of the bittern, resembling the tapping of a drum, on the one hand plays its last post for the rebel hero, and on the other, together with other images, "constitutes a nature trail which will continue the war effort manifest in snow's 'shrill fanfare' and the flame of many an 'upset daffodil'" (Helmers). Here, Helmers contends, the resurgent March flowers (note its military pun on marching) also connote the rebirth of the spirit (McDonagh's) into eternal life. Ledwidge's conviction that "[a] noble failure is not vain./But hath a victory of its own" ("O'Connell Sreet," CP 249) seems to be corroborated by the closing stanza of the ode, suggesting that McDonagh might, after all, hear the lowing of the dark cow (a symbol of Ireland) "lifting her horn in pleasant meads," thus symbolising the triumph of finally won independence.

Nevertheless, apart from the (ever more distant) echoes of the Insurrection, not even murmurs of the War are heard in his late poems sent from the western front. "Soliloquy," composed in France 1917, seems to register the increasing "tiredness of the pain and drudgery of the experience" (Johnson 2003: 130). On a furlough before the battle ("To-morrow will be loud with war" CP 238), Ledwidge's persona wonders how he, "a helpless child of circumstance," will be "accounted for" (CP 238). The soldier poet perceives himself as a loser, "a victim of the War's corruptibility, more than certain that his 'fallen' dream of fame will never come true" (Forrester 2012). Whilst simultaneously acknowledging the bravery of the individual soldier, he realises that his fate, as it were, is directed towards anonymity ("a name unmade"), and bound to the facelessness of those who have died and who keep dying (Forrester 2012).

[…]
It is too late now to retrieve
A fallen dream, too late to grieve
A name unmade, but not too late
To thank the gods for what is great;
A keen-edged sword, a soldier's heart,
Is greater than a poet's art.
And greater than a poet's fame
A little grave that has no name. (CP 238)

His resting place thus defined, Ledwidge, perhaps sensing his end, seems determined to revisit his "old walks" so that they can be imprinted in his soul forever. In "The Lanawn Shee," one such path follows the elusive muse whom he is compelled to pursue. The poet goes from hill to hill, "on through dangerous zones, [crossing] dead men's bones" (CP 261) and braving the stormy seas.

12 The Third Ypres

Ledwidge made it "Home" in his last poem, where, by "an act of emotional and aesthetic transference," the ravaged Belgian countryside is replaced in the poet's mind's eye by his memories of the Irish Elysium" (Brearton and Gillis 2012: 64–5). Nevertheless, the ghostly image of a "broken tree," the sole survivor of, and witness to, the atrocities of battle, alerts one to the presence of other disquieting evidence of its horrors, augmented by, among other things, "a song a robin sang" about the desire for happiness that can be fulfilled only "across the world":

> A burst of sudden wings at dawn,
> Faint voices in a dreamy noon,
> Evenings of mist and murmurings,
> And nights with rainbows of the moon.
> And through these things a wood-way dim,
> And waters dim, and slow sheep seen
> On uphill paths that wind away
> Through summer sounds and harvest green.
> This is a song a robin sang
> This morning on a broken tree
> It was about the little fields
> That call across the world to me. (CP 257)

Indicative of the menace which is dormant yet lurking in this mock pastoral, are the "faint noises," an echo of the whispers of the dying. The "rainbows of the moon" may reflect the spectacular rocket explosions at night, whereas the dimness spreading over wood-ways and waters may anticipate the darkness of death lying in wait on "uphill paths," where "a burst of sudden wings at dawn" brings to mind shell explosions or the rattling of machine guns (Dawe 2015). Instead, the bird's song offers a brief respite. Translating the song, the poet, himself the "poor bird-hearted singer of a day" (CP 168), realises only too well how cruelly the war has robbed him: of his land and home, and the dear people whose memories he struggles to preserve. People who, as it were, bind him to his "home," keeping him sane and safe, sustaining him, like his mother, with their kind hearts and strength and giving him the courage to go on.

Commenting on Ledwidge's status as a "war poet," Heaney argued that it "emanates from the combination of 'the tendermindedness towards the predicaments of others with an ethically unsparing attitude towards the self'" (Johnson 2003: 129). This attitude permeates such superb elegies by Ledwidge as "A Little Boy in the Morning" and "To One Dead," a poetic miniature dedicated to his beloved Ellie Voughey, whose unrequited love, some argue, may have hastened Ledwidge's decision to enlist, and of whose death he learnt while recovering from war wounds in the hospital in Cairo:

A blackbird singing
On a moss-upholstered stone,
Bluebells swinging,
Shadows wildly blown,
A song in the wood,
A ship on the sea.
The song was for you
and the ship was for me.
A blackbird singing
I hear in my troubled mind,
Bluebells swinging,
I see in a distant wind.
But sorrow and silence,
Are the wood's threnody,
The silence for you
and the sorrow for me. (CP 148)

Even though the poem is Ledwidge's last gift to Ellie, given the context of the war, its title could express the feelings of anyone who lost a loved one during that time. More importantly, "this potential openness of address together with the unspecified gender of the poem's "you" and "me" gives the poem its power as a lament; it goes beyond a specific time and place to represent the feelings of anyone who has suffered from heartbreak and loss" (Helmers, "To One Dead").

13 Conclusion: War with a Human Face

In the light of the poems discussed above, it seems rather surprising that "[n]ot much from this varied map of his soldiering [on the three fronts] made its way to his poetry. More significantly, it had no discernible impact on him as a poet" (Johnson 2003, 130; Smyth) – a poet who, given to the evocation of pastoral images rather than a display of the gruesomeness and brutality of the war, would, above all, be remembered for the pity of war, made gentler "by often just alluding to it or by emphasizing his more subtle suffering through his poems about home" (Johnson 2003, 130).

Paradoxically, the only theatre of the war that moved him deeply enough to affect his poetry was that of the Easter Rising, in which he was not given a chance to participate. Paradoxically, too, it is only on this Irish plane that Ledwidge, occasionally, ceases to deploy indirectness, which, elsewhere, serves to distance him from, and eclipse, the fighting. He would seldom lament soldiers, the victims of specific combat situations but in fact, many of his works written in the years 1914–1917 may be viewed as elegies in which an experience of personal, individualised loss acquires a universal dimension. Whenever an odd reference to the war did somehow manage to find its way into his works, "it still retained a rather human face, allowing the readers to believe in and hope for the survival of goodness and justice, and the return home" (Kennedy 7).

The singer of Érin sang his final song in a letter to Katharine Tynan to whom he sent his poetic testament ("In the Shadows"):

> THE silent music of the flowers
> Wind-mingled shall not fail to cheer
> The lonely hours
> When I no more am here.
> Then in some shady willow place
> Take up the book my heart has made,
> And hide your face
> Against my name which was a shade. (CP 183)

Bibliography

Baxter, Pearl. "Francis Ledwidge. Soldier. Poet." *Corncrakemagazine.com*. 2017. http:/www.corncrakemagazine.com/wp-content/uploads/2017/07/Ledwidge-Soldier-Poet.pdf. (2 May 2017).

Bolger, Dermott. *Walking the Road*. Dublin: New Island, 2007.

Brearton, Fran and Allan Gillis, eds. *The Oxford Handbook of Modern Irish Poetry*. Oxford: Oxford University Press, 2012.

Brown, Terence. *The Literature of Ireland: Criticism and Culture*. Cambridge and New York: Cambridge University Press, 2010. Kindle.

Crossman, Virginia. "Review of Ireland and the Great War." Reviews in History. 2001. http://www.history.ac.uk/reviews/review/218/ (13 Jan. 2018).

Curtayne, Alice. *Francis Ledwidge: A Life of the Poet*. London: Martin, Brian, & O'Keefe, 1972.

Dawe, Gerald. "An Affirming Flame." *Culture Northern Ireland.org*. 2015. http://www.culturenorthernireland.org/features/literature/affirming-flame/ (5 May 2017).

Forrester, A.J. "Soliloquy. Francis Ledwidge." *English Poetry Revision*. 2012. http://upthelinetodeathrevsion.blogspot.com/2012/05/soliloquy-francis-ledwidge.html (12 Mar. 2017).

Haughey, Jim. *The First World War in Irish Poetry*. London: Bucknell University Press, 2002.

Heaney, Seamus. "In Memoriam: Francis Ledwidge." In: *Field Work*. London: Faber and Faber, 1979.

Helmers, Marguerite. "'Lament for Thomas MacDonagh' by Francis Ledwidge." *Poem Analysis*. 2017. https://poemanalysis.com/lament-for-thomas-macdonagh%E2%80%A8-by-francis-ledwidge-poem-analysis/ (3 Nov. 2017).

Helmers, Marguerite. " 'To One Dead' by Francis Ledwidge." *Poem Analysis*. 2017. https://poemanalysis.com/to-one-dead-by-francis-ledwidge-poem-analysis/ (13 Nov. 2017).

Jeffery, Keith. *Ireland and the Great War*. Cambridge: Cambridge University Press, 2000.

Johnson, Nuala C. *Ireland, the Great War and the Geography of Remembrance*. Cambridge: Cambridge University Press, 2003.

Kennedy, Ian. "'Passive Suffering is not a Theme for Poetry.' A Representation of Suffering in Irish Poetry of the First War." http://www.academia.edu/9713708/Passive_Suffering_is_not_a_theme_for_Poetry._A_Representation_of_Suffering_in_Irish_Poetry_of_the_First_World_War/ (20 Apr. 2017).

Ledwidge, Francis. *The Complete Poems*. Ed. Liam O'Meara. Newbridge: Goldsmith, 1997.

O'Connor, Norreys Jephson. "In Memoriam: Francis Ledwidge." http://www.bartleby.com/272/69.html/ (10 May 2017).

O'Connor, Ulick. "Ledwidge: a fine lament for MacDonagh." Independent.ie. https://www.independent.ie/entertainment/books/poetry-ledwidge-a-fine-lament-for-mcdonagh-31239338.html/ (24 May 2015).

O'Gara-Kilmurry, Miriam. *Ėire's WWI War Poet: Francis Ledwidge*. Dublin: CreateSpace. Independent Publishing Platform, 2016.

O'Meara, Liam, ed. *Francis Ledwidge. The Complete Poems*. Newbridge: The Goldsmith Press Ltd., 1997.

O'Meara, Liam, ed. *Francis Ledwidge: Poet Activist Soldier*. Dublin: Riposte Books, 2006.

O'Meara, Liam, ed. *To One Dead, A Play on The Life of Francis Ledwidge*. Dublin: Riposte Books, 2013.

Phillips, Terry. "Enigmas of the Great War: Thomas Kettle and Francis Ledwidge." *Irish Studies Review*, Vol. 16, No. 4, 2008, pp. 385–402.

Romp, Charlotte. "'Am I not of those who reared/The banner of old Ireland high?' Triumphalism, nationalism and conflicted identities in Francis Ledwidge's war poetry." BA thesis, Radboud University Nijmegen, 2017.

Russell, Arthur. "Francis Ledwidge – The Poet of the Blackbird." English Historical Fiction Authors. 2013. http://englishhistoryauthors.blogspot.com/2013/11/francis-ledwidge-poet-of-blackbird.html/ (10 June 2016).

Smyth, Gerard. "The Call of the Fields." *Dublin Review of Books*. 2017. http://www.drb.ie/essays/the-call-of-the-fields (13 May 2017).

Stallworthy, Jon. *Anthem for Doomed Youth: Twelve Soldier Poets of the First World War*. London: Constable & Robinson, 2005.

Thurbidy, Jean. "Crossing Paths with Meath Poet-Soldier Francis Ledwidge." *The Wild Geese*. 2013. http://thewildgeese.irish/profiles/blogs/crossing-paths-with-meath-poet-soldier-francis-ledwidge/ (10 May 2017).

Townshend, Charles. *Ireland: The 20th Century*. London: Arnold, 1999.

Ward, Thomas Barrett. "The Easter Rising: Pearse, Print, and the Modern Irish Elegy." MA, University of Texas. 2012. https://repositories.lib.utexas.edu/bitstream/handle/2152/22784/Thomas%20B%20Ward%20MA%20Final%20Draft.pdf;sequence=1 (16 July 2016).

Brian Ó Conchubhair

The Polish Origins of Irish-Language Modernist Fiction? Joseph Conrad & Pádraig Ó Conaire

"Where exactly is the line between homage, reference, fair borrowing, and plagiarism? And is acknowledging such debts enough – or necessary?" (Gavron, 2018).

Abstract: Did Joseph Conrad, famously writing in his second language, pave the way for non-native speakers of Irish to write in *their* second language? This chapter explores the influence of Conrad on the Irish writer Pádraig Ó Conaire. Ó Conaire knew of Conrad and wrote a number of articles on him but the evidence presented here is mostly text-internal, involving comparisons of motifs in Ó Conaire's *Deoraíocht* and Conrad's earlier work, specifically *Almayer's Folly* (1895), *An Outcast of the Islands* (1896), *The Nigger of the "Narcissus"* (1897) and *Lord Jim* (1900). Ó Conchubhair argues that Conrad played an important part in Ó Conaire's development as a writer.

Keywords: Pádraig Ó Conaire, Joseph Conrad, *Deoraíocht*, Irish literature, Modernism

The Polish novelist Henryk Sienkiewicz received the Nobel Prize for literature in 1905 in large part due to his renowned novel *Quo Vadis*. Born during the Irish Famine in 1846, Sienkiewicz ironically died in 1916, another landmark in Irish history. The Quo Vadis – Henryk Sienkiewicz Festival in Galway, described by the Polish Embassy in Ireland as "the biggest ever celebration of Polish novelist Henryk Sienkiewicz in Ireland," celebrated his legacy from 10–17 September 2016. His connection to modern Irish literature, however, stems less from the translation of his work from Polish into Irish, than from its translation into English by the Irish-American folklorist Jeremiah Curtin. Critics such as Jan Rybicki have asserted that Poland's first literary Nobel Prize winner, Henryk Sienkiewicz, owed his great if short-lived fame to the very numerous, if very mediocre, translations by Jeremiah Curtin. Born on the 6 September 1835 in Detroit, Michigan, to Irish parents, Curtin spent his early years on a farm in Greenfield, Milwaukee, Wisconsin. Educated at Milwaukee University, and afterwards at Harvard, he graduated to join the staff of the

American embassy in St. Petersburg as Secretary (1864). His knowledge of Russian and the works of Tolstoy made him popular in the both aristocratic and administrative circles. His career faltered, however, when he ran afoul of Cassius Clay, the United States Ambassador to Russia, who destroyed the young man's diplomatic career. With his political livelihood in ruins, he visited Ireland in 1871, 1872, 1887, 1891, and 1892–93. During these trips, he collected folklore in south-west Munster and the Aran Islands that he subsequently published as *Myths and Folklore of Ireland* (1890). This book ranks among the first accurate collections of folk material and was an important source for W.B. Yeats when writing *Cuchulain's Fight with the Sea*. Curtin also published *Hero Tales of Ireland* (1894) and *Tales of the Fairies and Ghost World: Collected from Oral Tradition in South-west Munster* (1895). Other ethnographic publications include *Creation Myths of Primitive America in Relation to the Religious History and Mental Development of Mankind* (1898), *Myths of the Modocs* (1912), and *Myths and Folk-tales of the Russians, Western Slavs, and Magyars* (1890). Curtin, presumably, became aware of Sienkiewicz during his Russia sojourn and decided to translate – perhaps rewrite – his works into English. Among the books he published are *Children of the Soil* (1896), *Quo Vadis* (1897), and *The Teutonic Knights* (1900), as well as *The Argonauts* (1901) by Eliza Orzeszkowa and *The Pharaoh* (1902) by Bolesław Prus. These translations proved successful and provided a good income for Curtin, but were later criticised for their literalness, errors and unduly archaic tone and thought to be in part the work of his wife Alma Cardell Curtin, who posthumously issued *The Mongols in Russia* (1908) – now thought to be hers – with a foreword by Theodore Roosevelt.

In 1936 the Irish state publisher An Gúm issued the Rev. Aindrias Ó Céileachair's Irish translation of Sienkiewicz's *Quo Vadis* based on the Dent edition in the Wayfarer's Library rather than Curtin's American edition. A Cork-born priest, Ó Céileachair taught Irish at Liverpool University and, later, the University of Urbana-Champagne, Ohio. Nor was *Quo Vadis* the sole Polish text An Gúm issued. Seosamh Mac Grianna translated three of Joseph Conrad's novels that appeared as *An Máirnéalach Dubh/The Nigger of the "Narcissus"* (1933) which the *Irish Times* lauded (Nov. 4, 1933, p. 4); *Séideán bruithne/Typhoon*, which appeared in 1935; and *Díthchéille Almayer/Almayer's Folly*, which followed in 1936. Liam Ó Dochartaigh argues that Conrad's influence is evident in *An Druma Mór*, Mac Grianna's 1930 novel concerning a feud between two marching bands in Ros Cuain, a thinly disguised Rannafast in County Donegal in the North-West of Ireland in the years 1912 to 1922. According to Ó Dochartaigh

> má bhreathnaítear ar *An Druma Mór* mar chumasc cliste de mhúnla a fuarthas ó *Nostromo* agus d'ábhar a d'eascair as dúchas Gaeltachta an údair (an ghaisciúlacht agus téama an athrú saoil go háirithe) agus an t-iomlán scríofa i prós saothraithe Gaeilge nach bhfacthas a leithéid ag Ultach le trí chead bliain, tá mé cinnte go n-aithneofar gur úrscéal níos cumasaí é ná mar a mheastar go coitianta. (Ó Dochartaigh 1980: 23–24)
> [If *An Druma Mór* is viewed as a clever amalgam of strategies derived from *Nostromo* and material from the author's Gaeltacht heritage (heroism and the theme of modernisation) all written in polished Irish prose, such as was absent from Ulster for three hundred years, I am certain that it will be recognised as a more powerful novel than generally believed.]

But Polish literature in Irish is not confined to the 1930s. *Leabhar na Polainne*, Liam Ó Rinn's translation of Adam Mickiewicz's *The Book of the Polish Nation and Polish Pilgrimage*, originally published in December 1832 in Paris, was issued in Irish in 1920.

If the mid-1930s marked a golden age of Polish literature in Irish with Polish-language novels appearing in 1933, 1935 and 1936, what of the influence of Polish authors on Irish-language authors? This essay suggests that Ó Conaire's novel *Deoraíocht* draws heavily on Conrad's earlier work, specifically *Almayer's Folly* (1895), *An Outcast of the Islands* (1896), *The Nigger of the "Narcissus"* (1897) and *Lord Jim* (1900). It further suggests that Conrad's novels offered critical plot and stylistic devices that proved essential in Ó Conaire's development as a writer seeking to cultivate Irish-language fiction along contemporary European lines.

1 Pádraic Ó Conaire

Born in 1882 in western Galway, Ireland, Ó Conaire spent his adult years in London as a civil servant in the Ministry of Education. It was in the metropolitan centre that he joined the Gaelic League and expanded his literary and cultural horizons. As a young civil servant in the early 1900s, Ó Conaire taught language classes and lectured in Irish history for the Gaelic League. As a well-educated Irish-speaker (the product of Rockwell College and Blackrock College) living in the imperial capital, yet fully immersed in the cultural nationalist project of the Irish revival, he complicates the standard narrative that equates modernism with leaving Ireland and Irish things behind: a modernity epitomised in the multilingual *Finnegans Wake* and the Francophile Samuel Beckett (Quigley 2011: 171). Not only did he write in Irish while living in London, his novel *Deoraíocht* eschews nostalgic visions of a romantic return to Ireland and rejects the generic conventions of the folktale and the oral tradition so deeply intertwined in the Irish-language literary tradition. *Deoraíocht* deconstructs a first-person narrative recorded in a journal or diary and reconstructs it as a novel lacking a beginning and conclusion. In *Deoraíocht*, the antihero is deconstructed rather than monumentalised and the novel, like Conrad's *Lord Jim* rests on "an acceptance of simultaneity and multidimensionality wherein a protagonist can be 'both' and at the same time 'neither'" (Schlund-Vials 2009: 321–2). *Deoraíocht* is much less about what will happen next, the dramatic uncertainty demanded by most classic 19th-century novels, but rather what thoughts, ideas or mood will next grip its hero's fragile personality and mercurial temperament.

Deoraíocht may be read, as initial critics did, as a cautionary tale of the perils of emigration or as Ó Conaire's attempt to deal with human experience in the urban world and the impact of modernity on human dignity and sensibility. Set almost entirely in London, *Deoraíocht* details the exploits of Micheál Ó Maoláin, a Galwegian maimed in a traffic accident not long after his arrival in the capital. *Deoraíocht* is, arguably, the outstanding critique of modernity's impact on the Irish local organic community and the traditional coastal lifestyle. It captures an individual's alienating and alienated experience in a capitalist centralised bureaucratic system. While critics acknowledge the plot's "magic elastically" and the manner in which it "bends the realistic premise" (Cahalan 1988: 122), they concur that "it is much more a symbolic rendering of the fate of the Irish in exile than a documentary telling" (Titley 2006: 174). Cahalan considers it "the most innovative, forward-looking Irish novel in either language during this period before the arrival of Joyce as a novelist, rivalled in this respect perhaps only by James Stephen's *The Charwoman's Daughter* (1912)" (Cahalan 1988: 117).

Beginning *in medias res*, the novel startles the reader by starting with the aftermath of the dramatic accident that maimed the main character; this discombobulates the reader and initiates a process of confusion and uncertainty that is maintained throughout and underscored by the mysterious conclusion. The loss of a leg and a hand, as well as major damage to Ó Maoláin's face, mirror the psychological trauma he experiences as a rural emigrant in an urban setting. A grotesquerie of deformity and stripped of his identity (Cahalan 1988: 118), physically as well as culturally, he becomes a citizen of the modern world, confiding his jagged, confused emotions in his diary. Having frittered away the financial compensation he received as a result of his accident, Ó Maoláin begins performing as a freak in a travelling circus. During his time with the show, the circus manager, the "Little Yellow Man" – who is characterised by a peculiar laugh – contrives a marriage between Ó Maoláin and his daughter, the "Big Fat Lady." The "Little Yellow Man" treats his daughter as chattel. He displays her as a freak ("the most obese woman in the world") in his own show and, on learning of her engagement to Ó Maoláin, advertises them as a joint new attraction. Later, when the circus tours Ireland, Ó Maoláin encounters former friends in Galway. When his past and present collide, Ó Maoláin destroys the circus in a rage. Destitute, he returns to London, rejecting all efforts to rescue him. Once more, his past and present collide when the Fat Lady, the socialist Red-Headed Woman and his former romantic attachment from Galway gather to save him but, yet again, he cannot reconcile the various strands of his life and experience. Ultimately, he dies in a park in London under suspicious circumstances. Only them do we learn that the narrator, à la *The Third Policeman*, has been dead all along (Cahalan 1988: 118).

Deoraíocht depicts both the material reality of Ó Maoláin's immigrant experience and its emotional, physiological, and physical effects. In doing so, it abandons the decorum traditionally associated with depictions of Irish-speakers and promotes individual freedom without privileging any particular doctrine, dogma or method. Ó Conaire's impressionistic style and eschewal of a guiding authorial voice underscores his break with tradition. The voice here alternatively engenders sympathy and repulsion at equal turns. What results is a novel that presents perfervid but fleeting moments in the tragic life of an emigrant cast violently into modernity, where he experiences those "forms of psychic oppression and confinement" (Nicholls 1995: 165) so characteristic of metropolitan life in the first decade of the twentieth century. *Deoraíocht* is a fictional narrative without a clear start or end. It is an episodic novel based, we later learn, on a series of letters and diaries written by the main character and compiled for our benefit by an unknown friend. Wilkie Collins in *The Woman in White* (1859), Bram Stoker in *Dracula* (1897) and Joseph Conrad in *Lord Jim* (1900) employed a similar organising principle for their novels. Like *Lord Jim*, *Deoraíocht* comprises a fragmented series of events narrated by an unreliable, unpredictable, and unlikeable individual. The use of a narrator who finds the cripple's diary indicates a Conrad-like awareness of the limits of the novel and narrative structure as well as a clear rejection of the omniscient narrative voice. "The art of our century," says Katherine Kuh, "has been characterized by shattered surfaces, broken colour, segmented composition, dissolving forms, and shredded images" (qtd. in Hershman 2003: 431). Such literature avoids continuous narratives, fixed points of view and clear-cut moral positions in favour of paradox, irony and ambiguity. Fragmentation and decomposition, writes Amos Vogel, "denote less an escape from reality, but more an acute and penetrating analysis of human and social experience" (Vogel 1974: 19–20). A fragment, this argument continues, is "a part, broken off, something cut or detached from the whole, something imperfect. The modernist poets reinvented the fragment as an acutely self-conscious mode of writing that breaks the flow of time, leaving gaps and tears, lacunae. They created discontinuous texts, collages and mosaics, fragmentary epics such as Ezra Pound's 'The Cantos,' Louis Zukofsky's 'A,' and T. S. Eliot's 'The Waste Land'" (Hirsch 2014: 243). The beauty of Ó Conaire's novel and his contribution to Pre-World I modernism is not only that he anticipates the maimed soldiers returning from the Great War whose broken bodies carry their broken minds, but that in 1910 he marries a fragmented and fractured style and narrative style to a subject that was mentally and physically fractured.

The verbal and temporal swings that characterise the book's style embody the modernist attitude whereby style "is no longer merely the expression of meaning, but rather a process that makes meaning possible in the first place" (Hutchinson 2011: 35). If, as T.S. Eliot claimed, thinking in fragments is "the characteristic feature of the modern individual" (Moretti 1996: 186), then the novel's diaristic form may be seen as symptomatic of "the contemporary disorder" (Moretti 1996: 186; Bourke 2003: 54–67) wrought by modernity. Ó Conaire's narrator, unable to integrate life experiences into a unified whole, is himself a fragment, physically, emotionally, psychologically, linguistically. Division and duality shadow him throughout, whether in the form of his struggles to reconcile his present with his past or his bilingualism (he speaks both Irish and English in London and Galway). Amid resentfulness, anger and blind range, the elusive hope of a better life propels Ó Maoláin. He persistently shirks responsibility and continually embraces false hopes until finally, having eluded death by the accident that activates the narrative, death catches up with him in a public park.

When we glimpse the world through his bitter eyes and comprehend it through his tormented mind, what we see are flashes of a disturbing reality. This, to cite Jonathan Jones on Vincent Van Gogh, "is not an objective record of a misfortune but, in its hypnotic intensity, a portrait of the artist both martyred and liberated by madness" (Jones 2016). The novel's "untidiness" may therefore be read as a central element of its design rather than an unintended result of Ó Conaire's stylistic choices. Style, Remy de Gourmont suggested in 1902, is a question of physiology: "we write, as we feel, as we think, with our entire body" (Hutchinson 2011: 33). It follows that a one-handed, one-legged, unbalanced man will not provide a steady linear narrative. Rather, the textual gaps and omissions are features of form and personality. Ó Maoláin is, as Maud Ellmann says of Stephen Dedalus, "dismembering, not developing but devolving, not achieving an identity but dissolving into a nameless scar" (Ellmann 1981: 194). Louis de Paor underlines this link between form and theme when he says of the novel: "The physical disintegration of the central character is accompanied by an existential crisis of identity as he descends into the grotesque underworld of a travelling freak show. Despite the clumsiness of its structure, the novel's interrogation of dislocation and despair, of marginalization and isolation, is in keeping with the central preoccupations of European modernism" (de Paor 2014: 164). Ó Conaire's portrait of this crippled Irishman, then, represents the first effort, intellectually and stylistically, to engage with modernity and the concerns of modernism in the Irish-language novel. He finds beauty and humanity not in nature, history or myth, as favoured by folklorists and his fellow writers, but in ugly, degenerate London and its freak shows. As a novel marked by the stylistic, thematic, and generic concerns of early modernism, *Deoraíocht* offers what Conrad's co-author Ford Madox Ford called "the impression not the corrected chronicle" (Madox Ford 1964: 41). That is to say, it provides life as experienced in the moment rather than subsequently reordered, sequenced and intellectualised. The London of this book, and for that matter the Galway, lacks any sense of community. The temporary sanctuary provided for Ó Maoláin by the working men's hostel and the circus is illusionary. In this world, the past with its traditions and rituals are irrevocably sundered from the senseless disjointed present. As Schiller wrote: "Everlastingly chained to a single little fragment of the Whole, man himself develops into nothing but a fragment […] he never develops the harmony of his being, and instead of putting the stamp of humanity upon his own nature, he becomes nothing more than the imprint of his occupation or of his specialized knowledge" (Simpson 1988: 131).

While the novel shares similarities, mainly in tone and style, with Knut Hamsun's novel *Sult/Hunger* (1890), the constant anxiety that grips Ó Maoláin contains echoes of both Søren Kierkegaard's *The Concept of Anxiety* and Fyodor Dostoevsky's *Notes from the Underground*. For Ó Conaire, as for Lukács, the modernist experience is one of disconnection: the outer world of reality is unintelligible and in turns reinforces an internal sense of inalterability. Human action is both ineffectual and insincere. All that remains is an unpredictable world, a world dominated by angst, regret, fear and uncertainty (Lukács 2006: 36). Yet while *Deoraíocht* explores concerns that would later animate Joyce and Beckett, the novel is in some respects closer to the less formally experimental work of Conrad, Lawrence and E.M. Forster. Stephen Matthews argues that such authors, while pursuing a version of realism found in the nineteenth-century novel, and offering offered key insights into "the social, imperial and industrial realities of their time," also explored "the psyche of those entrapped by these modern realities" and "displayed a focus that they held in common with many more technically-experimental modernist writers and modernist thinkers" (Matthews 2008: 26). With *Deoraíocht*, Ó Conaire became part of this continuum of Edwardian writers who sought to capture and express the immediate impact of modernity on the individual, relying less on traditional plot and sentimentality – as understood in the English-language novel and the emerging

Irish-language novel tradition – and more on unreliable narration, and the emotional and intellectual impact of events as they occur. Whereas Ó Conaire's Irish-language contemporaries focused on linguistic preservation and were closely attuned to meeting readers' expectations, his novel marks the moment when the Irish-language author becomes aware of his alienation from dominant values of bourgeois culture and seeks to expand the reader's perceptual and symbolic horizon. *Deoraíocht* marks the advent of a critical self-consciousness within the twentieth-century Irish-language prose tradition.

2 Turning to Conrad. What has Conrad to do with all of this?

"Few problems can prove more vexing to the critic or historian of literature than the problem of influence" (Hassan 1955: 66). In what follows, I outline the possible connections, echoes, similarities, reverberations and parallels that occur in Conrad's novels and Ó Conaire's *Deoraíocht*. While direct evidence of clear influence is absent, the preponderance of indirect and supplementary evidence, nonetheless, indicates that *Deoraíocht* may owe a debt to Conrad's early novels. It is entirely possible that similarities and resemblances noted in what follows are merely coincidental. Possible, but unlikely. The number of the overlaps suggests not. If intentional, Ó Conaire is guilty of little more than participating in the long and honourable tradition of one author refashioning another's work as his or her own (Gavron 2018).

Many critics regard the Polish-British writer, Józef Teodor Konrad Korzeniowski, [aka Joseph Conrad] (1857–1924) as one of the greatest novelists to write in English. Born into the *szlachta*, a hereditary aristocratic class, in present day Ukraine, Conrad came of age in a divided nation with four languages, four religions, and a number of different social classes. His parents' early deaths led him to France and a career as a merchant seaman took him around the world. These formative maritime experiences in the West Indies and the Congo subsequently informed his most famous novels: *Almayer's Folly* (1895), *An Outcast of the Islands* (1896), *The Nigger of the "Narcissus"* (1897), *Lord Jim* (1900), *Youth* (1902), *Typhoon* (1902), *Nostromo* (1904), *The Secret Agent* (1907) and *Under Western Eyes* (1911). W.B. Yeats's winning of the 1923 Nobel Prize for literature came as a bitter blow to Conrad, whose growing renown and prestige among writers and critics had fostered his hopes for the award. In 1924, the year of his death, Conrad declined a knighthood as well as offers of honorary degrees from Cambridge, Durham, Edinburgh, Liverpool, and Yale universities.

Whereas only one of Ó Conaire's more than 400 essays deals specifically with Poland – "Cúigí Uladh na Polainn," ["The Polish Ulster Provinces"] published in

The Freeman's Journal (28 July 1919, p. 4) – Conrad figures in four essays: "Ceacht Conrad" ["Conrad's Lesson"] in *Fáinne an Lae* (22 November 1924), "Lón an Scríbheora: An Fada go mBeidh sé le fáil aige?" ["The Writer's Sustenance: How Much Longer"] in *An Claidheamh Solais* (10 March 1917), "An Fhírinne agus an Bhréag sa Litríocht" ["The Truth and the Untruth in Literature"] in *Fáinne an Lae* (12 May 1923) and "Conrad agus Smaointe Faoi Litríocht" ["Conrad and Thoughts about Literature"] in *Fáinne an Lae* (30 August 1924). Written shortly after Conrad's death on the 3 August 1924, the title of the final essay offers much but the body of the essay reveals little about Ó Conaire's feelings towards Conrad. In fact, as Philip O'Leary notes, "his principal point is that the work of Conrad (and others) proves that great art can be created in a writer's second language, an important and useful idea in the context of the revival, but not one that tells us much about Conrad or his influence on Ó Conaire" (O'Leary 1994: 68).

Repeatedly in these essays, Conrad serves as a model for aspiring Irish-language authors for whom Irish is not a first language and equally as a rebuttal to those who argue that a modern literature in Irish can only emerge from native-speakers. Ó Conaire's awareness of Conrad is unsurprising given the narrow degree of separation. T.P. O'Connor, the Irish reporter reviewed *Almayer's Folly* positively and selected it as "Book of the Week" in the Home Rule paper *The Sun*. He also serialised *Nostromo* in *T.P.'s Weekly* in 1904. R. Barry O'Brien, editor of *The Speaker*, London Gaelic League/Conradh na Gaeilge chairman (1892–1906) and president (1906–1917), not only hired Conrad as a reviewer but reviewed his work in 1904. W.P. Ryan, an Irish journalist and Gaelic Leaguer worked for the *Daily Chronicle* and *The Sun*, two newspapers that reviewed Conrad's work. Stephen Gwynn, who served an intermediary between Conrad and McClure, his U.S. publishers in 1900, attended Irish-language classes in London taught by Ó Conaire and, in 1913, wrote a letter of reference for Ó Conaire on House of Commons letterhead. Liam O'Flaherty, whom Ó Conaire mentored, was acquainted with Conrad through their shared literary agent, Edward Garnett. Roger Casement, a model for the *Heart of Darkness*, travelled with Conrad, was also a Gaelic Leaguer and, most likely, knew Ó Conaire.

Certain elements of *Deoraíocht* appear derived from Conrad's *Almayer's Folly*, *The Nigger of the "Narcissus:" A Tale of the Sea* (1897), *An Outcast of the Islands*, *Lord Jim* (1900) and *The Heart of Darkness*. In a 1996 article I laid out the similarities between Ó Conaire's canonical short story "Nora Mharcais Bhig" and Conrad's novel *Almayer's Folly*, most notable the concluding scene where Almyer, having lost his daughter, systematically removes all traces of her footsteps in the sand before obliterating her initials from the trunk case. Yet, as the narrator concludes, despite such acts of suppression he will never succeed in removing his daughter's name or memory from his heart. This act not only chimes with, but is replicated in Ó Conaire's story where Marcus's wayward daughter, having contravened social protocol by getting drunk and spending the night with a man in the village, is also exiled and sent back to London. The story concludes with Marcus on the pier, tarring over the name of his boat, named for his daughter and bought with the remittances she has sent – earned through prostitution. Like Almayer, the failed Dutch merchant stuck on a remote island, Marcus is a father who pinned his hopes and social aspiration on his daughter only to be disappointed. He too will eradicate her name from the record but will fail to erase her name and memory from his heart. Both stories feature cultural and social conflict, both tell of sexuality, independence and the daughters choosing their own destiny rather than fulfilling their fathers' social desires and ambitions.

Conrad's novella, *The Nigger of the Narcissus*, offers possibly the clearest evidence of influence. Published in the United States as *The Children of the Sea: A Tale of the Forecastle*, it concerns James Wait, a black West Indian sailor dying aboard the Narcissus as it sails to London. After a while at sea, the first mate remands Wait, who has tuberculosis, to his bunk. Some sailors grouse that his illness is a sham to evade work. Off the Cape of Good Hope, the ship capsizes. The crew survive by clinging onto the ship. Five men, on realising that Wait is missing, rescue him at their own peril. The storm passes and the crew right the ship. The crew, however, hold Wait to be the cause of their misfortune Aware of their suspicions, Wait suspects they will throw him overboard. The subplot – of an invalid who considers himself a burden on the collective and fears that the group will blame him for their misfortune and ultimately seize the opportunity to sacrifice him – appears in *Deoraíocht*. Ó Maoláin, in the workman's home, a large building that houses some one hundred men, notes the habit sailors have of throwing overboard the one who brings misfortune on the ship:

> B'fhacthas dom nach raibh uatha ach mé a dhíbirt as an teach. Iad siúd a bhí ar a n-aimhleas (agus bhí an-chuimse acu siúd ann) cheapas go m'fhéidir go sílidís gurb é an bacach duairc ba chiontach leis; gurb é a thug an mí-ádh ina dtreo. Chuimhnínn ansin ar ar chualas riamh de scéalta faoi mhairnéalaigh a chaith duine a thug an mí-ádh ar a long isteach san fharraige. An ndéanfaí mar sin liomsa? (Ó Conaire 1980: 9)

> [It appeared to me that they wanted nothing other than to evict me from the house. Those that were down on their luck (and they were many) I thought they might believe that it was the dour cripple that caused their misfortune; that I was the source of their woes. I then recalled what I had heard about sailors who threw over broad the one who brought bad luck on their vessel. Would that be my lot?]

Published in 1896, Conrad's second novel, *An Outcast of the Islands*, details Peter Willems's downfall. A disreputable individual, he embezzles his employer's money in the hope of becoming a partner in the company. Hudig, his employer, only tolerated Willems as he sees a relationship budding between him and his less than attractive daughter – a relationship of which Willems is unaware. Those familiar with *Deoraíocht* will recognise not only plot similarities in the case of Ó Maoláin's pseudo-romance with the Obese Woman who is Alf Trot's estranged daughter. In both cases, fathers – Alf Trot and Hudig – encourage less than desirable suitors – Ó Maoláin and Willems – to pursue their somewhat orthodox relationships to rid themselves of suitorless daughters. When the deceit becomes public, both men are incensed at the deception and the women are embarrassed. In both cases the implication is that the daughters were fathered in extra marital relationships and their fathers feel some obligation to "care" for their offspring. Both see in the unfortunate Ó Maoláin and Willems an opportunity to rid themselves of their burdens. Just as Willems flees the island and his wife, Ó Maoláin flees the circus and his fiancée. In both instances, they establish new relationships: Willems with Aissa and Ó Maoláin with the Red-Headed Woman. In both cases, their former love-interest reappears and they are forced to confront their past. A second connection between *An Outcast of the Islands* and *Deoraíocht* concerns the faulty pistol. Prior to meeting Alf Trot – the Little Yellow Man – for the second time, Ó Maoláin encounters a sailor from whom he purchases a pistol with a silver handle in the hope that it will save him in a moment of crisis. Among the items found at the novel's conclusion on Ó Maoláin's body is a silver-handed pistol that had never been fired. It is, in reality, a toy pistol. The novel concludes that the pistol failed the cripple, just as life had failed him. The motif of a faulty gun also appears in *An Outcast of the Islands*.

Heart of Darkness, despite its Irish overtones and the centrality of Roger Casement, bears less obvious similarities to *Deoraíocht*. Yet the emergence of the plot from "a packet of papers and a photograph, the lot tied together with a shoe string" which Kurtz bequeaths to Marlow resonates with *Deoraíocht* where the narrative is based on papers found in the victim's pocket. The narrative device of letters and documents composed by a person, now dead, is also present in *Lord Jim*. In *Lord Jim*, writes Linda Dryden, as in many of his fictional works, Conrad treats of "themes that touch upon the hopes and aspirations, the delusions and self-deceptions, the successes and failures of individuals everywhere" (Dryden 2009: vi). Here the titular character acts as a mirror image of Ó Maoláin. Neither can return home; both are disgraced and bear the scars of accidents. Both seek understanding and company while simultaneously shunning such invitations. Both inhabit the past, unable to forgive or forget not so much what happened as what they lost – the chance at happiness. Both benefit from acts of kindness from unexpected sources: Ó Maoláin from the men in the hostel, and Jim from

Marlow and Stein. Both men are prone to outbursts of laughter. Finally, both have to deal with angry revengeful fathers who feel the younger men owe them a debt.

Jim, disabled by a falling spar spends "many days stretched on his back, dazed, battered, hopeless, and tormented as if at the bottom of an abyss of unrest" (ch. 2).[1] He secures a position as first mate aboard the *Patna*. After several days sailing, the ship collides with a wreck; the crew fear the ship's destruction is imminent and abandon ship with little concern for the 800 pilgrims aboard. On being rescued, they learn that not only did their ship survive adrift, but a passing vessel had also rescued its passengers. The crew, fearing prosecution and indignity for dereliction of duty, abscond again. Jim alone stands trial. Marlow encounters this "malevolent soul in a detestable body" (ch. 2) at the public enquiry. Jim emits a loud outburst of laughter, reminiscent of Alf Trot: "He had never himself back and was shaking with laughter. I had never in my life heard anything so bitter as that noise" (ch. 8); it is later described as "a Homeric peal of laughter" (ch. 27). Marlow secures Jim a position in a distant port, but he invariably flees once conversation turns to the *Patna*. Jim, like Willems in *An Outcast* and Ó Maoláin in *Deoraíocht*, "is exiled from his preferred society [...] betrayal and retribution, thwarted ambition and self-delusion are key themes in both novels" (Dryden 2009: vii). Stein, a friend of Marlow, obtains another job for Jim in Patusan, a village on a remote island. "He had indeed jumped into an everlasting deep hole. He had tumbled from a height he could never scale again" (ch. 10). Acting "in the similitude of a corpse" (ch. 23), his hopelessness was such that his advisors opined that "to bury him would have been such an easy kindness! It would have been so much in accordance with the wisdom of life, which consists of putting out of sight all the reminders of our folly, of our weakness, of our mortality; all that makes against our efficiency – the memories of our failures, the hints of our undying fears, the bodies of our dead friends" (ch. 15).

Nonetheless, Jim earns the respect of the native people by freeing them from Sherif Ali, the bandit and protecting them from Rajah Tunku Allang, the corrupt local Malay chief. He falls in love with Jewel, a young woman of mixed race, whose mother had married a man named Cornelius. Despite his despicable treatment of his stepdaughter, Cornelius, once her relationship with Jim develops, demands compensation. Cornelius, "malevolent, mistrustful, underhand," who

1 In view of the numerous editions of Conrad's works, references are given to chapters only, rather than pages.

harbours an aggrieved sense of legal paternity over Jewel, is described – in terms reminiscent of Alf Trott, the Little Yellow Man – as screaming, "shaking a little yellow fist" (ch. 30) and having a "sour yellow little face" (ch. 34). Gentleman Brown, a pirate, arrives in Patusan; he deceives Jim and in a raid on the village kills his friend Dain Waris, among others. Humiliated and dishonoured, Jim takes responsibility for the death of Dain Waris, whose father shoots Jim with a flintlock pistol given to him by Stein.

The novel comprises two parts. Firstly Jim's cowardice aboard the ship and his consequent trial, and secondly an account of Jim's adventures in Patusan. The first four chapters are anonymously narrated. The end of Chapter Four introduces Marlow as the narrator, but there is also another narrator, one who listens to Marlow's account and to whom Jim writes at the end (Mongia 1992: 173–186). "But there was only one man of all these listeners who was ever to hear the last word of the story. It came to him at home, more than two years later, and it came contained in a thick packet addressed in Marlow's uprights and angular handwriting" (ch. 36). These yellow frayed letters are authored by one who "put it down here for you as though I had been an eye witness. My information is fragmentary, but I've fitted the pieces together, and there is enough of them to make an intelligible picture. I wonder how he would have related it himself" (ch. 36). This aspect of the narrative where the story is revealed via letters sent by the protagonist to the narrator is replicated in *Deoraíocht* where, at the novel's conclusion, the reader learns that the events are based on papers and documents found on Ó Maoláin's body.

3 Conclusion

The parallels are striking. It is clear that Ó Conaire knew of Conrad and felt strongly enough to write of him and about him. Drawing inferences from the commonalities outlined above, it appears that as a creative writer, Ó Conaire engaged with, and borrowed from, Conrad. As is true of Picasso and T.S. Eliot, such conversations between authors and texts "should be celebrated not hidden" (Gavron 2018). Pádraic Ó Conaire belongs to mainstream European Modernism. It is the literary, cultural and intellectual context that shapes the discussion of his work and links him with later Irish-language modernist writers such as Mac Grianna. He rejected the mode of writing – as demanded by An tAthair Peadar – that tells a smooth story with a beginning, middle and end that reassures and assuages. Being modern, according to Barthes, means knowing that some things can no longer be done. Ó Conaire recognised and felt that reality; consequently, his styles and mode of writing differ radically from those that preceded him, and ironically, many that directly followed him. Rather, he retreats from the polemics of cultural nationalism, rural linguistic purity and cultural certainty to the uncertainty and doubt of nonpartisan reality and interiority. His novels refuse to perpetuate the marginal as the ideal through affirmations of sacrifice and suffering. Instead of retreating into a past that never was, he opens his veins and confused mind to us. Schlund-Vials opines that *Lord Jim* "anticipates in form and content the psychological turn in modernism toward individual agency, existentialism, and trauma. The ostensibly eternal and certainly ambiguous question of Jim's 'soul' – constitutive of related queries about motivation, personal demons, and redemption…." (Schlund-Vials 2009: 320). For Dryden, however, this is "a modernist tale in which nothing can be taken for granted, no 'truths' relied upon, and no romantic closure assumed" (Dryden 2009: xii). *Deoraíocht* is deeply implicated in the advent of a critical self-consciousness within the Irish-language prose tradition. In contrast to almost all other prose texts of the period 1880–1940, it returns the reader to life more violently, more aware and alert to the moment and the experience of modern living (Bacon quoted in Josipovici 2011: 79).

I have argued that Ó Conaire was inspired and influenced by Joseph Conrad. Such an argument lacks conclusive evidence, a smoking gun, a letter of admission but I would argue that the mutual acquaintances, the four essays and what appear to be glaring similarities in their works suggests a link. Proving literary influence is a difficult task. We may never know if Conrad influenced the Unabomber ("Joseph Conrad…" 1996) but when examining Ó Conaire's work in connection to Conrad there is no doubt that these deep currents have a strong pull. If Ó Conaire learned anything from Conrad it was that the old style of storytelling no longer sufficed. From Conrad he acquired:

> […] this shifting narrative style, that resists the simple linear development of the popular realist novels of the preceding century, that has marked Conrad out as a distinctly Modernist author within an accepted literary canon. Conrad's stylistic experimentation enables him to interrogate, re-evaluate and question perhaps his most recurrent thematic interest: morality. However, though early literary critics turned to Conrad as a sort of moral sage, his fictional interrogation of morality, on closer inspection, rejects outright the simple preaching of moral sentiments and "truths." Conrad is instead interested in setting up fictional scenarios in which an apparently obvious set of values, or accepted belief system, is thrown into question – Conrad forces his readers to acknowledge the limitations of their own knowledge, and the historical and geographical specificity of their values and behavioural habits. In doing so, he exposes their relativity and, most importantly, their fragility. (Davies 2017)

From Conrad he arguably acquired not only this literary sensibility but also elements from his plots that he intricately wove into his own novel. His 1924 essay, despite not dealing with Conrad *per se*, may be seen as a tribute to the master's passing and an acknowledgement of his own debt. When we teach and critique *Deoraíocht*, and "Nora Mharcais Bhig," not to mention *An Druma Mór* and *Mo Bhealach Féin*, we might pause to consider that not only are we celebrating the origins of Irish modernism, but perhaps the Polish origins of Irish-language modernist fiction.

Note: *Deoraíocht* was published in Irish in 1910 and reprinted by Conradh na Gaeilge in 1916; by the Educational Company of Ireland in 1920, 1944 and 1994; by Cló Talbot in 1973, with a foreword by Micheál Mac Liammóir; and by Helicon, Dublin, in 1980. Gearailt Mac Eoin's English translation appeared in 1994 with subsequently editions in 1999, 2001 and 2009; it was translated into Danish as *Emigrantliv* in 1999; into German as *Exil* by Gabriele Haefs (2000); into Czech as *Vyhnanství* by Daniela Theinova (2004); into Vietnamese as *Tha hương* in 2007; into Greek as *Tha klápsei kaueís yia tou Máikel* (1999) and into Faroese as *Útlagin* by Angar Artúvertin (2012).

Bibliography

Bourke, Angela. "Legless in London: Pádraic Ó Conaire and Éamon a Búrc." In: *Éire-Ireland*, Vol. 38, No. 3–4, 2003, pp. 54–67.

Cahalan, James M. *The Irish Novel: A Critical History*. Boston: Twayne Publishers, 1988.

Casanova, Pascale. *The World Republic of Letters*. Trans. M.B. DeBevoise. Cambridge: Harvard University Press, 2004.

Conrad, Joseph. "Author's Note." In: *Lord Jim*, ed. Joseph Conrad. New York: Penguin Putnam Inc, Signet Classics, 2009, pp. xv–xvii.

Curtin, Jeremiah. *Myths and Folk-Tales of the Russians, Western Slavs, and Magyars*. Boston: Little & Brown, 1890.

Curtin, Jeremiah. *Creation Myths of Primitive America in Relation to the Religious History and Mental Development of Mankind*. London: Williams and Norgate, 1898.

Curtin, Jeremiah. *Myths of the Modocs*. Boston: Little & Brown, 1912.

Davies, Dominic. "Great Writers Inspire: Joseph Conrad." http://writersinspire.org/content/joseph-conrad. (Accessed 9 July 2018).

de Paor, Louis. "Irish Language Modernisms." In: *The Cambridge Companion to Irish Modernisms*, ed. Joe Cleary. Cambridge: Cambridge University Press, 2014, pp. 161–173.

Dryden, Linda. "Introduction." In: *Lord Jim*, ed. Joseph Conrad. New York: Penguin Putnam Inc, Signet Classics, 2009, pp. v–xiii.

Ellmann, Maud. "Disremembering Dedalus: *A Portrait of the Artist as a Young Man*." In: *Untying the Text: A Post-Structuralist Reader*, ed. Robert Young. London: Routledge and Kegan Paul, 1981, pp. 189–206.

Gavron, Jeremy. "The highest form of flattery? In praise of plagiarism." In: *The Guardian*, February 24, 2018. Online: https://www.theguardian.com/books/2018/feb/24/straightjacket-originality-homage-plagiarism

Hassan, Ihab H. "The Problem of Influence in Literary History: Notes towards a Definition." In: *The Journal of Aesthetics and Art Criticism*, Vol. 14, No. 1, 1955, pp. 66–76.

Hershman, Lynn. "Touch Sensitivity and Other Forms of Subversion: Interactive Artwork." In: *Women, Art, and Technology*, eds. Roger F. Malina and Sean Cubitt. Cambridge: MIT Press, 2003. pp. 431–436.

Hirsch, Edward. *A Poet's Glossary*. Boston: Houghton Mifflin Harcourt Publishing Company, 2014.

Hutchinson, Ben. *Modernism and Style*. Basingstoke: Palgrave Macmillan, 2011.

Jones, Jonathan. "The whole truth about Van Gogh's ear, and why his 'mad genius' is a myth." In: *The Guardian*, July 12, 2016. Online: https://www.theguardian.com/artanddesign/jonathanjonesblog/2016/jul/12/vincent-van-gogh-truth-about-ear-exhibition-on-verge-of-insanity-amsterdam. (Accessed 23 Nov 2018.)

"Joseph Conrad Novel May Have Influenced Alleged Unabomber." In: *Spokesman Review*, Associated Press, July 9, 1996. Online: http://www.spokesman.com/stories/1996/jul/09/joseph-conrad-novel-may-have-influenced-alleged/ (Accessed 23 Nov 2018.)

Josipovici, Gabriel. *What Ever Happened to Modernism?* New Haven: Yale University Press, 2011.

Lukács, György. *The Theory of the Novel*. Trans. Anna Bostock. Monmouth: Merlin Press, 2006.

Madox Ford, Ford. *Critical Writings*, ed. Frank MacShane. Lincoln: University of Nebraska Press, 1964.

Matthews, Steven, ed. *Modernism: A Sourcebook*. Basingstoke: Palgrave Macmillan, 2008.

Mongia, Padmini. "Narrative Strategy And Imperialism in Conrad's Lord Jim." In: *Studies in the Novel*, Vol. 24, No. 2, 1992, pp. 173–186.

Moretti, Franco. *Modern Epic: The World System from Goethe to Garcia Marquez*. Trans. Quintin Hoare. New York: Verso, 1996.

Nicholls, Peter. *Modernisms: A Literary Guide*. Berkeley: University of California Press, 1995.

Ó Conaire, Pádraig. *Deoraíocht*. Baile Átha Cliath: Helicon, 1980.

Ó Dochartaigh, Liam. "Fear Eile ón bPolainn." In: *Irisleabhar Mhá Nuad*, 1980, pp. 9–24.

O'Leary, Philip. *The Prose Literature of the Gaelic Revival, 1881–1921: Ideology and Innovation*. University Park: Penn State University Press, 1994.

Quigley, Megan. "Ireland." In: *The Cambridge Companion to European Modernism*, ed. Pericles Lewis. Cambridge: Cambridge University Press, 2011.

Schlund-Vials, Cathy. "Afterword." In: *Lord Jim*, ed. Joseph Conrad. New York: Penguin Putnam Inc, Signet Classics, 2009.

Simpson, David. *The Origins of Modern Critical Thought: German Aesthetic and Literary Criticism from Lessing to Hegel*. Cambridge: Cambridge University Press, 1988.

Titley, Alan. "The Novel in Irish." In: *The Cambridge Companion to the Irish Novel*, ed. John Wilson Foster. Cambridge: Cambridge University Press, 2006, pp. 171–188.

Vogel, Amos. *Film as a Subversive Art*. New York: Random House, D.A.P./C.T. Editions, 1974.

Breandán Ó Cróinín

A Portrait of the Artist in Late Modern Munster Irish

Abstract: This chapter is a study of cross-linguistic influences and connections. To mark the re-issuing of the autobiographical novel, *An Gealas i Lár na Léithe* [*The Brightness Out There*], by Pádraig Ó Cíobháin, a writer from the West Kerry Gaeltacht, in its 25th anniversary year, this chapter looks in particular at the influence of Joyce's *A Portrait of the Artist as a Young Man* on the later novel. Exploring the linguistic virtuosity of the novel, it shows that Ó Cíobháin's *Bildungsroman* withstands comparison, on more than one level, with that of his illustrious predecessor.

Keywords: James Joyce, Pádraig Ó Cíobháin, *Bildungsroman*, Irish literature

The autobiographical novel, *An Gealas i Lár na Léithe*, by the West Kerry Gaeltacht writer Pádraig Ó Cíobháin, was first published in 1992, and it has recently been reprinted in a revised edition to mark its twenty-fifth anniversary.[1] It was, in fact, one of three early books by the author which we can say took the world of Irish-language literature by storm with the publication of a thousand or so pages of startling prose in a remarkably short period of time, heralding the arrival of an important new voice in Irish fiction: *Le Gealaigh* a collection of short stories was published in January of 1991 and reprinted in October of the same year, followed by this novel *An Gealas i Lár na Léithe* (*An Gealas* henceforth), in the spring of 1992 and this, in turn, was followed by a second collection of short stories *An Grá Faoi Cheilt* in the autumn of the same year. Ó Cíobháin has gone on to publish a further four novels which can be said to be modern or even post-modern novels in the European tradition, a novella, two further collections of short stories, and a volume of retellings of some of the great stories of Old-Irish Literature.[2]

As is the case with many prose writers in Irish, however, there has been very little in terms of what we might call a critical response to much of this remarkable body of work, and I hope that this short essay will go some way towards

1 *An Gealas i Lár na Léithe* (2018) in fact just missed the cut-off date for publication in 2017, the intended year of its publication, which would have made it a twenty-fifth anniversary edition.

2 See Ó Cróinín (2015) for a brief overview of Ó Cíobháin's works to date.

demonstrating that Ó Cíobháin's work is deserving of proper critical analysis and commentary, and that it can in fact withstand comparisons with acknowledged classics of literature, as suggested by the title of the paper. However, *An Gealas* itself, it should be said – whatever about subsequent novels – would seem to have attained the status of a classic work overnight as it was received enthusiastically, not only by the Irish language reading public, but also by some of the more discerning members of our *aos liteartha*. For instance, Liam Ó Muirthile, himself a master craftsman in Irish prose and poetry, wrote in the *Irish Times* shortly after the novel's publication, describing it as follows:

> Odaisé chomhaimseartha déagóra a tharlaíonn a bheith lonnaithe i gCorca Dhuibhne nó idir an Ghráig agus Cill Airne, é *An Gealas i Lár na Léithe*. Pribhléid dúinn an éachtaint a thugann Pádraig Ó Cíobháin ar a mhuintir féin, ar a thírdhreach inmheánach féin, a roinnt leis. Tá gnéithe den úrscéal seo, blúiríocha scríbhneoireachta, a sháraíonn aon phrós Gaeilge nó Béarla, Duibhneach nó neamhDhuibhneach, dá bhfuil foilsithe le tamall fada. Tá a *métier* agus a chanfás aimsithe ag an gCíobhánach. (Ó Muirthile 2014: 126)

> [*An Gealas i Lár na Léithe* is a contemporary odyssey of a teenager which happens to be situated in Corca Dhuibhne [the West Kerry Gaeltacht], or between An Ghráig [the author's place of birth] and Killarney. Pádraig Ó Cíobháin's depiction of his own people, and the sharing of his own internal landscape with us is a privilege. There are aspects of this novel, passages of writing, which surpass any prose in Irish or English, from within Corca Dhuibhne or without, which has been published for a long time.][3]

Furthermore, the eminent scholar and critic, Gearóid Denvir, in an important article on Ó Cíobháin's early work in which he examines various aspects and themes of the early short stories together with the novel presently being discussed, described *An Gealas* in equally glowing terms:

> Ainneoin gur de dhlúth is d'inneach shaol Chorca Dhuibhne ina thréithe tuairisciúla é *An Gealas i Lár na Léithe*, ní creidheall ná caoineadh ná ceiliúradh iardhearcach ar an seansaol atá ann, ach cuntas réalaíoch gan mhaoithneachas, áibhéil ná bréagrómánsúlacht iardhearcach, ar odaisé phearsanta inmheánach duine óig ag éirí aníos, agus na cúinsí éagsúla pearsanta a théas i gcion air. (Denvir 1997: 19)

> [Although *An Gealas i Lár na Léithe* is deeply rooted in the world of West Kerry in its descriptive characteristics it is not a (death)knell or a lament or a pseudo-romantic backward look at times past, but rather a realistic and largely unsentimental depiction of the personal internal odyssey of a young person growing up, and of the personal and community circumstances which influence him.]

3 This and all subsequent translations from Irish to English in this essay are my own.

The first chapters of the novel excel in their descriptions of the author's traditional surroundings, and of his own family, friends and relations, and there are a number of youthful adventures involving the smoking of tea in clay pipes beneath old naomhóga [currachs], bloody encounters with pigs, and dogs with distemper, and so on, leading one to suspect that perhaps this is just another traditional Gaeltacht autobiography – an error Denvir (1997: 18) himself made initially by his own admission. Certainly, an autobiography of this type would be of great interest to advanced language learners and to scholars of Munster Irish due to its richness of idiom and dialect, but as we have already seen, Ó Muirthile and Denvir have both suggested that there is far more to *An Gealas* than this, and it is undoubtedly the quality of the prose and the philosophical, discursive voice which is apparent from the beginning which mark *An Gealas* out as something far more ambitious. The following passage is a good example of the author's style, and indeed his ambition, as he recreates in his mind's eye the scene at milking time when the narrator is left at home with his grandfather in the evening and they are suddenly bathed in brilliant sunlight – the shifting from darkness to light and back, a recurring motif throughout the book:

> Tá fhios agam go bhfuil an léas solais céanna i mbothán na mba ag doirteadh isteach tríd an bhfuinneoigín chúng thiar. Tá teas ag éirí ós na ba agus teas ag éirí ón mbainne ag doirteadh isteach sna bucaoidí. De réir a chéile téann an bainne nuathálaithe cliatháin na mbucaoidí ailimíne agus téitear ar an gcuma san gabhal an chrúdóra fé gach bó atá dá gcrú. Iann siad a súile, míogarnach chodlata thaithneamhach ag teacht orthu agus a gceannaíocha buailte suas go compordach le baotháin na mba acu, tinneas ina méireanta righnithe ag an síortharrac siní agus ag an sniogadh roimh dheireadh táil. Tá prioslaí teo ag sileadh le clab gach bó agus í ag cogaint a círe fén staic, tar éis di a raibh bailithe ina bolg aici d'fhéar a bheith curtha aníos aici agus í ag meilt an fhéir bhoirb léi arís, a súile dúnta le háthas. Cloisim crónán an chait i mbéal dorais an bhotháin, é suite ar a thóin i dteas na gréine, a dhá chois deiridh mar phrapa leis agus é ag leadhbadh fé ioscad cheann dá lapaí tosaigh. Ag súil le pláta dhen mbainne te atá sé chomh luath is a bheidh an chéad bhó eile crúite. Is maith le hidir ainmhí agus dhuine bailiú chun a mhuilinn fhéin. (Ó Cíobháin 1992: 56)

> [I know that the same beam of light is pouring through the narrow window behind in the cow shed. Heat rises from the cows and from the milk pouring into buckets. Gradually, the newly yielded milk warms the sides of the aluminium buckets and in the same way warms the groin of the milker beneath each cow being milked. They close their eyes, a pleasant drowsiness coming over them, their heads pressed comfortably against the flanks of the cows, their fingers painfully stiffened by the constant pulling on teats and the final stripping before the end of the yield. Hot saliva falls from the mouth of each cow as she chews the cud beneath the stack having brought up all the grass she has collected from her stomach as she grinds

away on the coarse grass, her eyes shut with delight. I hear the purring of the cat at the door of the shed, sitting on his backside in the heat of the sun, his two hind legs propping him up and licking the hind part of one of his front paws. He is expecting a plate of hot milk as soon as the next cow is milked. Both man and animal like to draw to their own mills.]

Even in translation, I would argue, this excerpt gives us a fairly good idea of Ó Cíobháin's mastery of language, and his sinewy prose style is also to the fore here, as indeed it is throughout the novel. And, perhaps not surprisingly, these early chapters are full of the wonder of "laethanta bánte diamhra na hóige" ["the incredible white-hot days of youth"], or as the narrator puts it elsewhere, when "iontas ab ea gach cor dá gcuirfeadh an lá dhe" ["every moment of the day was a cause of wonder" (Ó Cíobháin 1992: 8, 3). As the novel progresses, however, and the narrator's internal philosophical voice takes more of a hold on the proceedings, the reader is left in no doubt as to the scale of the author's ambition, and eventually some of his literary sources of inspiration become apparent.

The particular source of literary inspiration to which I have referred in this essay's title is quite obvious I would think, and it is even possible that the milking parlour scene just discussed may well remind us of the "once upon a time […] moocow coming down along the road" to meet "a nicens little boy named baby tuckoo" to quote the opening lines of Joyce's famous *A Portrait of the Artist as a Young Man* (2000: 3), but as we shall see, *An Gealas* has more than moocows in common with Joyce's famous self-portrait, despite the obvious differences between these two authors.

Ó Cíobháin has previously described himself as being from "búndún Chorca Dhuibhne" or, to translate that phrase discreetly, "the very extremity of the West Kerry peninsula." His home place, An Ghráig, lies between Dún Chaoin and Baile an Fheirtéaraigh and is about as far away on the map from the capital city of "Poblacht na hÉireann" as it is possible to get without leaving the island of Ireland. I mention this for two reasons: firstly, since Ó Cíobháin can be said to be a writer on the periphery in the geographical sense, as well as a writer in a minority language – albeit Ireland's first official language – and secondly, since I have nonchalantly referred to Ireland's most famous prose writer in an indirect manner in the title of this essay. Joyce, as is well known, hailed from Ireland's capital city and wrote in English, Ireland's other official language, although it is equally well known that this second fact caused him to engage in much soul searching, as we shall have occasion to mention.

Joyce's *A Portrait of The Artist as a Young Man* is probably the most celebrated example of the *Bildungsroman* or the "coming of age" autobiographical novel (or perhaps more accurately *Künstlerroman* – a novel describing the coming of age of the artist),[4] certainly in Ireland if not internationally, and it is probably safe to say that any aspiring young Irish writer in either of our official languages will at some stage fall under his spell. In fact, Ó Cíobháin in his introductory essay in the new edition of this novel (2018: xxvii–lxvii) specifically mentions Joyce and *A Portrait of the Artist* as being one of his influences when he began writing *An Gealas*, but he also mentions Joyce's *Ulysses*, Dylan Thomas's *A Portrait of an Artist as a Young Dog*,[5] and many other influences as diverse as Milan Kundera, J.P. Donleavy, and even D.H. Lawrence's *Lady Chatterley's Lover*.

However, Ó Cíobháin's voracious literary appetite notwithstanding, it would seem that comparisons with Joyce's *Portrait* in particular are as inevitable as they are obvious and we might do well to very briefly summarise the pertinent – for us here now – aspects of this celebrated work first published just over a hundred years ago: a *Portrait of the Artist* purports to be an account of the early life of Stephen Dedalus from his earliest memories through his school years in the Jesuit run private school at Clongowes Wood (where corporal punishment is at times fiercely meted out) and later after his family fall on hard times in the slightly less prestigious Belvedere College where he is identified as a possible candidate for the priesthood, although by this time he has been attracted to the world of sensual pleasures and has, in fact, begun to visit prostitutes in Dublin's red-light district. Famously, however, Joyce's Stephen re-embraces the church after listening to sermons on the four Last Things – Death, Judgement, Hell and Heaven – whilst on a school retreat, and contemplates a life of religious devotion. The zeal of the reconverted is short-lived however and an epiphany he experiences on Dollymount Strand where he watches a beautiful young woman at the water's edge leads to his final abandonment of the church and his famous declaration to "fly the nets" of "nationality, language and religion" – and to a resolve to live the life of an artist with "cunning, exile and silence" as his weapons. Throughout the novel, Joyce's or rather Stephen's respectable middle-class family looms large in the background, and his relationship with his profligate father is a particularly troubled one. Finally, it should be said that Joyce's obsession with

4 See Titley (1991: 427–47) for a definition of the "Bildungsroman" genre in relation to the Irish-language prose tradition, and Ó Cíobháin (2018: lviii) for a discussion of related terms.

5 The influence of this collection of short stories (Thomas 2001) is worthy of another study, particularly in relation to the earlier chapters of *An Gealas*, and also with regard to some of Ó Cíobháin's earliest short stories in *An Gealaigh* (1991), and in *An Grá Faoi Cheilt* (1992).

language is apparent throughout and, of course, his comments on the English language in Ireland being the language of the oppressor are often quoted:

> The language in which we are speaking is his before it is mine. How different are the words home, Christ, ale, master, on his lips and on mine! I cannot speak or write these words without unrest of spirit. His language, so familiar and so foreign, will always be for me an acquired speech. I have not made or accepted its words. My voice holds them at bay. My soul frets in the shadow of his language. (Joyce 2000: 205)

As we shall see, there are many echoes of Joyce's *Portrait* to be found in *An Gealas i Lár na Léithe*, but at the same time there is much else which would seem to be its diametrical opposite. We might start with the language of the novel: obviously given Ó Cíobháin's background, the novel is written in Irish, and it is Irish – and a distinct dialect of Irish at that – which is to the fore as a theme itself throughout *An Gealas*. Most of the action of the novel takes place in and around the author's home place of the West Kerry Gaeltacht in the late 1950s and through the 1960s, at a time when the language was clearly in the rudest of health there. Also, most of the characters in the novel are either contemporaries of Ó Cíobháin's narrator or, more often, much older than he himself, and for that reason we may well refer to the language of the novel as *An Nua-Ghaelainn Rí-Dhéanach* or, if you prefer, *Very Late Modern Munster Irish*, which is the author's own description of the kind of Irish spoken by himself and his contemporaries.[6]

An Gealas, then, can be said in one sense to give us an accurate description of this Gaeltacht community as it was over 50 years ago now, a community which is linguistically self-sufficient yet aware of the threat, the power and, indeed, of the practical necessity of English in the outside world. Whilst Irish is the lingua franca of the world of Ó Cíobháin's narrator – and it should be pointed out that Irish is spoken even by the shopkeepers in An Daingean or Dingle at this time – the advice given to the narrator of *An Gealas* in relation to his study of English in the local primary school is telling: "[C]oimeád leis an mBéarla, mar chomh luath is a chuirfir barra an Daingin soir duit ní mór an mhaith dhuit do chuid Gaelainne" or to translate this piece of stock advice: "Stick with English because as soon as you are on the other side of Dingle your Irish will not be much good to you" (Ó Cíobháin 1992: 14).

As well as this Killarney, which is described elsewhere in the novel as a dirty or contemptible foreign town ("baile suarach Galltachta") might even be one of the torments that life has in store for the young narrator as is perhaps augured

6 See Ó Cróinín (2014) for a discussion of Ó Cíobháin's use of this particular type of language in his novella, *Novella Eile*.

by the metaphorical description of the crows which he sees loitering with intent in the potato field at home:

> Tagann agus scaipeann na faoileáin ina rabhaiteanna. Tagann agus fanann na crothóga dubha, a gclúmh agus a sciatháin dhubha leo síos fé mar a bheadh sútáin ar shagairt i gcliarscoil, a lapaí atá ag faire ar a méireanta a shnapadh i bhfolach i bpócaí a sútán. Fanaid san ar leathimeall nó go n-imíonn a namhaid – mise agus an chuid eile againn atá mar dhaoine sa ghort – abhaile i gcomhair na bprátaí i lár an lae sara ndéanfaid slad ar na prátaí nuashaolaithe pince. (Ó Cíobháin 1992: 40)

> [The seagulls come and go in great waves. The crows come and stay, their black plumage and wings hanging down like soutanes worn by priests in a clerical school, their hands waiting to snap their fingers hidden in their soutane pockets. They wait on the outer edges until the enemy disappears – myself and the rest of us people in the field – off home for the spuds in the middle of the day, before they slaughter the newborn pink potatoes.]

A clerical school is indeed what is in store for our young hero. After passing his entrance exams, he is sent to *Coláiste Bhréannain* [*St. Brendan's College*] in Killarney from where suitable candidates were at the time given what could be called a vigorous classical education and encouraged to enter the priesthood. As daunting as boarding school can be for a young teenager, it is the added linguistic complication which makes things much worse for our protagonist, and he soon realises that he is undergoing what he understands to be a process of anglicisation behind the ivy-covered walls where he is now obliged to learn and speak English, and to deal with an authoritarian clergy in the stifling atmosphere which prevails. The narrator's initial impressions of this boarding school prove to be only too accurate as much of the time he will spend in what, for him, is a rather forbidding institution will appear to him as a nightmare:

> Cím go bhfuil clúmh eidhneáin ar gach aon fhalla anso. Tá trí phríomhfhoirgneamh sa choláiste ar fad, an clúmh san ar gach ceann acu fé mar a bhéidis ar fad tagtha in inmhe, agus gan mise agus mo chomhaoistí a bhí ag dul isteach sa chéad bhliain ach barrathagtha, an clúimhín go gioblach neamhdhíobhálach tosnaithe ar fhás orainn, ag cur lenár gceal tuisceana ar an saol.
>
> Meileann gach aghaidh dá bhfeicim sa tsuanlios an chéad oíche seo isteach ina chéile, go ndeineann aon aghaidh amháin chomónta díobh uile: aghaidhín bheag phingine bhricní tar éis ghrian an tsamhraidh, an ghruaig bearrtha isteach go dtí an gcnámh ag meaisiní gruaige ár n-aithreacha i mbotháin bha ar fuaid Chiarraí; deireadh an tsamhraidh, gan na ba istigh fós istoíche nuair a deineadh an lomadh; scuabfaí an ruaimneach gruaige amach san aoileach le bruis thigh na mba.
>
> Deifríonn aon dream amháin linn, agus sin iad muintir Thrá Lí. Tá bearradh gruaige le dealramh fachta acu san: *crew cut*, an ghruaig sa stíl-sean ina mbíonn sí ina coilgsheasamh ar a gceannaibh ar nós na gráinneoige. Cuimlím féin lámh bhuartha siar

de mo phláitín ar thóir *crew cut* ná fuil agam. Ní mór ná go ngoilim. Féachaim ar leaid atá le beith sa leaba in aice liom agus é a d'iarraidh a chulaith oíche a tharrac anairde air féin, gan aon cheann dá dhá chois a ardach ró-ard. Dúirt sé liom anois díreach gur duine de mhuintir Dhonnchú ó Oileán Bhéilinse é: Mícheál a chéad ainm. Agus tá a fhios agam, dá raghainn amach ar an leaindeáil mar a bhfuil na báisíní níocháin, agus dá bhféachfainn orm féin i gceann de na scátháin, nach mé a bheadh in ao' chor ann, ach íomhá Mhaidhc Uí Dhonnchú ag féachaint thar n-ais orm. Táim bailithe ó bheith 'om fheiscint féin i ngach aon áit ar fuaid an tsuanleasa; beidh tromluí siúrálta agam anocht. (Ó Cíobháin 1992: 102–3)

[I see that every wall here is covered with an ivy down. There are three main buildings in the college in all and they are all covered with the same down as if they had all reached maturity, while myself and my peers who were just going into first year are only just beginning, the harmless tattered down starting to grow upon us, adding to our ignorance of the world.

Every face that I see in the dormitory melts into one common face: a small freckled penny face after the summer sun, the hair shorn to the bone with our fathers' hair clippers in cow sheds throughout Kerry; the end of the summer and the cattle not yet indoors at night when the shearing was done; the long horsehair would be swept into the dung with the brush from the cow house.

There is one group who are different from us and that is the Tralee contingent. They have all gotten decent haircuts: *crew cut*, the hair in that style where it stands up in spikes on their heads like that of a hedgehog. I rub a worried hand over my own pate searching for a crew cut that I haven't got. I almost start to cry. I look at the lad who is supposed to be in the bed beside me trying to put his pyjamas on without raising either of his legs too high. He said to me just now that he's an O'Donoghue from Valentia Island: Mícheál was his first name. And I know that if I went out onto the landing, where the wash basins are, and looked in one of the mirrors, that it wouldn't be myself that I would see at all but the image of Mike O'Donoghue looking back at me. I am sick of seeing myself everywhere around the dormitory; I'll surely have a nightmare tonight.]

The narrator soon comes to the conclusion that he is being treated as a second class citizen due to the fact that he is a native Irish speaker and he comments – in an exaggerated fashion it must be said – that his plight is the similar to that of a black person in Alabama in 1964.[7]

The contrast between this *coláiste cónaithe* or boarding school in Killarney on the one hand and An Ghráig and Dún Chaoin on the other could not be greater; Killarney is bleak, oppressive and *gallda* – "Anglo" or "foreign" – while the West Kerry enclave to which the narrator belongs, and to which he returns during his

7 "[N]íl aon oidhre air ach a bheith i do dhuine den gcine gorm in Alabama i mbliain seo an Tiarna 1964" ["'It is just like being a black person in Alabama in this the year of the Lord 1964"] (Ó Cíobháin 1992: 109).

holidays, is described as a kind of Gaeltacht utopia where the inhabitants are not beholden to any foreign laws or institutes. The local personalities, both old and young, are fishermen, small farmers, musicians and in some cases reprobate rakes who gather in Kruger's pub in Dún Chaoin in the evenings where they celebrate their way of life in music, song and dance and mingle with the visitors many of whom are there to learn the language – which of course is itself a process of de-anglicisation.

This vision of a Gaeltacht paradise, which is indeed hard to resist and provides many of the finest passages in the novel, is presented to us in the narrator's discursive philosophical voice which matures as the novel progresses, mirroring his growing realisation that he himself will perhaps go on to become a writer who will be able to give a voice to his own people. Along with his gradual discovering of himself as an artist, his physical maturation and his growing attraction to young women is given prominence, and this sexual awakening of the young teenager is, in fact, one of the main themes of the novel. Whilst home for the summer holidays the now sixteen-year-old narrator meets and falls in love for the first time with Sándra, a young girl from Cork, who along with many of her friends is sojourning in the Gaeltacht for much of the summer improving her language skills and learning about life in general. The young couple meet in Kruger's public house while dancing a set together, and later retire to a house in the nearby townland of An tSeantóir where an after hours party is in full swing. Indeed, the magical night time journey on foot from Kruger's back to An tSeantóir provides another fine example of Ó Cíobháin's muscular prose style:

> Tagaimid go bun an bhóithrin a shíneann é fhéin suas i gcoinne an chnoic go dtí an Seantóir. Ciúnaíonn an mathshlua againn, toisc sinn a bheith ag imeacht de bhóthar an rí agus ag tabhairt fé bhóithrín cnoic. Tá diamhaireacht ar an gcnoc fé chlóca na hoíche ná beadh riamh ar an bhfarraige istoíche dhúinne nár chaith oíche riamh amuigh ag iascach, agus ná caithfeadh leis, mar nár ghá dhúinn é. Súnn an cnoc i dtreo bhun a bhoilg sinn – ó sin é an scailéathan atá orainn. Luíonn an ceo mar bhrat ar an dtalamh – na goirt féir ghlais máguaird – mar bíodh go bhfuilimid ag éirí i gcoinne an aird, talamh saothraithe folláinithe ag dea-fheirmeoireacht é seo a thugann barraí maithe coirce, féir, prátaí, meangalsaí is tornapaí de shíor. Agus leanann rian lámha neamhdhíomhaoine na bhfeirmeoirí beaga gur leo an talamh so air le feiscint go mbainimid amach an barra mar a bhfuil tigh na Seantórach. Fáiltím fhéin roimh dhoircheacht agus thaisreacht an bhóithrín seo mar gurb ina leithéid is treise a thuigtear dhom ealaín Dhún Chaoin a bheith. Bolathaím Dún Chaoin im thimpeall, ag teacht fén áit ag an síorcheofrán anocht. Tá sceacha sleaiseálta sciotaithe le feiscint ar éigean ar chliatháin na gclaitheacha, boladh na fiúise – a sligiríní go trom fé ualach boilgíní uisce – á shú isteach i bpolláirí mo shróine agam. Sleamhnaím ar na bollairí i lár an bhóithrín, agus éistím le glór an fhéir ag fás in úsc an fhliucháin. (Ó Cíobháin 1992: 162–3)

[We come to the end of the boreen which stretches itself up against the hill towards An tSeantóir. The crowd quietens since we are leaving the king's highway and are facing into a mountain boreen. There is a mysteriousness about the hillside under the cloak of night which we would never imagine was the case on the sea, never having spent a night fishing as we never had need to and never would. The hill draws us towards the bottom of its belly or at least that is how we wildly imagine it. A fog covers the ground like a carpet – the fields of green grass all around – for although we are going upwards against the hill, this land has been well farmed and cultivated and always produces good crops of oats, grass, potatoes, mangles and turnips. And the mark of these never idle farmers stays with us the whole way until we reach the top where the house at Seantóir is to be found. I myself welcome the darkness and the dampness of this boreen as it is in this kind of place that I understand the true essence [or art] of Dún Chaoin to exist. I smell Dún Chaoin around me soaking into the place with the constant drizzle tonight. You can barely see the slashed and cut hedges on the edges of the fences, the scent of fuschia – its hanging flowers heavy with the weight of rain drops – I breathe in through my nostrils. I slip on the rounded stones in the middle of the boreen, and I listen to the sound of the grass growing in the oozing dampness.]

The party or *bálnight* in An tSeantóir provides the opportunity for our unnamed narrator and Sándra to begin their love affair, as it would appear that this is a case of love at first sight and, unsurprisingly then, the young lovers succumb to their natural desires over the course of a passionate summer of love. It may be, in fact, that the year in question is 1967 – although this is not made clear – and the love scenes which, while they are intense, are artfully handled, and perhaps even bear the influence of Lawrence's *Lady Chatterley's Lover*, which we have mentioned previously. Naturally, however, this whirlwind romance must come to an end as Sándra must of course return home at the end of the summer, while our narrator must return, yet again, to Killarney. It is interesting to note, however, that he himself comments, even at the time of this love affair – or so we are led to believe – while reflecting on what he already knows will be a short-lived love story, that come what may, this relationship will enrich his soul in time to come.[8]

Although he is indeed proved to be correct with the passing of time, things do not look the same when he returns to what for him is the purgatorial, puritanical Anglo-Irish Catholic world of his Killarney boarding school where he soon learns that Sándra has moved on so to speak and, tormented by thoughts of her going to dances with young Corkmen, and by his own lustful thoughts and dreams he lapses into sloth and a kind of teenage depression. He finds himself in the company of outsiders – those who are shunned by the majority of the school

8 "I bhfad ina dhiaidh seo a shaibhreoidh an coidreamh so m'anam" ["It is much later on that this relationship will enrich my soul"] (Ó Cíobháin 1992: 178).

population – and even loses interest in football, which for a Kerryman is a sure sign that things are not right. In many ways he is the archetypal troubled and angst-ridden teenager, uncertain of his place in the scheme of things, afflicted by acne and all the time tortured by thoughts of the terrible sin which he convinces himself that he has committed with Sándra.

It is clear however that it is only when he is in the grey world of the boarding school that his relations with Sándra seem to him to be sinful – here he is convinced of it because of the process of anglicisation which he has undergone, and as a result of the force-fed diet of a religion which sees the sin of lust as the greatest of all sins, or perhaps the only sin. This is in stark contrast to the way in which he sees and understands the world when at home where his own role models are portrayed as free and unbothered by men of the cloth or by other authority figures as we have already seen, and, although his Gaeltacht people are portrayed as a people of faith theirs is a faith rooted in folk tradition rather than one controlled by the dictates of any oppressive institution.

It would seem to me that the inescapable conclusion for the reader here is that it is precisely because the tormented youth is set adrift from his own culture and language that he suffers these pangs of conscience, and it is whilst he is in this state of confusion that he turns to the institutional religion which presents itself as being his *Gealas i Lár na Léithe* or "Brightness in the Midst of the Greyness," to give the novel's title a rather too literal translation. The brightness he sees in the midst of the greyness around him is the brightly painted college chapel (Ó Cíobháin 1992: 204–5) where he seeks solace, firstly by attending daily mass and secondly, when this seems futile, by attending a spiritual retreat where he listens intently to the fierce words of Father Ó Cadhla whose final sermon on the pains of hell awaiting those who do not repent is more than a match for Joyce's sermon on the same theme. Denvir has suggested that this part of the novel is perhaps a little too obviously based on Joyce's *Portrait*, but we might look at this another way and suggest that Ó Cíobháin outdoes Joyce here, as an analysis of this sermon would seem to suggest that he has gone as far as back as the eighth century Old-Irish religious text *Fís Adamnáin*[9] or *The Vision of Adamnán* for inspiration – an intertextual sleight of hand which has since become a trademark of Ó Cíobháin's.

At any rate, inspired by this final sermon of fire and brimstone the by this time desperate youth resolves to confess his sins, and having done so is so overjoyed that he experiences a kind of religious ecstasy, proclaiming himself ready

9 See *Fís Adomnáin* edited by Whitley Stokes in *Irische Texte*, Leipzig, 1880, pp. 165–96.

to worship God with his whole heart and soul, but also tellingly, through, as he says, "urlabhra mo bhréagchráifeachta" ["my sanctimonious speech"] (Ó Cíobháin 1992: 236). It is interesting to note that his experience in the confessional is made easier by his inadvertent use of his native language which, fortunately, is allowed by the priest who we learn speaks Irish and has a rather naive view of the Gaeltacht people as being paragons of Catholic virtue to a man and a woman.

As we might suspect, however, this new religious fervour does not last and before long it is clear that our hero has become the master of his own destiny, and even before he returns home for the summer he knows that the life of a priest, which has already been ruled out for him in the confessional, is not for him since the celibate life is evidently not one that he can endure, or as he says "[n]í hann a mheasfainn dhom fhéin mo shaol a chaitheamh gan cuimhneamh ar bhean" ["I surely don't intend to spend my life without ever thinking of a woman"] (Ó Cíobháin 1992: 260).

Although he is treated with suspicion by many of his contemporaries when at home, some of whom feel that he is perhaps no longer one of them, his solution to his problems is the very opposite of Joyce's Stephen Dedalus, who famously sought the life of an artist in exile where he could "forge in the smithy of his soul the uncreated conscience of [his] race." In *An Gealas*, however, the narrator's instinct is to return home and reconnect with his native culture. He develops an even closer relationship with his father during the final summer holiday described here, and visits to his grandparents' home – where snuff, sherry and tobacco are always to be had – are akin, he says, to "returning to the womb."[10] Here he is impervious to the Anglo-Irish world without as he luxuriates in the comfort of his home place, surrounded by the mellifluous sounds of the Old-Irish or SeanGhaelainn of Cloichear and of Baile Reo – the native townlands of his grandfather and grandmother, respectively.

He is aware now that he will most likely have to live outside this community – not by choice however – and his desire to become a writer and to speak on behalf of his own people strengthens as he realises that he may yet act as "an interpreter who will express in print the matters which are of concern, interest and regret to them, those things which are of profit, pleasure and of value to them, when [he] is ready to face that challenge [himself]."[11] He is aware that none of this remarkable

10 "[Is] geall le dul thar n-ais 'on bhroinn é" (Ó Cíobháin 1992: 249).

11 "[I]m theanga labhartha a chuirfeadh i bhfriotal an chló scríte na nithe is cíos, cás is cathú dhóibh, na nithe is sochar, sonas is séan dóibh, nuair a thiocfadh sa tsaol go mbeadh de choinníoll ionam an triailsean a chur orm fhéin" (Ó Cíobháin 1992: 290).

community will live forever but he is determined that "their vitality, thoughts, speech and opinions, things that are more important than flesh and blood"[12] will live on in himself and in his writings, which he hopes will come in time.

One of the final scenes in the book, when the narrator returns home late at night from a tryst with his new love, Rosailí, paints a picture of a youth who is full of hope for the future, at ease with himself and his place in the world, and full of love for his own people and his native place:

> Cím solas i seomra codlata m'athar agus mo mháthar taobh thiar dár dtighne uaim soir. Tá barra na fuinneoige oscailte, sioscadh suaimhneasach na trá isteach chucu. Tá scáth m'athar agus é ar a ghlúine ag bonn na fuinneoige le feiscint, ag rá a phaidreacha, nó ceann éigin é ag feitheamh go dtiocfainnse abhaile mar táim déanach. Líonann mo shúile de dheora, a mblas im bhéal mar go sileann siad anuas ar mo leicne agus go leadhbaim d'uachtar mo bheol iad. Deora paisiúnta buíochais. Grá do m'athair, grá do mo mháthair, grá do mo mhuintir uile; grá don áit seo ó bhun Chnoc Bréanainn go Ceann Sléibhe, grá do Rósailí go bhfuilim ina croí istigh agus í sin im chroíse. Titeann ceo draíochta i gcoim oíche orm, anois is gan mé a thuilleadh ar strae. (Ó Cíobháin 1992: 336–7)

> [I see in the distance a light in my father and mother's bedroom at the back of our house to the east. The top of their window is open to the soothing whispering from the strand. My father's shadow can be seen where he kneels at the bottom of the window as he says his prayers, or perhaps he is just waiting for me to come home as I am late. My eyes fill with tears, their taste in my mouth as they trail down my cheeks and I lick them from the top of my lip. Passionate tears of joy. Love for my father, love for my mother, love for all my people; love for this place from the bottom of Cnoc Bréanainn to Ceann Sléibhe, love for Rosailí who is in my heart and I in hers. A magic mist descends upon me in the middle of the night, now that I am no longer astray.]

An Gealas, is in the end – much like Joyce's *Portrait* – a hopeful or an optimistic book, despite the trials and tribulations suffered by the narrator in his youth. It is in my opinion the finest *Bildungsroman* written in Irish in modern times, and we are certainly not short of them. It can also withstand comparison, as I hope is evident, with anything in the genre written in the Anglo-Irish literary tradition. In truth, if the author had stuck with one of his original working titles, "Portráid den Ealaíontóir agus É go Cabanta" ["A Portrait of the Artist when He was a Precocious Brat"] (Ó Cíobháin 2018: xxviii), few would have thought him to be over ambitious. And perhaps one of the most extraordinary things about Ó Cíobháin's early work, in addition to his great ambition, is how outward looking he is. His models are not, as we might expect, the writers of the Great Blasket

---

12 "[M]airfidh a mbeocht, a gcuimhnte, a gcainteanna, a dtuairimí, rud[aí] is tábhachtaí ná feoil is fuil" (Ó Cíobháin 1992: 332).

Island, and of Corca Dhuibhne in general, but the great writers of Europe, some of whom we mentioned earlier and many more of whom he mentions in his own introduction to *An Gealas*. Of course, much of the pleasure of reading *An Gealas* is due the author's absolute mastery of the idiom of his native Munster Irish, and he has gone on to become one of our major – and most challenging – prose writers. Pádraig de Paor has written of the "martyrdom" of Irish prose writers in general, and specifically of Ó Cíobháin as a prose writer who has written one stunning work after another, quietly and without much recognition, and the same can be said, of course, of several other prose writers in Irish.[13]

This may be about to change for Ó Cíobháin, however: Gearóid Denvir, in a recent essay published in *Úrscéalta na Gaeilge*, writes as follows in his discussion of another novel of Ó Cíobháin's – *Desiderius a Dó* – published in the year 1995:

> Úrscéal é *Desiderius a Dó* le Pádraig Ó Cíobháin a d'eascair as zeitgeist na linne agus as cúraimí leanúnacha aeistéitiúla agus smaointeoireachta is féidir a rianú aniar trí shaothar a údair ó foilsíodh a chéad úrscéal, *An Gealas i Lár na Léithe*, sa mbliain 1992. Rianaítear ann oilithreacht anama an té a fáisceadh as cruinneshamhail dorcha Ríordánach na 1950idí in Éirinn, ach a tháinig in inmhe i ndomhan úrnua réabhlóideach na saoirse pearsanta i ndeireadh na 1960idí agus tús na 1970idí. Is é an focal, arna ionramháil, go cruthaitheach ag an saor focal, maille le próisis chruthaitheacha eile mar an ealaín, an ceol, an fhealsúnacht, an reiligiún fiú, a shoilsíos an ród le linn na hoilithreachta. (Denvir 2018: 247)
>
> [*Desiderius a Dó* by Pádraig Ó Cíobháin is a novel which has sprung from the *zeitgeist* of the times and from ongoing aesthetic and reflective concerns which can be traced back through the work of its author since the publication of his first novel, *An Gealas i Lár na Léithe*, in the year 1992. In it we follow the spiritual pilgrimage of one who was moulded in the dark Ó Ríordáin-like world of 1950s Ireland and who came of age at the end of the 1960s and in the early 1970s. It is language itself, having been manipulated creatively by the wordsmith, together with other creative processes such as art, music, philosophy, and even religion, which light the road during the pilgrimage.]

An Gealas is, as we have already seen, perhaps best described as an odyssey rather than a pilgrimage but this description of another outstanding novelistic achievement by Ó Cíobháin could obviously just as easily be applied to the work under discussion here. It is quite clear to the present writer in any case, that Ó Cíobháin's entire body of work is deserving of this kind of scholarly attention and intellectual criticism, and what better place to start than with this early

---

13 Here, I paraphrase from de Paor's original text: "Is liosta le háireamh sa Ghaeilge na scríbhneoirí fónta nach bhfaigheann mórán aitheantais, scríbhneoirí próis ach go háirithe, Pádraig laochúil Ó Cíobháin a bhfuil éacht i ndiaidh éachta curtha i gcrích go ciúin aige, gan ach sampla follasach amháin a lua" (de Paor 2014: 127).

autobiographical novel? The present essay, of course, is an attempt to investigate just one aspect of what is, in many ways, quite a complex work, but I would hope that *An Gealas* will yet get the recognition it deserves from Irish language scholars.

In conclusion, I should briefly mention the book's title and the new edition: *An Gealas i Lár na Léithe*, as I have already suggested can be literally translated as "The Brightness in the Midst of the Greyness," but that would be a poor translation indeed. The author has informed me that the expression relates to a certain point in the sky out to sea visible from his parents' home in An Ghráig where a brightness can be seen when poor weather is about to clear – when, as is often said metaphorically "tiocfaidh aimsir bhreá fós" ["fair weather will come yet"]. The translation "The Brightness Out There" has, I believe, been suggested by the poet Liam Ó Muirthile and I think this might not be too far off the mark. Other translations have been suggested by scholars who have mentioned the novel *en passant* elsewhere: Sewell (2004: 471) suggests "The Gleam Amid the Grey" while Máirín Nic Eoin's "A Gleam of Light Across the Grey" (2007: 152) is not bad at all.

I suggested to the author some time ago that a new edition of *An Gealas* would be a good idea, but he took a little persuading, tending as he does now, to look forward rather than back. Fortunately, however, he was convinced in the end, and I have been privileged to work with him on the new edition and, indeed, to write a short introduction to the novel (Ó Cróinín 2018). More importantly, the author's own lengthy introductory essay (Ó Cíobháin 2018: xxvii–lxvii) will be of great interest to those who have followed his career. This new edition has been carefully revised, and in fact destandardised to a certain extent; errors have been ironed out, and the author has made some subtle changes to the text here and there which will give scholars plenty to think about in years to come when arguments will no doubt rage over the definitive text of *An Gealas i Lár na Léithe*. As, of course, is the case with many a classic novel.

Bibliography

Denvir, Gearóid. "Ár Leithéidí Arís? Léamh ar Shaothar Phádraig Uí Chíobháin." *Oghma*, 7, 1995, pp. 17–32.

Denvir, Gearóid. "Desiderius a Dó (1995)." In: *Úrscéalta na Gaeilge*, eds. Ronan Doherty, Brian Ó Conchubhair and Philip O'Leary. Indreabhán: Cló Iarchonnacht, 2018, pp. 247–67.

de Paor, Pádraig. *Áille na hÁille*. An Daingean: An Sagart, 2014.

Lawrence, David Herbert. *Lady Chatterley's Lover*. London: Harper Press, 2013.

Nic Eoin, Máirín. "Twentieth Century Gaelic Autobiography." In: *Modern Irish Autobiography: Self, Nation and Society*, ed. Liam Harte. Basingstoke, Hampshire and New York: Palgrave MacMillan, 2007, pp. 132–55.

Ó Cíobháin, Pádraig. *Le Gealaigh*. Baile Átha Cliath: Coiscéim, 1991.

Ó Cíobháin, Pádraig. *An Gealas i Lár na Léithe* (An Chéad Eagrán). Baile Átha Cliath: Coiscéim, 1992.

Ó Cíobháin, Pádraig. *An Grá Faoi Cheilt*. Baile Átha Cliath: Coiscéim, 1992.

Ó Cíobháin, Pádraig. *An Gealas i Lár na Léithe* (An Dara hEagrán). Baile Átha Cliath: Coiscéim, 2018.

Ó Cróinín, Breandán. "Leabhar na Míosa." *Comhar*, Meán Fómhair, 2014, pp. 25–27.

Ó Cróinín, Breandán. "Brolach." In: *De Chion Focal*, ed. Pádraig Ó Cíobháin. Baile Átha Cliath: Coiscéim, 2015, pp. xiii–xxvii.

Ó Cróinín, Breandán. "Laethanta Bánte Diamhra na hÓige." In: *An Gealas i Lár na Léithe*, ed. Pádraig Ó Cíobháin, Baile Átha Cliath: Coiscéim, 2018, pp. ix–xxvi.

Ó Muirthile, Liam. "An Ghréig ar an nGráig." In: *Rogha Alt*, ed. Liam Ó Muirthile. Baile Átha Cliath: Cois Life, 2014, pp. 124–126.

Sewell, Frank. "James Joyce's Influence on Writers in Irish." In: *The Reception of James Joyce in Europe, Vol. I: Germany, Northern and East Central Europe*, eds. Geert Lernout and Wim Van Mierlo. London: Thoemmes Continuum, 2004, pp. 469–81.

Thomas, Dylan. *A Portrait of the Artist as a Young Dog*. London: Phoenix, 2001.

Titley, Alan. *An tÚrscéal Gaeilge*. Baile Átha Cliath: An Clóchomhar, 1991.

Mark Ó Fionnáin

Rats, Wraiths and Railways – The Irish Language in Science-Fiction and Fantasy

Abstract: This chapter brings us to the final frontier as it takes off after traces of the Irish language to be found in modern science fiction by authors as diverse as Harry Harrison, Tim Armstrong and Andrzej Sapkowski in locales as varied as the island of Sodor and Mega City One. Along the way there is space to explore the linguistic politics of the cosmos – why *do* aliens speak sometimes English, sometimes Scottish Gaelic? Although there is not much science fiction in Irish, Ó Fionnáin shows there has been a surprising amount of Irish in science fiction.

Keywords: science fiction, literature, Irish language

1 Introduction

A brief glance at the range of literature available in the Irish language today reveals that there are many genres and types to sate the appetite of its readership: biographies, short stories, novels, poetry, plays, but a closer examination reveals that there is little or no science-fiction or fantasy.[1] True, there are translations, including those from the 1920s and '30s which were produced under the Irish Free State's *An Gúm* translation scheme, such as *The First Men on the Moon* (translated as "An Chéad Chuairt ar an nGealaigh") and *The War of the Worlds* [*Cogadh na Reann*], and more recent efforts, such as the first *Harry Potter* "Harry Potter agus an Órchloch," *The Hobbit* "An Hobad," the two *Alice in Wonderlands* "Eachtraí Eilíse i dTír na nIontas" and "Lastall den Scáthán agus a bhFuair Éilís roimpi,"[2] and the first book of the series *A Song of Fire and Ice*, namely *A Game of Thrones* "Cluiche na Corónach."[3] In addition to these, there

1 It is beyond the scope of this paper to enter into a discussion about what constitutes science-fiction or fantasy, especially in an Irish-language setting. The interested reader is directed to Fennell (2014) and O'Leary (2005, 2011).

2 These two are modern translations by Nicholas Williams, who also translated *The Hobbit*. The original 1927 translation of *Alice* by Pádraig Ó Cadhla has also been recently reissued.

3 The translator of *Cluiche na Corónach*, Oisín Ó Muirthile, has announced that he has started on the second book, and that there are other fantasy texts he would also like to work on, including some by Terry Pratchett (http://tuairisc.ie/tus-curtha-le-haistriuchan-gaeilge-ar-an-dara-leabhar-sa-tsraith-game-of-thrones/). Whilst this is

are those not done directly from English, such as the first book in Isaac Asimov's *Foundation* trilogy from Swedish entitled "An Fhondúireacht" and Viktor Pelevin's *Омон Ра* "Amón-Rá" from the Russian.

There are some native works which could indeed be classified as science-fiction or fantasy, but they are few and far between, for example the novella *Pax Dei* from the 1980s but which has only just over 60 pages in it, and the occasional fantastical or sci-fi-ish short story by the likes of Alan Titley, Mícheál Ó Conghaile or Daithí Ó Muirí. It would be outlandish to claim, however, that Irish has anything approaching a sci-fi genre, never mind fantasy.[4] This means that not only is Irish lagging behind its much more powerful linguistic neighbour, but also behind its sister languages, Scottish Gaelic and Manx: the Scots have published their first proper hard-core sci-fi novel – *Air Cuan Dubh Drilseach* – and first fantasy – *An Sgoil Dhubh*[5] – and Manx its first fantasy novel as well, *Droghad ny Seihill*.[6]

This lack of sci-fi in Irish made the author of *Air Cuan Dubh Drilseach*, the American Tim Armstrong, ask on his blog why there is so little sci-fi material in Irish. There are several suggestions: according to Philip O'Leary, in the new Catholic Ireland that arose after the founding of the Free State, there was not much interest in science generally (following on from the Catholic Church's

good news for Irish language fans of fantasy, it again underlines the paucity of native sci-fi/fantasy texts. It further raises the question of whether it is worth setting about translating a whole series of (very sizeable) books if the translations are to rely on the translator's own goodwill and free time.

4 This is not to ignore the output of the prolific Cathal Ó Sándair (1922–1996), who wrote many books in many genres in Irish, including several space adventures with An Captaen Spéirling (see Fennell 2014: 140–47).

5 There is also the novel *Gormshuil an Rìgh* by Fionnlagh MacLeòid which could be classed as fantasy in that "kings and heroes can encounter fabulous creatures with unlikely abilities," but in Watson's opinion it is more of an "allegorical novel," where there is no attempt made to set the scene or offer any explanations (Watson 2011: 180–81).

6 Regarding Scottish Gaelic, the online Gaelic bookshop run by *Comhairle na Leabhraichean* ("The Gaelic Books Council" www.gaelicbooks.org) has a section dedicated solely to sci-fi/fantasy books. At the time of writing, during Glasgow's planned Book Festival in March 2018 (www.ayewrite.com) there will be a discussion specially dedicated to "The New Wave of Gaelic Sci-Fi" featuring Tim Armstrong (*Air Cuan Dubh Drilseach*), Iain F. MacLeòid (*An Sgoil Dhubh*, and his latest *An Taistealach*) and Dàibhidh Eyre (*Cailèideascop*). In comparison to Scottish Gaelic, Irish does not even have an old wave of sci-fi. As for Manx, the author of *Droghad ny Seihill*, Christopher Lewin has also written a "fantasy" short story entitled *Jough-Laanee Aegid* "An Elixir of Youth" in his collection *Jough-Laanee Aegid as Skeealyn Elley*.

lead), never mind sci-fi (O'Leary 2005; 2011: 117–125). Jack Fennell, drawing on O'Leary's works, reiterates the opinion that Irish speakers were too obsessed with issues of dialect and orthography, literary language, fonts etc. to be bothered with inventing new words and genres (Fennell 2014: 121; O'Leary 2010: 35–40). But another opinion also expressed by O'Leary might be truer, in that sci-fi and fantasy were never really considered proper literature to begin with.

Armstrong says that he cannot comment on the first opinion of O'Leary's, i.e. that there was no interest in science generally, but regarding "proper" literature he has this to say:

> Nuair a leughas mi ficsean saidheans, chan eil mi an dùil ri sgudal, ach cuid dhen litreachas as dùbhlanaich agus as inntinnich a leughar anns an latha an-diugh, agus gu dearbh, tha mi a' smaoineachadh [...] anns an t-saoghal nuadh anns a bheil teicneòlas a' toirt buaidh nas treasa air beatha mhac-an-duine le gach latha, tha ficsean-saidheans a' sìor fhàs nas cudromaich mar *genre*. Agus am fianais Mary Shelley gu Kazuo Ishiguro, an robh daoine inntinn-fhosgailte a-riamh fo amharas gum b' urrainnear litreachas le "L" mòr a sgrìobhadh ann am ficsean-saidheans? Ach chan eil teagamh gu bheil cuid mhòr ann fhathast nach cuir mòran diù anns an *genre*, agus is dòcha gu bheil am beachd staoin sin a' claonadh sgrìobhadh ann an Gàidhlig na h-Èireann agus Gàidhlig na h-Alba fòs. (Armstrong 2015)
>
> [When I read science-fiction, I'm not hoping for cheap rubbish, but some of the most challenging and intellectual literature which is being read today and, I think [...] in the new world in which technology is influencing people's lives more and more each day, science-fiction is continually growing as a genre. And in the light of [writers from] Mary Shelley to Kazuo Ishiguro, was any open-minded person ever in doubt that science-fiction was not literature with a capital "L"? But there is no doubt that there are still many today who have no interest in the genre, and it is likely that that that shallow opinion is still biasing writing in Irish and Gaelic (my translation).]

He asks his blog's readership why there is no sci-fi in Irish, but he gets no worthwhile answer. One reader does suggest the author Tomás Mac Síomóin, but when asked what sci-fi he has written, the respondent falls silent.[7]

---

7 Of course, several reasons why there might be no sci-fi/fantasy in Irish is that writers have no interest in the topic, no imagination, no time, or a myriad of other reasons. Regarding Mac Síomóin, he has written several books that are fantastical, e.g. *An bhFuil Stacey ag Iompar* "Is Stacey Pregnant?" about a traffic jam the length of Ireland, where people have to struggle to survive in their cars which are going nowhere, in a type of Irish-language "Lord of the Flies," but, again, it would not be considered sci-fi or fantasy *per se*. Armstrong is also doing his bit by rescuing lesser-known Scottish Gaelic science-fiction short stories (the "old wave"?) from obscurity and discussing them on his website, for example *Oirthir Tìm* by Cailein MacCoinnich, *An t-Adhar Ùr* by Dennis

Thus, it would appear that apart from translations and the occasional short piece here and there if one can find it,[8] sci-fi and fantasy does not exist as a genre in Irish. But that is not to say that the Irish language itself does not exist in a science-fiction or fantasy setting. The aim of this paper is to therefore take a look at some of the references and usages of Irish in sci-fi, and to comment on how successful they were in creating the worlds of tomorrow.[9]

2 Judge Dredd

The latest notable usage of Irish is in a recent edition of the British comic *2000AD*. *2000AD* is a science-fiction/fantasy comic that has been coming out each week since 1977. One of its mainstay characters is Judge Dredd, who polices the futuristic Mega-City One in post-apocalyptic America, and who is, depending on the circumstances and the criminal, judge, jury and executioner. In the story *Blood of Emeralds* that ran in Progs (Issues) 1934–1939 in 2015, Dredd and his Irish partner Judge Joyce end up in Murphyville (the Ireland of the future),[10] and in Prog 1938 they can be seen heading towards the local spaceport. Down in the corner of the last picture on the page there is a standing stone with a Celtic swirl and the words "Spásfort Bhaile Átha Cliath." The English for this is "Dublin City Spaceport," but there is no English offered in the frame.

King, *Mr. Universe* and *An Duine Ùr* by Rob Shirley, and *An t-Eilean Cèin* by Garbhan MacAoidh.

8 Other occasional sci-fi pieces that are very much under the radar but which have been brought to my attention are *In Inmhe* by Eoin P. Ó Murchú in *Misneach 6*, and (the beginning of) *Scéal an Spásgharda*, on Panu Petteri Höglund's website https://irishforenglishspeakers.blog/2017/06/06/sceal-an-spasgharda-tus/. Ó Murchú is currently in the process of working on an Irish translation of Armstrong's novel, and Höglund is the translator of *An Fhondúireacht* from Swedish.

9 This article makes no claims to be in any way comprehensive, as it would be impossible to read every single word in English sci-fi or fantasy to see if there is any use of Irish. The following examples are merely those the author has managed to find and deemed relevant. Others have been excluded, for example the series *The Navigator Kings* by Garry Kilworth, where Polynesian seafarers capture a Gaelic-speaking Scot. There are some sentences and words in Gaelic in the series, but this would probably be expected, due to its premise.

10 Murphyville was originally introduced in Progs 727–732 and was created by Northern Ireland writer Garth Ennis (*Hellblazer*, *Preacher*, *Punisher*, etc.) to parody and send up Ireland and its stereotypes. Carroll has rooted Murphyville more in reality as opposed to jokiness.

The writer of this particular Judge Dredd story, Michael Carroll, is himself Irish, and he is not the first Irishman to write or draw for the comic, but he would seem to be the first to make the effort to put some Irish, however brief, into a story, and correctly too, as can be seen by the use of the genitive case (i.e. *Bhaile* and not *Baile*), and the recently composed neologism *spásfort* "spaceport." It might be tempting to see this just as a case of the typical "cúpla focal" "couple of words/ lipservice" that is frequently paid to Irish, even in Ireland, although in itself this is to be welcomed in an English-language comic. This could be understood, however, as Carroll making a discrete statement about Ireland's still independent culture and heritage. As the story is concerned with the animosity between Murphyville and Brit-Cit (the England of the future), this simple use of Irish – without an accompanying English explanation – could also be read as a political statement, in that, despite everything – and especially the fact that Murphyville only exists because of Brit-Cit's financial aid – the Ireland of the future is still culturally distinct from its larger, more powerful neighbour. For a comparison with this use of Irish, in more recent issues (Progs 2055–2060, November-December 2017), Judge Dredd goes to future-Siberia, where he encounters Sov (i.e. Soviet, i.e. Russian) judges. Despite this story also being written by Michael Carroll, the Sov judges, and the local Siberian hostiles, all speak impeccable English, even amongst themselves, their badges have their names written in English and not Cyrillic (e.g. *Zima* instead of *Зима*), and even when they curse (which is in Russian, despite their fondness for the Queen's English), it is given in Roman letters as opposed to Cyrillic (e.g. *yebena mat'* and not *ебена мать*), all of which makes it easier for the English-language reader to know what is going on. It should be noted that this is generally the case, regarding Sovs and others, and as the comic is English it of course makes sense that foreign languages and alphabets would be avoided. As such, however, it puts into context Carroll's decision to make the effort to use some untranslated Irish in his story.

3 The Stainless Steel Rat Wants You!

Whilst one might reasonably expect the Ireland of the future to still be (at least officially) bilingual, and thus an encounter with Irish is nice, but not necessarily totally unexpected, when we move further afield and out into the cosmos the issue of language becomes more complicated: so many aliens and races, each with their own language and method of communication. Of course, one could ignore these problems and make everyone a linguistic expert, *à la* Han Solo in *Star Wars* who effortlessly communicates in English with Wookies, Rodions, Hutts, etc. Another path was taken in *The Hitchhiker's Guide To The Galaxy*, where a Babel

Fish is inserted in the ear and you instantly understand all languages. But the American author Harry Harrison chose a different route.

Harrison fought in the Second World War, and whilst in the army became interested in Esperanto as a universal language, learnt the language, became a member of the Esperanto Society, and eventually President of the Irish Esperanto Association for a period, when he settled there in the 1970s.[11] He wrote several series of sci-fi books, and frequently in his universes he gets around the language issue by making Esperanto the universal language, which every technologically advanced race speaks. This holds true for his series about The Stainless Steel Rat,[12] otherwise known as "Slippery" Jim diGriz. Originally a thief (a Stainless Steel Rat), Jim has a heart of gold and is thus frequently called upon to save the world – or, indeed, the galaxy.

In one of the stories, *The Stainless Steel Rat Wants You!*, aliens are waging war on our galaxy and Jim goes undercover to thwart them, heading for the latest planet they have taken over and which they are now using for their base. Whilst doing so, he encounters the original inhabitants of the planet, who are called *Cill Airne*, which is the original Irish of the Anglicised placename "Killarney." And in order to show that the Cill Airne do not possess technology, and thus do not speak in Esperanto, what language does Harrison give them?

> "*Estas granda plezuro renkonti vin*," I said, but they were unmoved. "If they don't speak Esperanto what do they talk?" I asked Angelina.
> "Their own language of which I have learned a few words. *Do gheobhair gan dearmad taisce gach seoid*," she added. They nodded in agreement at this, clattered their weapons and emitted shrill war cries.
> "You made quite a hit with them," I said.
> "I told them that you were my husband, the leader of our tribe, and you had come here to destroy the enemy and lead them to victory." (Harrison 1985: 64)

And later on:

> There was instant agreement on the plan. In the diGriz family we are used to making our minds up rather quickly, while the Cill Airne had learned to do the same in their constant war against the enemy. Some moldering floor coverings were thrown back to reveal a trapdoor that was levered up. I was beginning to think that the aliens were not very bright if they let this sort of thing happen under their very noses, or smelling tentacles, or whatever. Bolivar and James dropped into the opening followed by our allies who exited with many shouts of *Scadan, Scadan*! (Harrison 1985: 66)

---

11 See his autobiography for a detailed look at his life-long love for Esperanto (Harrison 2014: 281–294).

12 And the *Deathworld* series.

The Irish used in the first quote is, in fact, a line from a poem by the Munster poet Eoghan Rua Ó Súilleabháin (1748–1784), and it is most unlikely that Ó Súilleabháin ever thought that he would be quoted billions of years into the future. It is worth noting, however, that Angelina's translation is not too far off: the original line means "You will get without fail the best of all jewels" and if freedom from the aliens is indeed what the Cill Airne desire and what they are fighting for, and this is what they will achieve under Jim, then her words actually do make sense in this context. It is clear, therefore, that Harrison did not choose this line at random, and that he must have had some interest in Irish. He could have chosen a language – any language – at random, opened a dictionary and taken the first words that came to hand, or, indeed, put down the first random collection of letters that entered his head. Instead, he carefully chose something that actually makes sense in context.

Regarding the shout of encouragement "*Scadan, Scadan*!" (= *scadán*) "Herring, herring!" there would therefore seem to be deliberately chosen nonsense here, as opposed to randomly chosen nonsense, as it were, in that he could have chosen an Irish word that actually makes sense in the context, but he opted not to do so. Except that, on further consideration, maybe it does, in fact, make some sort of sense, as in English "herring" and "hurry(ing)" are quite close phonetically, and so it is entirely plausible that he deliberately chose a word that is similar in translation, and thus there is actually deliberate sensible nonsense in this little word here.

And if Harrison did indeed have such an interest in Irish that he carefully and deliberately chose his words, a line from Eoghan Rua Ó Súilleabháin is probably not the first thing an American or any foreigner would learn, unless they have in their possession a copy of the old *Teach Yourself Irish*,[13] which contains the words *Cill Airne* and *scadán*, and in which Ó Súilleabháin's lullaby, along with an English translation, is given as a piece of reading at the end of the book. Did Harrison have a copy of *Teach Yourself Irish* and use it? If so, how far did he get (*Cill Airne* appears at the end of Chapter 4, *scadán* further on, and Eoghan Rua's poetry at the back)? It is an intriguing thought, and might explain Harrison's interesting choice of Irish vocabulary for his book.[14]

---

13 That by Dillon and Ó Cróinín.

14 His fun with languages expressed itself in other ways as well. In the same book it is stated that "dup" is an insult on the planet Blodgett, which is phonetically the same as the Welsh word "dwp" meaning "stupid." He also apparently used some Cornish in one of his books, but at the time of writing I have failed to locate it. The website sciencefictionobserver.blogspot.com has an entry from 8/06/2016 on the foreign

Another point of interest is what happens to Irish when it has to be translated into other languages. If a language has a Latin alphabet, then there is no problem in merely writing out Ó Súilleabháin's words, except for spelling the Irish correctly, which the Polish translator failed to do:[15]

- *Estas granda plezvro renkonti vin* - oświadczyłem, ale nie wykazali żadnych oznak zrozumienia. Spytałem więc Angelinę: - Jeśli nie znają esperanto, to jak się z nimi dogadałaś?
- Ich własnym językiem, nie jest trudny. *Dpo gheobhai gaii dearmand taisco gach seoid* - dodała.[16]

Skinęli potakująco, schowali broń i wydali przenikliwy i przejmujący okrzyk wojenny.

- Chyba się lubicie - mruknąłem.
- Powiedziałam im, że jesteś moim mężem i że przybyłeś tu, aby zniszczyć naszych wspólnych wrogów i poprowadzić nas do zwycięstwa. (Harrison 1994)

But if the language in question does not employ the Latin alphabet, the Irish has to be dealt with and transcribed into the target language's system of writing. There follows here the Russian version of the first quote given above:

- Очень рад приветствовать вас, – произнес я на эсперанто, но они даже не пошевелились.
- Если они не понимают эсперанто, то на каком языке они говорят? – спросил я у Анжелины.
- На своем собственном. Я уже выучила несколько слов.
- *Ду геобхайр деармад тайше Гош сеонд*, – сказала она.

Они закивали и стали потрясать оружием, испуская воинственные крики.

- Здорово ты с ними общаешься, – заметил я.
- Я сказала им, что ты мой муж и глава племени. И прибыл сюда, чтобы уничтожить врагов. (Harrison 1998; emphasis added)

---

placenames and vocabulary used in *The Stainless Steel Rat's Revenge*, which it turns out are mainly Serbian on one planet and Turkish on another.

15 And the German, and the Czech, amongst others. Kotarski also manages to make a mistake in the Esperanto. In addition to his inability to transcribe other languages correctly, Kotarski expresses his own opinion about the incomprehensibility of Irish, although he gives the reader the impression that it is diGriz's. After the expression "Scadan, Scadan!" the translator adds in brackets "cokolwiek to znaczy" "whatever that means" (Harrison 1994).

16 Italics mine.

The actual phonetic transcription of the Irish sentence, and of the words *Cill Airne* and *scadan* into Russian is as follows:

> Ду геобхайр деармад тайше Гош сеонд
> Du gyeobkhayr dyearmad tayshye Gosh syeond
>
> силайрины
> silayriny
>
> скадан
> skadan

As can be seen, the Russian translators had to make a guess as to how to represent the letters, and based their version on their understanding of English phonetics. The end result is, therefore, even more of an incomprehensible mess than that by Kotarski. The word "gan" is absent, and "gach" has now been turned into a person, as evidenced by the capital letter. The hard /x/ of "gach" has also been softened into a /ʃ/, whilst the hard /k/ of *Cill* has been replaced by the typical soft English /s/.

But not every Russian is at such a loss. On one discussion board,[17] someone complained about this, stating that such sentences and words should not have been translated into Russian as they are not in English, and that they should have been left as they were in the original text. They refer to the "идиот-переводчик" "idiot-translator," and go in search of the original English. They not only find the original text, but also give a passable translation of the line of poetry. Before doing so, however, they describe the unknown Irish as

> ...тяжёлая химия с потерей целых слов и появлением из ниоткуда букв там, где им быть не положено по любым правилам хоть и английским...
>
> "...black magic in which whole words are missing and there are letters from who-knows-where in places where they should not be according to any rules, even those of English..."

They go on to translate Eoghan Rua's quote as "вы сделали правильный выбор купив наши драгоценности," "You chose well when you bought our jewels," which is not too far off the mark, but then ruin it by saying it is probably taken from a tourist guidebook or phrase book. As for *scadán*, which they translate as "cod," they feel that the Cill Airne are so taken with this fish that it has become their battle cry. Fascinatingly, however, despite this close approximation of the meaning of the Irish words, there is absolutely no mention of Eoghan Rua, Ireland, Irish or, indeed, of the source for this information itself, which leaves one wondering how and where they came upon it.

---

17 https://dvinetz.dreamwidth.org/202650.html.

4 Air Cuan Dubh Drilseach

In the universe of *Air Cuan Dubh Drilseach* by Tim Armstrong, we have the same solution to the issue of language as proposed by Harrison, just with a different language as the universal method of communication. In this case it is Scottish Gaelic which is the language of everybody and everything.[18] This was done, according to Armstrong, because:

> When you write a realistic novel set in the present, you have to deal with the language question; will you write the dialogue as if everyone's speaking Gaelic when, realistically, it would mostly be in English, and then just write the scaffolding language in Gaelic? In this novel, I was able to create [a] world where Gaelic is the default language. (Cockburn 2013)

As such, everything in this universe is seen through Gaelic, including, much to our subversive joy, English, as in the following phonetically rendered examples (Armstrong 2013: 87–88, 141, 165):

> "Dhì-ha! [...] a bheibidh. Ù hù!"
> "Yee-ha! [...] baby. Woo hoo!"
>
> "Dur taugan babhd as [...] Uads goan oin?"
> "They're talkin' 'bout us [...] What's goin' on?"
>
> "Ìbheil's eact ual eags param eands aidh eag speact"
> "Evil sexual experiments I expect."
>
> "Man, teg aut al da èilidh uns ... Fugan frìogaidh."
> "Man, check out all the aliens. Fuckin' freaky."

But there is also variety to be seen here in the Gaelic itself, and there is a small incident in a restaurant on the planet Neasg where the cook speaks Irish, and which in itself illustrates that this universe, unlike that of Harrison's Esperanto-speaking worlds, also has some variety when it comes to language and language use. In this section, the description is in Gaelic, the conversation (in italics) in Irish (Armstrong 2013: 206):

> Bhruidhinn A-Hiom an toiseach: "*An bhfuil sibh oscailte?*"
> Thoinn gaotharan màirnealach os cionn a' chòcaire fhad 's a ghabh e beachd air Sàl agus air A-Hiom. [...]
> "*Tá, gan amharas. Céard ba mhaith libh anocht a chairde?*"
> "Sú-sí glasraí más é do thoil é," arsa A-Hiom.
> "*Go hiontach. Tae?*"

18 See Ó Fionnáin (2016) for a more detailed analysis of Armstrong's use of Gaelic in the novel.

> "*Sea, go raibh maith a'd.*"
> Shuidh A-Hiom agus Sàl nan tost, an còcaire ag obair gu gleusta romhpa [...]
> "*Rud ar bith eile a chairde?*"
> "*Tá muid ceart go leor leis seo. Iontach uilig. Go raibh maith a'd.*"
> Rinn an còcaire faite-gàire eile riutha agus dh'fhalbh e air ais dha na soitheachan.[19]

This little snippet of Irish would not be too complicated for a Scottish Gaelic speaker to understand, and Armstrong subtly introduces it without drawing attention to it, but it does give a layer of depth to his Gaelic universe, in that not only is Gaelic the universal language, but there are "dialects" as well. Indeed, if it is not a typo, the spelling of "amharas," which is Gaelic,[20] could illustrate that the majority Gaelic language is influencing the minority Irish language, which again adds to the linguistic and cultural layers. Moreover, this small use of Irish gives rise to a range of questions regarding the use of languages in Armstrong's universe: is Irish the language of Neasg itself? Or of a community on Neasg? Is the cook an immigrant from somewhere else? Is Irish spoken by, for want of a better description, the working class and Gaelic by the more advanced, more prosperous, space-travelling, upper-class, *à la* Esperanto for Harrison? Is Manx possibly spoken somewhere in Armstrong's universe? Here we can see that not only has Armstrong poked fun at English – now reduced to a minority mode of communication – but he has also subtly rewritten the history of the Gaelic languages, by implying that Scottish Gaelic is the major language and Irish is an offshoot "dialect" of it. It is to be hoped that some of these linguistic conundrums will be addressed in the sequel(s).[21]

5 Wiedźmin

Leaving the world of English behind, we turn to *Wiedźmin* "The Witcher" by the Polish writer Andrzej Sapkowski, a series of fantasy novels and short stories whose titular hero – Geralt of Rivia – gets to grips with various monsters and demons, his body specially mutated for such tasks. In creating his world for *Wiedźmin*, which is heavily influenced by Polish and Slavic mythology, Sapkowski invented a language called *Starsza Mowa* "Older Speech." For this, Sapkowski took words from various real languages and combined them into his "Older Speech," and fans of *Wiedźmin* have long wondered what these sources are. Attempts at

---

19 Italics mine.

20 The Irish is *amhras*.

21 At the time of writing, the follow-up *An Luingeas Dorcha Air Fàire* "The Dark Ship on the Horizon" is being serialised in the magazine *Steall*.

putative dictionaries can be found online,[22] but their efforts are not helped by the fact that no-one is sure what the correct pronunciation of any particular word is, and Sapkowski is not saying. In any case, amongst the source languages, there are words from French, English, Latin, Sanskrit and Irish, amongst others. Some of them are probably correct in their choice of source, for example:

- *dice* – to speak (Spanish *decir*, French *dire*, Latin *dicere*)
- *fen* – fen (AngloSax. *fen*, *fenn*, Dutch *veen*, German *fenne*, Gothic *fani*)
- *cáemm* – to go, come (for example English *come*)
- *laeke* – lake (French *lac*, English *lake*)
- *shaent* – to sing (French *chanter*)

In the case of Irish, there are also words which an Irish speaker would instantly recognise, and which are correctly accredited to Irish (or "Gaelic"), although sometimes their purported meanings are a bit imprecise. Amongst these are:

- *ard* "height"
- *beann'shie* "banshee"
- *aevon* "river"[23]
- *blath* "flower"
- *caer* "city"[24]
- *ceádmil* "welcome"
- *deireadh* "end"
- *gleanna* "glen"
- *sidh/seidhe* "elf"

However, some of those amateur lexicographers' attempts would seem to have gone a bit astray, ascribing sources to some words purely on the basis of a very tenuous link, if such a one even exists. For example:

- *addan* "dancing" (from the French *danser*?)
- *a'taeghane* "today" (akin to the French *aujord'hui*)

---

22 For example http://wiedzmin.wikia.com/wiki/S%C5%82ownik_Starszej_Mowy, https://wiedzmin.gamepedia.com/S%C5%82ownik_Starszej_Mowy and http://hl.wz.cz/polhl.html. As these are written in Polish, I have translated them in the examples given above. Any errors are those of the original authors.

23 Although one can see the Irish word *abhainn* in *aevon*, it is also possibly from the Welsh *afon*, even though only the Irish is offered as a possible source. It is noted, however, that there is the river Avon in England, but not that it is closer to Wales than to Ireland.

24 Possibly also from the Welsh. The meaning of *caer* is explained as "house, cottage, also a place," but not "a city" as it does mean in Irish.

Amongst these are some Irish words that would seem to have also defeated Sapkowski's fanbase, including this prime example:

- *dh'oine* [din/duan] = person (probably from the French *homme*)

Dh'oine's link with *homme* would seem to be so tenuous that it is non-existent, but the Irish word *duine* "person," on the other hand, would seem to be an incredibly strong candidate as the source for this Older Speech word. Amongst other Irish claims to be the source for Older Speech vocabulary, but which have stumped our researchers, are:

- *aine* "light" = Áine (personal name, originally meaning "bright")
- *beanna* "woman" = bean
- *dhu* "black" = dubh[25]
- *elaine* "beautiful" = álainn
- *Imbaelk* = Imbolc (the traditional Irish feast day on 1st February)
- *Belleteyn* = Bealtaine (the traditional Irish feast day on 1st May)
- *Saovine* = Samhain (the traditional Irish feast on 31st October – 1st November)
- *feainne* "sun" = fáinne "ring"

Irish can also be seen in placenames, such as *Ceann Treise*, the name of a waterfall, or *Ard Gaeth* "The Height of the Winds," but meaning in Older Speech *Wrota Światów* "The Gates of the Worlds."

Unfortunately, whilst the previous examples from other authors and Sapkowski himself are correct in their Irish, some of the Irish used in *Wiedźmin* leaves one with the urge to reach for a red pen, and such mistakes have to be laid at the door of Sapkowski himself, not his fanbase. The name of the land of the elves – *Tír ná Lia* – would seem to mean "The Land of the Doctors," a strange name in itself, but the accent over ‹a› implies a comparison or contradiction, as in "(neither) country nor doctor." An even stranger placename, indeed. Although adjectives follow nouns in Celtic languages, Sapkowski ignores this in examples such as *elaine deireadh* "beautiful end," instead of the correct *deireadh elaine*. On the other hand, the city Muirehen "Old Sea" seems to be an attempt at correct Irish syntax with the adjective after the noun this time, except that the word "old" in Irish is a prefix and thus the correct version should be *henmuir* (or even *henvuir*, depending on Sapkowski's choice of spelling). A further example of the puzzling nature of this *Starsza Mowa* is *Dearg Ruaidhrí* "Red Riders," a band of wraiths

---

25 Although possibly from the Scottish Gaelic *scian dubh*, the black dagger worn with a kilt, which is usually anglicised as *skeean dhu*.

who travel on skeletal horses looking to capture people to use as slaves. Their name, however, literally means in Irish "The red [colour] of Ruaidhrí." There is no-one in their group called Ruaidhrí, nor or they in the pay of someone called Ruaidhrí. It again would seem that Sapkowski merely liked the words and their appearance, but it does take away somewhat from the enjoyment of seeing Irish used in a text if the words and phrases are littered with inconsistencies and mistakes, unlike the other examples given previously from other sources.

6 Thomas the Tank Engine

As a final example of the use of Irish in a somewhat fantastical setting, we cannot ignore those talking trains who inhabit the Island of Sodor. The creator of Thomas the Tank Engine, the Rev. Wilbert Awdry, published a book in the 1980s giving the history of the Island of Sodor on which Thomas lives, helping to flesh out his stories for children, which had been in print since the 1940s, by listing historical events, persons and places and the history of the railways themselves. Since Sodor is located next to the Isle of Man, he also gives the inhabitants their own Gaelic-based language called Sudric, but unfortunately the only words he offers in Sudric are "Nagh Beurla," translated as "I don't understand English" (Awdry 1987: 5). The book is a slim volume, about 160 pages all told, including several maps, but amongst the placenames mentioned in the history of the island, as can be seen on any map of Sodor, are examples such as these:[26]

- *Shane Dooiney* (mountain) "Old Man"
- *Shan Ven* (mountain) "Old Woman"
- *Cas-ny-Hawin* (place) "Foot of the River"
- *Ballamoddy* (place) "Farm of Dogs"
- *Rheneas* (i.e. "divide" + "waterfall") "Divided Waterfall"
- *Benglas* (i.e. "white" + "stream," river) "White Stream"

These Sudric placenames might be rare enough in the book, and frequently there is no translation given of them, but the Irish-speaker is left with a feeling for a deeper understanding of the history of the island, and a richer picture of the "historical" development over the centuries than the English speaker.

26 As the Island of Sodor is "located" between the Isle of Man and England, Awdry used Manx as the basis for his local language and placenames. However, Manx (and Scottish Gaelic) are "really dialects of Irish" (Dillon and Ó Cróinín 1961: ix), and Manx has thus been included here, as the few basic words used in the placenames etc. will not cause any trouble to an Irish speaker.

7 Conclusion

All of the preceding is proof that even if Irish writers themselves are not too interested in sci-fi or fantasy, there are those who are interested in Irish itself and who have used the language, be it words, whole sentences or even conversations, to add depth to the worlds they have created. When successful, they can add a whole extra layer of culture and understanding to the newly-invented world(s) in question, but when unsuccessful they sadly tend to distract from the effort made by the author. In any case, even if sci-fi/fantasy has a limited place in Irish, at least the examples given above have shown that Irish has a place, however small, in sci-fi/fantasy itself.

Bibliography

2000AD

Armstrong, Tim. *Air Cuan Dubh Drilseach*. Inbhir Nis: Clàr, 2013.

Armstrong, Tim. "Ficsean Saidheans ann an Gàidhlig na hÈireann." 2015. http://drilseach.net/2015/03/09/ficsean-saidheans-ann-an-gaidhlig-na-h-eireann/ (9 Nov. 2017).

Awdry, Wilbert. *The Island of Sodor: Its People, History and Railways*. London: Kaye & Ward, 1987.

Cockburn, Paul. "We're talking to Tim Armstrong, author of *Air Cuan Dubh Drilseach*." 2013. arcfinity.tumblr.com/post/50642045399/were-talking-to-tim-armstrong-author-of-air-cuan (9 Nov. 2017).

Dillon, Myles, and Donncha Ó Cróinín. *Teach Yourself Irish*. Bristol: Hodder and Stoughton, 1961.

Fennell, Jack. *Irish Science Fiction*. Liverpool: Liverpool University Press, 2014.

Harrison, Harry. *The Stainless Steel Rat Wants You!* London: Sphere, 1985 [1978].

Harrison, Harry. *Stalowy Szczur i Piąta Kolumna*. Trans. Jarosław Kotarski. Warsaw: Amber. 1994. https://doci.pl/uzavrano/harry-harrison-cykl-stalowy-szczur-06-stalowy-szczur-i-piata-kolumna+f15n1m (9 Nov. 2017).

Harrison, Harry. *Ты Нужен Стальной Крысе!* Trans. Syergyey Konoplyov and Irina Konoplyova. Moskva: Eksmo, 1998. http://loveread.ec/read_book.php?id=646&p=1 (9 Nov. 2017).

Harrison, Harry. *Harry Harrison! Harry Harrison! A Memoir*. New York: Tor Books, 2014.

Ó Fionnáin, Mark. "Freedom, real and unreal, in Air Cuan Dubh Drilseach." In: *Scottish Culture: Dialogue and Self-Expression*, eds. Aniela Korzeniowska and Izabela Szymańska. Warsaw: Wydawnictwo Naukowe Semper, 2016, pp. 277–286.

O'Leary, Philip. "Science Fiction and Fantasy in the Irish Language." 2005. http://archive.today/imbyE#selection-31.0-457.14 (9 Nov. 2017).

O'Leary, Philip. *Irish Interior: Keeping Faith with the Past in Gaelic Prose 1940–1951*. Dublin: University College Dublin Press, 2010.

O'Leary, Philip. *Writing Beyond the Revival: Facing the Future in Gaelic Prose 1940–1951* Dublin: University College Dublin Press, 2011.

Watson, Moray. *An Introduction to Gaelic Fiction*. Edinburgh: Edinburgh University Press, 2011.

Internet Sources

https://dvinetz.dreamwidth.org/202650.html

http://wiedzmin.wikia.com/wiki/S%C5%82ownik_Starszej_Mowy

https://wiedzmin.gamepedia.com/S%C5%82ownik_Starszej_Mowy

http://hl.wz.cz/polhl.html

Pádraig de Paor

Aspects of Seán Ó Ríordáin's Poetic Idiom

Abstract: This is a close reading of the poem "Adhlacadh Mo Mháthar" ["My Mother's Burial"] by Seán Ó Ríordáin, arguably the greatest Irish language poet of the 20th century. The poem is revisited and reassessed and it is argued that a cluster of sometimes misunderstood words, such as "peaca" ["sin"], "geanmnaíocht" ["chastity", "purity"], "drúis" ["lust", "concupiscence] and "paidir" ["prayer"], make more sense when read as part of a "poetics of not being sick."

Keywords: Seán Ó Ríordáin, poetics, Irish literature, Adhlacadh Mo Mháthar

Seán Ó Ríordáin (1916–77) was arguably the greatest poet writing in Irish during his lifetime, and has influenced most poets composing in the language after him. Outside the Irish language world, he has been mostly ignored, due in large part to the lack of satisfactory translations. Almost half a century had passed before Frank Sewell, working with other poet-translators, published *Seán Ó Ríordáin: Selected Poems* (2014), a dual language selection of his poems. Bit by bit, Ó Ríordáin's poetry is gaining a wider readership.

In 1945, at the age of 28, Ó Ríordáin published possibly his most famous poem "Adhlacadh Mo Mháthar" ["My Mother's Burial"] in a journal called *An Iris* [*The Journal*]. While some were aghast at Ó Ríordáin's non-traditional poetics, many others responded appreciatively to his rather idiosyncratic use of the Irish language. This poem is credited by Seán Ó Tuama as having created an exciting new and modern "*frisson*" in Irish language literature similar to Baudelaire's effect on French about a century earlier (Ó Tuama 1978: 5). Ever since this early poem, Ó Ríordáin has achieved high canonical status within the Irish language world.

The first monograph on his work was published just five years after his death. In 1982 Seán Ó Coileáin published his important *Seán Ó Ríordáin: Beatha agus Saothar* [*Seán Ó Ríordáin: Life and Work*] (Ó Coileáin 1982). Although fitting that Seán Ó Ríordáin should have his work considered in such a sustained and sympathetic way, it is arguably worth asking whether Seán Ó Coileáin chose to read the poet's work in an overly autobiographical fashion. Perhaps it is both an advantage and disadvantage that the first monograph on the first truly great modern Irish language poet of the 20th century should have been written by a scholar who both knew the poet and had access to his diaries. I admit to feeling a little uneasy with references to diary entries being described as prose versions of poems (Ó Coileáin 1982: 219). An over-emphasis on a poet's life as a key to understanding his poetry can reduce it to a social or historical document rather than something which is primarily creative and imaginative. At stake is a most basic irony at the heart of all literature: the understanding that the author is not the same as his character, that the poet is not the same as the persona who speaks in his poem. The reader must respect this basic ironic distinction even in the case of a poem like "Adhlacadh Mo Mháthar" which has a clear autobiographical dimension. However, it is not a diary entry, or a letter, or report of a personal conversation, but a creative act of the imagination. In this poem, Seán Ó Ríordáin, whose mother had recently died, creates a persona who speaks about his experience of losing his mother. It is not Seán Ó Ríordáin who speaks in the poem but a created persona, an alter ego perhaps, but most certainly a creatively altered ego. In this essay, I ask whether the overly autobiographical approach might have led to a misunderstanding of some aspects of Seán Ó Ríordáin's idiom, in particular, a cluster of words borrowed from religion and sexuality: especially "drúis" ["lust"], and "geanmnaíocht" ["chastity"], but also "peaca" ["sin"], "faoistin" ["confession"] and "paidir" ["prayer"]. Like Joyce with "epiphany," Ó Ríordáin borrows prestigious words from religion and sexual morality, and gives them a new aesthetic reading. Ó Ríordáin does not necessarily eradicate the original meaning entirely, but rather palimpsests his new metaphorical meaning over the old.

A poem, like all creative literature, can be seen as a ladder of articulacy. The poem has its first rung in the ordinary lived experience of the poet. This real life experience is then, consciously and/or unconsciously, figured through creative use of language to give rise to a symbol or a metaphor which can generate new meaning. The final rung on the ladder of articulacy is the movement from that symbol to thought, a new thought enabled by the symbol or metaphor (Ricoeur 1967: 25–29, 347–357; Taylor 2016: 129–176). For example, one can start with the outer experience of physical dirt, "matter out of place" in Mary Douglas's definition (Douglas 1966: 35). Physical dirt is commonly figured as a symbol of invisible metaphysical dirt (Douglas 1966). This symbolic dirt then allows people to express a range of thoughts about inner realities, such as "impurity," "uncleanness," "sin" etc., or to describe, for example, how one can feel "defiled" or "polluted" after sexual abuse (Scruton 2006: 143–144). This articulation of metaphysical "dirt" allows us to think new thoughts about the world, thoughts that once thought, cannot perhaps be unthought again. That is to say that one can ascend the ladder of articulacy from outer physical reality to abstract thought, from the lived experience of a poet to his poetry, but one cannot descend again, or retrace one's steps. Charles Taylor, following Ricoeur in this train of thought, draws attention in particular to the figuring of "integrity," a concept important to Seán Ó Ríordáin's poetry: "ionraic" ["integral"]. Again this concept starts with a physical experience of something like a plate or a jug being broken or fractured (Taylor 2016: 226–250). This outer reality is then figured, through the creative use of language, to talk about an inner reality, moral integrity or metaphysical wholeness. Alternatively, in reverse, it can articulate a state of emotional or psychological brokenness.

There is another such ascent of the ladder of articulacy in Seán Ó Ríordáin's poetry around the concepts of contagion and empathy. I posit that O Ríordáin made a metaphorical move from physical experience to psychic contagion, from physical touching to emotional or psychological "touching." The experience of being infected with a contagious disease, as Seán Ó Ríordáin was with tuberculosis, is likely to make one consider how we "touch" one another, how we infect and affect one another. A communicable disease here is the first rung on a ladder of articulacy that ascends to thinking about our experience of the communal. I suggest that Seán Ó Ríordáin's experience of being ill with a contagious illness led him to ponder deeply the questions of sentient contagion, on the one hand, and of the more "healthy" empathy, on the other hand. Sentient contagion, something we have in common with animals, is, in Ó Ríordáin's idiom, mere "prós" ["prose"]. Sentient contagion is an unconscious imitation of the other (like yawning or the child's adoption of an accent unbeknownst to himself) (Lebech 2004: 57–58; Hatfield et al. 1994). Contagion leads to a crowd mentality whereby one can be infected by another through, for example, the second-hand "ideas" of groupthink. For Ó Ríordáin, this contagion is not just prosaic and quotidian but also inauthentic (see his ironic poem "Saoirse" ["Freedom"]).

By contrast, "filíocht" ["poetry"], for Ó Ríordáin, is born of a deep empathy with the other. Empathy is the act in which foreign experience, the experience of another, is experienced by the subject, in a secondary way, following Edith Stein's understanding (Stein 1986). For Ó Ríordáin the act of empathy is itself potentially poetic, and true poetry is a deeply empathic exploration of foreign experience. Ó Ríordáin declares this explicitly in his poem "Malairt" ["Switch"] and his introduction to his first collection *Eireaball Spideoige* (1952) – now available in translation (Sewell 2014: 231–242).[1] There are few experiences more foreign to us, perhaps, than that of death. Could "Adhlacadh Mo Mháthar" be read as

1 All references to "Adhlacadh mo Mháthar" are to Sewell's bilingual edition (Sewell 2014). Where Sewell is not credited the translation used is mine.

an attempt to experience another's death, in a secondary way, through empathy? While some, like Heidegger, would deny the possibility of such an act, against that, Edith Stein, for one, holds that death can be indeed be experienced through empathy, indeed even from seeing the deceased, however unsatisfactorily (Stein 2007: 75–77; Lebech 2015: 163–164).

The opening stanza of "Adhlacadh Mo Mháthar" finds the speaker physically sitting in the June evening sun, but mentally lost in a recollection of his mother's burial day back in mid-winter. His retrospective attempt to be fully present to the harrowing occasion, which he had been perhaps too numb to experience, is described as follows: "Bhí m'aigne á sciúirseadh féin ag iarraidh/An t-adhlacadh a bhlaiseadh go hiomlán,/Nuair a d'eitil tríd an gciúnas bán go míonla/spideog a bhí gan mhearbhall gan scáth" ["I was beating my brains in an attempt/to fully taste the occasion when there flew/through the stilly brightness/a robin, unruffled, completely without rue"] (Sewell 2014: 46–49). The robin here is the inspiration and the image needed for the poetic ascent. And as birds can leave the earth at will and fly up to the heavens, they are almost universally symbols for the spirit, and for inspiration, the ability of the imagination to soar to higher regions (Eliade 1964: 98). They are also often associated with death in various ways, including incarnations of the spirit of the deceased. Irish folk belief provides widespread evidence of a variety of similar beliefs (Ó Dochartaigh 1987).

In the next stanza, the robin seems to me to be a psychopomp, an intermediary between heaven and earth. The robin could be read as the liminal being who will accompany the deceased mother's soul up to heaven. Later in the poem, when the speaker admits that he would like to catch the robin's tail ("Ba mhaith liom breith ar eireaball spideoige"), he is saying two things: that he would like to follow his mother to heaven, and that he would like to capture the experience of her burial in poetry. Both of these attempts are about as possible as catching the robin's tail: "Ranna beaga bacacha á scríobh agam,/Ba mhaith liom breith ar eireaball spideoige" ["Writing lame little stanzas/I'd like to catch a robin's tail" (translation mine)]. The poem is, nevertheless, an attempt to touch his mother. He touches the letter that she had handwritten him: "Seanalitir shalaithe á léamh agam,/le gach focaldeoch dár ólas/Pian bhinibeach ag dealgadh mo chléibhse,/Do bhrúigh amach gach focal díobh a dheoir féin." ["I'm reading a grubby old letter./With every word-sip a spear/ of sorrow piercing my ribcage./ Each word wringing out its own particular tear"] (Sewell 2014: 46–47). The third stanza refers to the touch of her hand: "Do chuimhníos ar an láimh a dhein an scríbhinn,/lámh a bhí inaitheanta mar aghaidh,/Lámh a thál riamh cneastacht seana-Bhíobla,/Lámh a bhí mar bhalsam is tú tinn." ["I thought of the hand that wrote the letter./A hand as recognizable as a face./A hand that yielded Biblical charitableness./A hand which was like balsam when you were sick" (translation mine)]. Even if her hand can no longer touch her son, her words certainly can still. But is the reverse also true? Can he touch her now through his words? How does one communicate with or "touch" the deceased? Chastely, is the poem's answer, in my reading.

This poem, and perhaps all Seán Ó Ríordáin's work, understands "chastity" to be a pre-requisite for empathy and thus for poetry, in my reading. The truly empathic "I" does not allow itself to be infected by the other, to succumb to the contagion of the other's experience, to allow itself to be fused with the other; the truly empathic "I" does not let itself be submerged in the other or succumb to the crowd mentality, but rather maintains a psychic chastity. It should be obvious that Seán Ó Ríordáin does not use "drúis" or "geamnaíocht" in his poetry only in their everyday senses, but in "Adhlacadh Mo Mháthar" this distinction is explicit: "Le cumhracht bróin do folcadh m'anam drúiseach,/Thit sneachta geanmnaíochta ar mo chroí" ["With a fragrant sorrow my lustful soul was cleansed/The snow of chastity fell on my heart" (translation mine)]. In our post-Freudian culture we have become used to understanding chastity in a reductive, indeed negative, way as the avoidance of sexual activity or even of desire. Ó Ríordáin would also have been aware of the older catholic, more positive, view of chastity as a virtue, as explained, say, by Dietrich von Hildebrand, the German philosopher who was writing in the 1920s with the intention of contradicting Freud (von Hildebrand 1927). Here chastity is the virtue that enables people to love fully in every relationship, in the fashion appropriate to that relationship. Therefore, understood in those terms, it is quite normal for the poem's speaker to talk about having a chaste heart in relation to his deceased mother (*pace* Riggs 2000: 331–335). In this context an unchaste or lustful heart is obviously not one filled with sexual desire, but rather one filled with a possessive clinging to his mother who is moving on to the next stage of her existence.

Where self-control is lost, empathic knowledge of the other *as other* is lost, and with it the possibility of poetry; instead, one ends up trying to possess, control, grasp or "comprehend" the other. Even the desire to "comprehend" the mother's death is "lustful" or domineering or controlling. (Here I am using "comprehend" in a negative sense, one of the original Latin's meanings: *comprehendere* "to capture, arrest, overwhelm, control," a negative sense with which Ó Ríordáin would have been familiar from the prologue from St John's gospel read at the end of Mass: *Et Lux in tenebris lucet et tenebrae eam non comprehenderunt*). To "comprehend" her death is to try to impose an identity on the other, rather than let her be what she really is. The deceased mother during her burial is still in the liminal stage of her final rite of passage during which she is shedding her old earthly identity before acquiring her new otherworldly identity. "Do thuirling aer na bhFlaitheas ar an uaigh sin,/Bhí meidhir uafásach naofa ar an éan,/Bhíos deighilte amach ón diamhairghnó im thuata,/Is an uaigh sin os mo chomhair in imigéin." ["The air of Heaven came down on the grave./The bird was in an awesome sacred ecstasy,/I, a layman, was excluded from the mysterious transaction,/ And the grave in front of me so far away" (translation mine)]. In this context, it is fitting that the son refers to some of his mother's previous rites of passage, encompassing three key stages in her life: as a girl, as young mother including her pregnancy with him, and now deceased: "Gile gearrachaile lá a céad chomaoine,/ Gile abhlainne Dé Domhnaigh ar altóir,/Gile bainne ag sreangtheitheadh as na cíochaibh,/Nuair a chuireadar mo mháthair, gile an fhóid." ["The brightness of a young girl on her first Holy Communion day,/The brightness of a host on the altar on a Sunday,/The brightness of milk escaping out of breasts,/When they buried my mother, the brightness of the sod" (my translation)]. Part of the son's empathic embrace of his mother entering her new state of existence without him is to imagine her as she existed as a young girl before him. As the ground is covered with snow, it is in terms of that image of brightness or radiance that he recounts a number of stages in his mother's life. The stanza refers to her first Holy Communion, or first intimate communication with God, her being "touched" by Him, but also alludes to both death and resurrection, as the second verse refers to the Host, which means "sacrificial victim"; the third verse refers to another intimate communication through touch and through consuming – the maternal nurturing of her baby. These images make it abundantly clear that the death of one who gave life to the speaker of the poem is a most sacred event. The speaker resents those at the burial who will not allow themselves to be touched in any way by the sacrality of the awesome event of death, a sacrality which is both blessed and accursed: "D'fhéachas-sa treo eile, bhí comharsa ag glanadh a ghlúine,/D'fhéachas ar an sagart is bhí saoltacht ina ghnúis." ["I looked in another direction, a neighbour was cleaning off his knee/I looked at the priest and there was worldliness in his face" (translation mine)]. They fail to empathise with the bereaved son; they fail to experience what he is experiencing. In Ó Ríordáin's idiom, they are prosaic.

"Prós" ["prose"] is always understood negatively in Ó Ríordáin's work as the failure of poetry. This is most explicit in "An Peaca" ["The Sin"]: "D'fhéachas arís ar lámhscríbhinn an dáin,/Ach prós bhí in áit na filíochta— /An ré is na scamaill is an spéir mar ba ghnáth—/Mar bhí peaca ar anam na hoíche." ["I looked again at the manuscript of the poem/but it was prose instead of poetry—/ the moon and the clouds and the sky as usual—/because there was sin on the soul of the night."] (Sewell 2014: 18–19). It seems to me that for Ó Ríordáin prós ["prose"] is "comprehending" something, comprehending in the negative sense already alluded to, a controlling possessive "grasping" of the other, thus allowing its essence to elude one – in the case of the poem "An Peaca" ["The Sin"], the experience of the awesome moonlit night. On the other hand, poetry, for Ó Ríordáin, if I "understand" him correctly, is a radical feeling into the other's experience which neither possesses or contaminates the other, nor is contaminated by the other. For this, poetry demands a form of discipline, of "chastity," a controlling of the self which desires to control the other.

It is clear in "Adhlacadh Mo Mháthar" that the mother's death is not the end of her being as such, but rather the painful occasion of the tearing asunder, "screadstracadh" ["scream-tearing"], of her spirit from her body. Pádraigín Riggs (Riggs 2000) notices a close relationship between Ó Ríordáin's unusual way of describing his mother's death "Mar screadstracadh ar an nóinbhrat" ["tearing the evening's mantle"] and the synoptic gospels' description of the tearing of the temple veil in two from top to bottom (Matthew 27:51, Mark 13:38, Luke 23:45–6). The same word "stracadh" is used in both Ó Ríordáin's poem and in Peadar Ua Laoghaire's translation of the gospels, a version very likely to have been read by the poet. There seems to be more to this allusion than Pádraigín Riggs lays out. The significance of those mysterious references in the gospels to that tearing of the veil is discussed in the Letter to the Hebrews (4:4, 7:25, 9:12–15). That explanation seems to me to be very relevant to Ó Ríordáin's poem. The holy of holies was separated from the rest of the Jewish temple. Inside the holy of holies was the Ark of the Covenant, so holy that it could not be touched, except by the High Priest once a year after elaborate purification rituals. The veil kept the holy of holies from being profaned and thus separates God from man. The veil of the temple is ripped in two when Christ, the true High Priest, died and entered the holy of holies, heaven. Thus the tearing of the veil of the temple refers to the tearing of the barrier between man and Heaven and means that our access to the holy of holies in heaven is now open. Of course, it is easy to see how this relates to the poem. The deceased mother is not just being buried but is entering heaven, into the holy of holies, a place where the this-worldly son cannot follow her. The first stanza, repeated in the penultimate stanza, with its arresting aforementioned "screadstracadh ar an nóinbhrat" ["tearing the evening's mantle"] also has other spiritual echoes. Rilke referred to poets as the "bees of the invisible." "We wildly gather the honey of the invisible, in order to store in the great golden hive of the Invisible" (Rilke 2011: 70). Ó Ríordáin, for his part, writes, "Beach mhallaithe ag portaireacht" ["An accursed bee bumbling"] – the bee is, of course, traditionally a symbol of the Blessed Virgin, as worker honeybees are "virginal" (having no part in the reproduction of their species); bees feature prominently too in the Holy Saturday liturgy on the eve of resurrection during the blessing of the paschal candle (made of bees wax).

This powerful poem is both about the death of one particular woman, but it also, as Máire Ní Annracháin has argued, lends itself to another reading: that of the death of Mother Ireland (Ní Annracháin 2012: 67–68). The oldest literary conceit in Irish is the imagining of the land of Ireland as a woman, alternately as a beautiful fertile young mother and as a wizened old crone. When the right ruler is in place, his "spouse," the land, is fruitful, radiant and nourishing; when a false ruler is in place, scarcity and death prevail. I agree with Máire Ní Annracháin that "Adhlacadh Mo Mháthar" stands alongside Máirtin Ó Cadhain's Caitríona Pháidín, cailleach [hag] extraordinaire, in her graveyard plot in the novel *Cré na Cille* (1949), as an expression of the post-revolutionary cultural depression of the 1940s Irish Free State. The poem also opens itself to a reading whereby the poet, by speaking truth is bringing the summer into being again. The penultimate stanza is a repeat of first stanza: "Grian an Mheithimh in úllghort…" ["The June sun on the apple orchard…"].

However, poetry that brings the world to life again is so powerful, that it can only be spoken by one who has a pure or "chaste" soul: "Thit sneachta geanmnaíochta ar mo chroí" ["The snow of chastity fell on my heart"]. The burial can only become "real," or rather realizable, if its is relived, or lived fully in time and in language. "Anois adhlacfad sa chroí a deineadh ionraic/Cuimhne na mná d'iompair mé trí ráithe ina broinn." ["Now I will bury in the heart made integral/the memory of the woman who carried me three trimesters in her womb" (translation mine)]. The chaste respect for the other extends to death itself, as argued above. Death is not, in this poem, to be mastered, controlled or "comprehended," but rather "felt into." This "feeling into," or empathy, requires both attentiveness and recognition. Seán Ó Ríordáin calls this attentiveness and recognition "paidir" ["prayer"] roughly corresponding to Gerard Manly Hopkins's "instress," the recognition of the other person's or thing's distinctive design or nature – "inscape" for Hopkins and for Ó Ríordáin "cló" ["impression", "type", "incarnation", "imprint"] (Nic Ghearailt 1988: 37–43). Failure to recognise the other's singularity or uniqueness results in "peaca" ["sin"] and "prós" ["prose"].

"Prose" or "sin" may also refer to the hypersemy of everyday chatter, the sick signs of everyday promiscuous discourse of the crowd. Here again the poetic meaning of "chaste" in Ó Ríordáin's poetry is clear. The poet must not forget that language is sacred and he must be able to resist the contagious clichés which are exchanged casually. The "chaste" poet tries to establish the right relationship with the other; he does not claim the power to name the other, does not spray his tag on her, or reduce her by a rude categorisation, but rather calls the other into being, by constructing symbols which allow the other to disclose herself.

If the experience of being ill and in danger of death tends to focus the mind on the question of existence, then the experience of contracting a contagious disease inevitably encourages one, especially one with a philosophical bent like Seán Ó Ríordáin, to contemplate both contingency as well as contagion. It is noteworthy that both "contingency" and "contagion" share similar etymologies (Latin *contingere*, *con*, *tangere* to touch together, touch closely). Contagion, physical or psychosocial, is one way to experience the communal, albeit, for Seán Ó Ríordáin, not a particularly healthy one. Psychic contagion can lead, as Edith Stein points out, to group behaviour and a crowd mentality (Stein 2010: 148). This type of experience of the communal can be regarded as a relatively low form of togetherness, purely on the animal level, and for Seán Ó Ríordáin, the crowd is inauthentic and threatens the self. In his ironic poem "Saoirse" ["Freedom"], Ó Ríordáin gives the example of such communality as experienced at "halla an rince" [the dance hall]. Dance is a particularly mimetic or imitative art form. The dance hall is the place where mimetic desire, in the Girardian sense, dominates, often unconsciously, a place of an animal *transe-en-dance*, to use Catherine Clément's phrase (Clément 2011), rather than the more spiritual transcendence of poetry. For Seán Ó Ríordáin, with his modernist leanings, the authentic individual, as he matures, stops imitating others and starts to think and speak for himself, and indeed, develop his own style, as original as possible. Romanticism's extreme emphasis on the originality of the writer living on the margins of society is resonant here in more ways than one. In the 19th century tuberculosis was a recurrent theme in art and literature (Mac Giolla Léith 2012: 48) and a disease often suffered by artists, including most famously Chopin (1810–1849).

Arguably, Seán Ó Ríordáin does not shun the experience of communality as such, but rather its base unconscious form. In Ó Ríordáin's poetry, readers follow a persona who is consciously working out his selfhood "in fear and trembling," and always anxious lest his singularity be mobbed by the crowd and his voice be lost amidst the chatter. However another form of experiencing communality is possible, a form higher than that of the animal contagion of the dance hall or of the "daoscarshlua" ["crowd", "mob"]. Such an experience of a higher communality is generated, for Edith Stein, when meaning is shared between conscious subjects or selves, and such a communality can be considered spiritual (Stein 2000: 133–166). What does this mean in practice? I argue that those of us who read Seán Ó Ríordáin's poetry and enjoy discussing its meaning experience a taste of precisely that spiritual communality. Here what we have in common is the experience of being seized by persona that interests or fascinates us. Paradoxically, it is around a persona who expresses grief at separation, marginalisation in the community and is tormented by loneliness, that we, the readers, experience "communality." However, this is only a paradox, and not a contradiction, because, even if the persona of Ó Ríordáin's poetry often feels excluded from the group, or excludes himself from the group, it is still against that same communal experience of the group that he makes sense of himself as an individual. This brings us to the other end of Ó Ríordáin's poetry: the reader. The reader experiences the foreign experience of the above mentioned persona. Reading Ó Ríordáin's poetry allows us to experience, in a secondary way, what another feels. Seán Ó Ríordáin's intention as a poet, while primary, is not the totality of his poetry. Our readings, though secondary, are an important part of the creative work. The reader can see something else in the work over and above the intention of the poet, just as an empathic listener sees aspects of his friend that she will not see herself. With this in mind, I am suggesting in this essay that it is time to look again at Ó Ríordáin's work, in particular aspects of his idiom, borrowed from religion and sexuality: especially "drúis" ["lust"], "geanmnaíocht" ["chastity"], but also "peaca" ["sin"], "faoistin" ["confession"] and "paidir" ["prayer"], and also at the theme of "contagion."

Bibliography

Douglas, Mary. *Purity And Danger: An Analysis of Concepts of Pollution and Taboo*. London: Routledge, 1966.

Eliade, Mircea. *Shamanism: Archaic Techniques of Ecstasy*. New Jersey: Princeton University Press, 1964.

Hatfield, Elaine, John T. Cacioppo, and Richard L. Rapson, eds. *Emotional Contagion: Studies in Emotion and Social Interaction*. Paris: Cambridge University Press, 1994.

Lebech, Mette. "Study Guide to Edith Stein's Philosophy of Psychology and the Humanities." *Yearbook of the Irish Philosophical Society*, Vol. 4, 2004, pp. 40–76.

Lebech, Mette. *The Philosophy of Edith Stein: From Phenomenology to Metaphysics*. Bern: Peter Lang, 2015.

Mac Giolla Léith, Caoimhín. "Seán Ó Ríordáin agus Aisling na Feola." In: *Fill Arís: Oidhreacht Sheáin Uí Ríordáin*, eds. Liam Mac Amhlaigh and Caoimhín Mac Giolla Léith. Indreabhán: Cló Iar-Chonnacht, 2012, pp. 47–57.

Ní Annracháin, Máire. "Seán Ó Ríordáin agus Fréamhacha an Dúchais." In: *Fill Arís: Oidhreacht Sheáin Uí Ríordáin*, eds. Liam Mac Amhlaigh and Caoimhín Mac Giolla Léith. Indreabhán: Cló Iar-Chonnacht, 2012, pp. 66–81.

Nic Ghearailt, Eibhlín. *Seán Ó Ríordáin agus "An Striapach Allúrach."* Dublin: An Clóchomhar, 1988.

Ó Coileáin, Seán. *Seán Ó Riordáin: Beatha agus Saothar*. Dublin: An Clóchomhar, 1982.

Ó Dochartaigh, Liam. "'Adhlacadh Mo Mháthar': Dhá léamh faoi anáil an Bhéaloidis." *Comhar*, Vol. 46, No. 2, 1987, pp. 20–24.

Ó Tuama, Seán. "Seán Ó Ríordáin agus an Nuafhilíocht." In: *Filí Faoi Sceimhle: Seán Ó Ríordáin agus Aogán Ó Rathaille*. Dublin: Oifig an tSoláthair, 1978.

Ricoeur, Paul. *The Symbolism of Evil*. Boston: Beacon Press, 1967.

Riggs, Pádraicín. "Adhlacadh Mo Mháthar." In: *Saoi na hÉigse: Aistí in Ómós do Sheán Ó Tuama*, eds. Seán Ó Coileáin, Breandán Ó Conchúir and Pádraigín Riggs. Dublin: An Clóchomhar, 2000.

Rilke, Rainer Maria. *Duino Elegies: A Bilingual Edition*. Trans. Edward Snow. New York: North Point Press, 2011.

Scruton, Roger. *Sexual Desire*. London: Continuum, 2006.

Sewell, Frank, ed. *Seán Ó Ríordáin: Selected Poems*. London: Yale University Press, 2014.

Stein, Edith. *On the Problem of Empathy*. Washington, DC: ICS Publications, 1989.

Stein, Edith. *Philosophy of Psychology and the Humanities*. Washington, DC: ICS Publications, 2000.

Stein, Edith. "Martin Heidegger's Existential Philosophy." Trans. Mette Lebech. *Maynooth Philosophical Papers*, Vol. 4, 2007, pp. 55–98.

Taylor, Charles. *The Language Animal: The Full Shape of the Human Linguistic Capacity*. Cambridge: Harvard University Press, 2016.

von Hildebrand, Dietrich. *Reinheit und Jungfräulichkeit*. Wien: Oratoriumsverlag, 1927/*In Defence of Purity: An Analysis of the Catholic Ideals of Purity and Virginity*. Steubenville: The Hildebrand Press, 2017.

Alyce von Rothkirch

Dragon Red in Tooth and Claw: Darwin, Nature and Morality in Niall Griffiths's *Sheepshagger*

Abstract: Niall Griffiths's novel *Sheepshagger*, set in the wilderness of West Wales, tells the story of a feral character called Ianto. Using a theoretical framework taken from Animal Studies and cognitive ethology, the chapter demonstrates that despite its hyper-realistic language, Griffiths's second novel is in fact a work rich in symbolism and an intricate analysis of the interconnectedness of man and nature. The moral aspects of Ianto's violent behaviour and his relationship with the animal world are read in the broader context of identity and Wales's colonial predicament.

Keywords: posthumanism, animal studies, Niall Griffiths, *Sheepshagger*

It is a gruesome ending. The Maenads, led by the King's mother Agave and high on Dionysian spirits, brutally kill Pentheus, King of Thebes. Once they wake up from their possession, they are appalled at what they have done. Agave, overcome by remorse, goes into exile. Or, in Niall Griffiths's ironic revision, a group of denizens of the fringes of Welsh society, high on magic mushrooms, kill Ianto, Iago Prytherch's bastard son, who, in turn has been responsible for the apparently motiveless killing of three English visitors to West Wales: a delinquent boy on an Outward Bound trip, and a hippy couple, who had come to Ceredigion on a holiday. Like Agave, the empathetic Gwenno has a breakdown and goes to live in exile (she moves to Surrey), and the rest of the group are left to ponder what exactly happened and who, if anyone, was to blame.

References to Greek tragedy abound in Griffiths's novel *Sheepshagger* (2001). For all the hyper-realism of the dialogue, this is not a realistic novel. Ianto's friends in Aberystwyth form a chorus, obsessively reviewing and analysing what happened (see Bednarski 2012: 63). Ianto himself is a tragic character who, according to the author, vainly seeks "cosmic significance" (Peddie 2008: 122). Bednarski has demonstrated how the novel's three structural levels go from documentary realism to a deeply fictional, mytho-poetic narrative level (2012: 66 ff.). By integrating mythical, historical and fantastic elements with more realistic-sounding plot elements, the novel draws attention to the power of narrative to shape us and sometimes to derail us.

Drawing on the raison d'être of the bundle of approaches collectively known as Animal Studies, namely the shift in perspective that demotes human beings from their place at the top of the evolutionary "chain of being" and emplacing them, as equals, among other animals (cf. Haraway 2008; Castricano 2008), this essay posits that, at the heart of the novel, there are two competing moral narratives, both derived from Darwin's theory of evolution. The first is that life is a continuous struggle for existence, which only the strong can, and indeed should, survive. The second is equally important but is often overshadowed by the first: it is that of a morality based on kindness, compassion, empathy and cooperation, which constitutes the other side of the "survival of the fittest." Fitness, after all, means "succeeding to reproduce," and recent studies in biology, ethology and related fields have shown that being nice is a viable survival strategy (see, for example, Bekoff and Pierce 2009).

In *Sheepshagger*, these moral narratives are juxtaposed. The novel dramatises the consequences of Ianto's central, tragic flaw, which is that he privileges the discourse of "might is right" over that of empathy and compassion, thus placing himself on a track of violence and counter-violence that can only end with his death. And, arguably, Ianto's fate has a symbolic function that goes beyond the characters in the novel. On the level of society and of the nation, too, the continued victory of the law of the strong is shown to be disruptive and destructive, whether we are talking about those who occupy the margins of society or whether we are considering the complex (post-)colonial relationship between England and Wales. In a discourse in which the strong invariably triumph over the weak, there is no room for the "other."

Ianto's otherness is made obvious from the beginning of the novel. Nobody really likes him. Out of the group of people associating with him only Danny and Gwenno reach out to him, but even they are ambivalent. One reason for this ambivalence is that Ianto regularly absents himself from human company. According to Danny, "out of every given month, Ianto would on average spend two weeks in-a town like, y'know in society, with people. Two weeks. That's half his whole fuckin life" (54). Ianto moves fluidly between the human world ("in society, with people") and the world of nature, where non-human animals live. His experience appears to be an example of what E.O. Wilson calls "biophilia," i.e. "the [connection] that human beings subconsciously seek with the rest of life" (1992: 350). John Bradshaw argues that this notion may be a "somewhat romantic idea" which is easily co-opted to support particular agendas, notably that of nature conservation (2017: 229). Having said that, Bradshaw also argues that "[i]nteractions with the natural world must have shaped our brains" (231) throughout our evolutionary history so that we, as a species, easily connect to the natural world and to other animals in it. Ianto yearns for contact with nature and regularly engages with it, becoming, in turn, more animal-like. At the beginning of the novel we see him traverse the coastal hills up to the isolated farmhouse that once belonged to his family: "Ianto climbs steadily up the steep slope using his feet and long hands, prehensile and balanced like one unused to other forms of locomotion, say bipedal, upright" (14). Sinuously and curiously ape-like, this apparently addled drug addict moves up the hill without so much as breaking a sweat, while his wheezing and spluttering friend Llŷr struggles to keep up. But there are limits to Ianto's biophilia. Despite his alienation from his own species, Ianto cannot simply, in Charles Foster's evocative phrase "be a beast" instead (2016). For one thing, non-human animals simply inhabit their *Umwelt* (von Uexküll's term for both an animal's habitat and its view of that world and its place in it) whereas humans are often not similarly at ease. While Ianto yearns to be equally at home in nature as other animals are, he has to return to the human world regularly, if only to eat (see 40–1) as he does not seem to be able to either hunt or forage successfully. In the end he is only half-feral and, more crucially, he retains a point of view which is firmly human.

Another reason for his friends' discomfort is that Ianto rarely speaks. He follows instructions, he trails other, stronger characters (97, 174), he swallows any drug or drink he is given (96), but nobody knows what he is thinking. Instead, he often communicates a range of emotions by grinning. He bares his teeth like a non-human animal would – in a display of submission (e.g. 129 or 132) like a chimpanzee (see *Scientific American* 1999) or, like a dog, as a precursor to aggression. For instance, just before the second murder he is shown standing "in wait behind the shower curtain, his hands curled into claws. His teeth bared in a grin" (200), resembling both the monstrous Norman Bates in *Psycho* as well as an anxious or angry dog, who shows his teeth prior to biting. His friends are repelled by Ianto, whether it is because he is as an animalistic and, indeed, atavistic degenerate (see Richter's discussion of the literature of atavism after Darwin, 2011: esp. 33) or whether it is merely because of his silence.

Especially at moments of crisis Ianto retreats into nature. Thus, after having been repulsed by the new inhabitants of his family's former farmhouse, he runs away and ends up in the peat bogs, where he "falls headlong over some log rotting beneath the knotted grass", landing face-forward in the watery mud. Nature appears to embrace and accept him: "[c]hickweed [binds] itself around his legs and toadflax [infiltrates] the laces of his trainers as if seeking a mate" (25). Similarly, when Llŷr shoots a kestrel, Ianto cannot bear this display of pointless cruelty and, "as he has done for years [he] just walks away into the place where the ground swells and swells," becoming part of the landscape, "the silent watcher on high and how really does he differ from bird, from bush?" (37). Florence Williams, among others, has shown that an engagement with nature has a healing effect (2017; see also Bradshaw 2017: 230–2). Until he has committed his second murder, Ianto can immerse himself in nature and emerge restored.

Ianto's isolated upbringing leads him to seek out the company of non-human animals. Closely observing them and interacting with them informs his moral universe. Initially, he explores his *Umwelt* with an open mind. At the age of seven, a viper coils around his arm, a touch they both appear to delight in: "*One chubby fingertip strokes the serpent's head; briefly the peppercorn eyes close, as if in feline pleasure*" (28). He is described as playing with "*the cubs of badger and fox*," he hunts with the polecat, races with the hare. "*Ianto it is who would soar wing-to-spread-fingered-wing with raptor, with passerine, low over the forest canopy*" (28). In the manner of children everywhere, Ianto empathetically imagines what it is like to be another animal. As an adult he retains some of that anthropomorphism and sees himself as, for example, a reptile "lying on his back in the bog. Snake-silent and lizard-still" (25), although his imagination now has limits, as we shall see.

Bednarski has argued that Ianto's experience of nature as a child symbolically represents a state "reminiscent of the paradisiacal unity between Man and Nature" (2012: 68). I would add that, if it is paradise, it is one which is no longer innocent. From the beginning, Ianto experiences the brutality inherent in the natural world. At the age of five he accidentally kills a lamb, whose eyes had been pecked out by a corvid. He is haunted by the cosmic unfairness of the situation: how something as symbolically innocent as a lamb could be so needlessly sacrificed, and how he becomes an unwitting instrument of death. At the age of eight, he comes across the larder of a butcher bird, whose grim habit it is to put still living prey on spikes. The boy imagines himself as one of the bird's victims and flees in terror (90–92). As an adult, Ianto feeds some ducks in a municipal pond. Even this turns into a dark experience as the adult birds ruthlessly push the ducklings aside and apparently drown one of them (44). Nature appears to be "red in tooth and claw." It seems that Thomas Hobbes was right: in the state of nature, lives are "nasty, brutish and short," and the only thing that saves humans from the violence of the fight for existence is civilisation, our ability to transcend instinct, a point more recently developed by Steven Pinker in *The Better Angels of Our Nature* (2012). Nature, apparently, has no use for kindness or empathy.

Thus, Ianto, who seems to be unable to differentiate between the necessary and impersonal violence of predation and a more generalised violence of the strong against the weak, begins to construct a moral universe for himself in which the law of the strong always prevails. Humans often perceive "wild nature" in this way, as Marc Bekoff argues when he looks at the narratives of nature documentaries:

> They concentrate on attention-seeking sex and violence, showing animals mating, being aggressive, and in acts of predation. The details may be correct, but the impression radically misrepresents animal lives and feeds the false notion that nature is a competitive, brutal game of "survival of the fittest." In fact, wild animals spend much of the time resting and being nice to one another, playing, sharing food, and cooperatively defending food and territory. Indeed, for all species that have been studied, more than 90 percent of their time is spent performing in positive and friendly ways, or what are called prosocial behaviours. (Bekoff 2014: 110)

Perhaps it is inevitable that we, who might easily be named *homo narrativus*, are drawn to the drama of sex and violence. Work by scientists, observers and science writers shows, though, how animals use appeasing behaviours and aggressive displays to avoid actual violence (see Lorenz on animal aggression, 2002; Balcombe on fish behaviours, 2017; or Elli Radinger on the harmonious relationships in wolf packs, 2017). Indeed, animals are frequently cooperative and friendly. Frans de Waal, for instance, notes the many ways in which primates cooperate to achieve common goals (de Waal 2016). Despite their well-documented capacity for aggression, chimpanzees "practice proactive peacemaking" to manage conflict (Balcomb: 2010, 124; see also de Waal 2016). Safina notes that the "second-most-common cause of wolf death in the Rockies is getting killed by other wolves" (the first is being shot by human hunters; 2015: 145) but clashes do not occur as a matter of course, and lead wolves, such as the famous 21, who "never lost a fight" and "never killed a vanquished wolf" (Safina 2015: 145), have been known to spare the lives of challengers (see also Radinger 2017: 39–41, 56–57). While the reality of predation is bloody (Blakeslee 2017: 113; Radinger 2017: 146), violence does not suffuse all areas of an animal's life.

Where does the idea of life as a struggle for existence come from? It was Charles Darwin, who, having been impressed by Malthus's pessimistic account *An Essay on the Principle of Population* (1798), posited that unceasing competition between individuals was the main motor for natural selection. Living beings, he proposed, always produce more offspring than can survive. Thus, individuals are pitted against members of the same species in competition for resources like food and shelter and have to be constantly on their guard not to become food for other species. For Darwin, the struggle for existence was a metaphor that encompassed "the whole economy of nature" (2009: 65). In this sense, the struggle between dogs for a piece of food is equal to the struggle for moisture of a plant living in arid conditions. Moreover, Darwin referred to the opportunity to reproduce. Thus, losing the struggle for existence does not necessarily mean a violent end, it merely means that an individual has not transmitted his or her genes to the next generation. It says little about quality of life.

However, Darwin found it hard to resist his own phrase. At the end of the relevant chapter in *On the Origin of Species*, he feels the need to console his readers with the reflection "that the war of nature is not incessant, that no fear is felt, that death is generally prompt and that the vigorous, the healthy, and the happy survive and multiply" (2009: 19). This has echoes of the Hobbesian view of the state of nature as an unregulated war of everyone against everyone else. Herbert Spencer turned his attention to the survivors of the struggle for existence, whom he termed the "fittest." In his view natural selection was a way to achieve a "self-acting purification of the species" by means of weeding out those "unfitted for living," i.e. the "diseased and feeble" (1864: 445). Social Darwinism was born, and with it the human tendency to celebrate the strong and to justify the annihilation of the weak by citing the "laws" of natural selection.

This compelling narrative of the "survival of the fittest" has been shown to be limited and biased, however. A case in point is that, contrary to Herbert Spencer's analysis, nature does not always efficiently remove the "diseased and feeble" for the benefit of the species in general. Social non-human animals perceive themselves and each other as individuals, and the idea that they act for the benefit of the species has been shown to be false (see Sapolsky on individual selection, 2013: Lecture 10). They care for the sick, the disabled and the elderly in their midst. Joanna Burger has observed that the chicks of seagulls suffering from lead pollution were weaker than other, non-disabled chicks. Nevertheless, they became healthy adults. Burger writes: "It turned out the parents didn't spurn their weak offspring; quite the reverse. In what we would think of as a very human gesture, they invested extra energy and attention to compensate for their chicks' disability, giving their weaker offspring [...] a helping hand" (2001: 205). Similarly, wolf packs do not abandon disabled pack members. The story of a wolf called Limpy, a son of 21, is a case in point: his back leg was broken by a stag when he was young, and the fracture never healed properly. The pack cared for him and he lived for many years (Radinger: 115 ff.). Wolves also care for the old by, for instance, regurgitating food for them as if they were pups (Radinger 2017: 77 ff.). Elephants also care for the disabled and the old (Safina 2015: 58–65). This list of other-regarding behaviours of non-human animals is not presented here to show how "human" animals are but, rather, to show that, as Darwin put it in *The Descent of Man* "the difference in mind between man and the higher animals, great as it is, certainly is one of degree and not of kind" (Darwin 2004: 151). Thus, the emphasis on conflict and violence as characteristic of life on planet Earth is misleading: "nature red in tooth and claw" is unquestionably one survival tactic of the selfish gene, but so are altruism, empathy, kindness and compassion.

Thus, to return to the novel, Ianto's focus on predation, violence and death, is tragically one-sided, with terrible consequences for his own life and for those of his victims. An example of how he internalises the morality of the law of the strong is his ongoing fascination with birds of prey, which he shares with the novel's author (Griffiths 2011). At the age of eight, Ianto watches an old tree being struck by lightning, and observes a hen harrier "*rising on the thermals above the flames long-tailed and lethal*" as if the bird had set fire to the tree. Ianto perceives a superior being in him, a leader: "*all the guidance he could comprehend ever and could want or pray for nothing more than this taloned plunger from wet skies or moonlight leading him in the dance on the slab of smashed bone, showing him on to the stone dark with blood long-spilled and he small boy following glad*" (52). At the age of nine and a half he observes a pair of peregrine falcons at their nesting site on the cliffs. They are both homing in on a seagull, the female merely chasing the gull and then, "[*a*]*s if drawn there by laser, some inexorable computerised mapping, the tiercel descends in a whistling stillness in which even the sea seems awestruck and at shocking speed towards the oblivious gull and gulps great gulfs of blue in its eye-searing stoop, young Ianto watches breathless its unstoppable descent and he sees the impact before he feels in his bones the sonic thump of that contact and hears the scream amid the white burst of feathers*" (218). Flying back to the nest, the two birds revel in their triumph: "*Wheeling and screaming between two blues the raptors revelling in murder*" (218). It is an awe-inspiring moment. Things about nature click into place for Ianto. Firstly, he no longer focuses on the victim of this interaction, as he had done when looking at the butcher bird's larder. Secondly, the birds appear to behave in an oddly gendered way, the female acting as helpmeet to the male. Simon Barnes has noted that birds of prey seem to us "as glorious symbols of manhood" (2016: 123), and certainly Ianto derives his understanding of masculinity from his interpretation of interactions such as this. Most importantly perhaps, these apex predators appear to be personifications of the success of the moral narrative of "nature red in tooth and claw": they appear to kill without remorse when they feel like it, and they glory in their power afterwards. It very clearly is not about food, which might have been a more realistic assessment of what occurred.

The fact that Ianto idolises raptors rather than, for instance, fluffy sheep or pretty songbirds, is in itself enlightening. Apex predators are amongst the so-called "charismatic species," whom humans either fear or admire. Simon Barnes has noted that: "We want to be hawks. We want to soar, we want to fly with power and purpose, but above all we want to kill: or, at least, to play our own part in the great dramas of the sky" (2016: 124). Wolves are apt to summon similar emotions in us:

> Here is an animal capable of killing a man, an animal of legendary endurance and spirit, an animal that embodies marvellous integration with its environment. This is exactly what the modern hunter would like: the noble qualities imagined; a sense of fitting into the world. The hunter wants to be the wolf. (Barry Lopez quoted in Blakeslee 2017: 105)

Ianto wants to be an apex predator: a charismatic animal who has the unquestionable right to inhabit his *Umwelt*, who effortlessly asserts himself, who has control over his life and acts as he sees fit without being beholden to anyone else. In reality, he cannot achieve any of this. He is hounded out of the place he thinks of as belonging to him as of right (see Bednarski on Ianto's attempts to defend his home territory, 2012: 61 ff, 72–73). He follows a group of people, who suffer his presence, and he seems to have no will of his own, no agency. His admiration of apex predators is undoubtedly why he attaches himself to the sociopathic, violent Roger, who engenders nervous fear in others, rather than to the more compassionate Danny. Roger simply assumes leadership and unhesitatingly fights those who cross him (173 f.). Ianto, after around the age of eight, has come to believe that Alpha violence wins and everyone else loses.

This is crucial to our understanding of the character. It is all too tempting to see the cause of the self-destructive and violent track of his life as the result of the vicious rape and mutilation he suffers at the age of ten. However, as gruesome as the rape is, it does not *engender* Ianto's belief that only the strong survive in this world. The rape serves to *confirm* this view. It suggests to him that in a dog-eat-dog world, one must at all costs avoid becoming a victim, which, in his logic means that he must turn predator. Thus, in the drug-induced haze that he will seek out again and again in later life to dull the pain of existence, the ten-year old boy, who is hospitalised after the attack, decides to "*wait like the spider unaccompanied except by an urge for murder for whatever the wind will bring to him, and for however long it takes*" (237).

In order to enact his revenge, the adult Ianto shape-shifts into his vision of what an apex predator looks like. As with the peregrine falcons he observed as a child, the victim is unimportant. Animal Ianto, who is still high on a cocktail of different drugs and has not eaten for a long time, is transfixed by the sandwiches of a teenager, who has become separated from his Outward Bound group and is wandering through the hills on his own. When the boy does not respond to his roughly barked command to hand over the food, Ianto imagines that he is a snake: he "rocks forward slowly until he is on all fours in the water and begins to slow-creep snake-bellied over the submerged rocks towards the boy. Staring at him with hooded eyes" (86). The snake recalls the viper he made friends with as a child, but this friendly image has been displaced by that of the snakelike arm of the rapist, "*the fang-like fingers grabbing the waistband of Ianto's shorts and yanking him roughly to the ground*" (232). The snake is powerful, fast, kills without compunction, and then devours its victim. Ianto does likewise. He kills the boy and then symbolically eats the boy's food off his dead body.

It seems appropriate that his attack on the teenager takes place in what many would call "wild Wales," the hinterland of Aberystwyth invoked in, among other representations, the TV drama *Y Gwyll* (S4C, 2013). Wild nature in *Sheepshagger* is a realm that is distinct from the realistic depiction of a largely down-at-heel Aberystwyth, where dole queues are joined and where people go for pints in pubs. Nature is a space in which a feeling of unreality can grab hold of the characters. Raves are held here, and it is also here that Ianto's friends come to search for magic mushrooms. Llŷr's cottage occupies a liminal space between civilisation and "wild Wales" and it is here that the group parties to Dionysian excess as the cottage is buffeted by equally excessive gale-force winds (101–151). This space is described by means of a lyrical register that is at odds with the realism of the dialogue. Here people are apt to lose their inhibitions, as if led astray by the *tylwyth teg*, the West Walian fairyfolk, described by Jan Morris as "unpredictable and often vindictive" creatures who were "able to change a man's character" and who "could play around with time" (Morris 2000: 86–87). The unreal quality of this wild space is underscored by the paradox that there are no genuinely wild spaces left in Wales – or, indeed, in Europe. Peter Wohlleben, a forester and vocal proponent of the campaign to rewild traditional forest landscapes, has shown that, in Europe, the last primeval forests had disappeared by the middle of the 19th century (2013: 43–44). Marc Bekoff agrees, saying that "[w]hat we consider 'wild nature' today is largely artificial" (Bekoff 2014: 22). The authenticity of wild nature that Ianto seeks, in which he can allow his true apex predator nature to emerge and take the life of another human being with efficient, cold-blooded cruelty, is therefore bogus.

On a symbolic level, the first murder might be interpreted as a predaceous act, as a hungry Ianto primarily wants to eat. The second murder is different: the act of killing becomes an end in itself. The landscape is full of traces of violence, like the "leftovers of fox or otter and the dark clotted spraints of a predator" (198). Welsh history touches the present: Ianto follows the path to "the Pumlumon valley where the Hyddgen plaque stands, monument to a battle in 1401 when men led by Owain Glyndŵr slaughtered 200 Saesneg regulars and Flemish mercenaries" (198–9). Everything in this landscape seems to propel him towards murder – and only then does he identify the couple, whom he had seen earlier on the bus, as his victims. Unluckily, the hikers resemble Ianto's rapist in several key aspects, and Ianto, who is grieving for his dead friend Roger as well as for his childhood self, determines to act. He merges with the landscape, becomes a "sprite" or "woodland imp," his eyes like those of a "cat at a hamster cage, focused with an intensity breakable not by thunderbolt nor earthquake" on his prey (200). The central stone of the circle of standing stones "has been used by a merlin and perhaps other raptors as a plucking block to strip their prey" (201) and seems to beckon to him. Even the fossils caught in the limestone speak to him: "the writhing runnel of a worm and the stippled tracks of a trilobite converging upon that vermiform trace and a gouged and flurried meeting of the two and then the worm track terminates and there is only the trilobite's trace, first and original predator father" (202), recalling that predaceous behaviour of animals began in what we term the Cambrian period (Godfrey-Smith 2017). Ianto, modern Cambrian predator, is prepared to follow suit.

But now we have reached the peripeteia in this tragedy. Ianto's idea of predaceous killing clashes mercilessly with reality. For one thing, the kill does not go smoothly. Despite observing animals all his life and despite having already murdered, Ianto has failed to realise how difficult it is to take a life. In his article on birds of prey, Niall Griffiths describes how long it takes a buzzard to kill a rabbit, the description echoing the action in the novel:

> The bird swooped. *Whack.* Climbed again and did it fourteen times, until the rabbit looked less like a rabbit and more like a jigsaw piece, yet still it twitched and flopped and it was at that point that the bird landed and fed [on] the rabbit's broken but still-struggling body. (Griffiths 2011: 39)

Even highly skilled predators like wolves fail to bring down elk and other big game 80 % of the time and have to work hard at perfecting the skill of hunting (Radinger 2017: 146–7). Ianto lacks both the practice of killing and the stomach for its goriness. As Radinger says: "death is no Disney movie. [...] Death is always bloody and chilling" (translation mine, 2017: 146).

Secondly and despite Roger's recent death, Ianto never realises that apex predators are not invincible. He instinctively understands that the sheep whom he sees mourning a stillborn lamb (151) is a victim of a sometimes cruel natural world. But apex predators, despite appearances, are also vulnerable – notably to human intervention: the same peregrine falcons that to him appear to be such symbols of ferocious power nearly died out in the mid-20th century (Lockhart 2017: 197–8; see also Baker 2017). Even raptors are not invulnerable, as Ianto discovers to his cost.

Thirdly, Ianto confuses predaceous killing with other types of aggression. To say it again, predators kill other animals to provide food for themselves and their young. There is no discernable purpose behind Ianto's intention to kill the hikers (beyond his "cosmic revenge"), but he trains his eyes on them and determines to see them as his rightful prey "with the lurching intent that the buzzard must feel when the rabbit breaks cover below" (199). He no longer sees the hikers as members of his own species. This might be a warped response to the racial abuse he and Llŷr were subjected to at the hands of the new English owners of Ianto's family's farmhouse (18–19), or, indeed, the rape he suffered as a child. However, Ianto instrumentalises what he believes to be the instinctive action of a predator to justify his desire for revenge.

Thus, despite Ianto's efforts to displace feelings of compassion and responsibility, the second murder is due to nothing other than his desire to kill. Afterwards, realising the enormity of his crime, he tries to run away in order to seek forgiveness. He comes upon a lonely cottage in the hills in which an elderly, monolingual Welsh woman resides – clearly a figure born of his imagination, potentially a personification of the kind of authentic Welsh identity that he has no access to, an authenticity which may never have existed and which certainly does not exist now. At first she engages, as Bednarski describes, in an act of ritualistic purification (2012: 88), but rejects him as soon as she realises that the blood on his face is not his own. She, and indeed nature herself, will not accept his abasement this time (214–15). Now exiled from nature as well as from the world of human beings, he does not have long to live.

Ianto's end seems to arrive with the inevitability of a tragic fall – inevitable because "[i]diopathic Ianto" (38) carries the seeds of his destruction in him from birth. Yet, he did have a choice. As a young child, a holistic appreciation of the complexity of nature, which includes lighter as well as darker shades, was open to him. As he grows up, though, he becomes increasingly blind to the side of nature that is not "red in tooth and claw" and, fatally, decides to model his behaviour on this misapprehension. To be sure, his awareness of virtuous behaviour is not totally extinguished. We witness him hesitatingly question Roger's decision to send an acquaintance to a drug dealer, who means him harm, for "a good fuckin larf" (167), as well as Roger's sexual harassment of two trainee nurses (185). However, in his craving for revenge, he allows the moral narrative of "might is right" to drown out his awareness that there is another way.

The struggle of the two moral narratives – of "might is right" against kindness, compassion, and empathy – goes beyond Ianto's story. It is at the heart of the meandering choric discussion that Ianto's friends have about his and their crime. Indeed, its importance transcends the characters. The novel suggests that it also informs the colonial violence Wales suffered and continues to suffer at the hand of its stronger English neighbour, a violence conceived of in terms of rape and mutilation, which leaves the victim disturbed and without a clear sense of identity. It also describes the loss of a home territory – lost this time not by means of war, but by a more insidious display of financial muscle, which displaces a rural Welsh population from their homes and destroys communities. It presents homelessness and rootlessness as causing a mental disassociation, in which victims are no longer sure who they are. Most recently, this experience of mental disassociation and of powerlessness (which was shared by many English regions, which have a history of feeling disconnected from the metropolitan centre) may have led to the ultimately self-destructive Brexit vote in Wales: to a more or less feeble attempt to "take back control." Ultimately, it is a disastrous moral narrative, especially for its victims. But the novel also shows that we have a choice. Despite the seemingly overwhelming evidence to the contrary, we do not have to accept that life is merely a matter of the survival of the strongest, with the concomitant consequences for the losers in this story. If we open our eyes to the fullness and the richness of the lives of other animals, we may be able to learn what our place in our *Umwelt* really is.

Bibliography

Baker, John Alec. *The Peregrine*. 1967. London: William Collins, 2017.

Balcombe, Jonathan. *Second Nature: The Inner Lives of Animals*. Houndmills: Palgrave Macmillan, 2010.

Balcombe, Jonathan. *What a Fish Knows: The Inner Lives of our Underwater Cousins*. London: Oneworld, 2017.

Barnes, Simon. *The Meaning of Birds*. London: Head of Zeus, 2016.

Bednarski, Aleksander. *Inherent Myth: Wales in Niall Griffiths's Fiction*. Lublin: Wydawnictwo KUL, 2012.

Bekoff, Marc. *Rewilding Our Hearts: Building Pathways of Compassion and Coexistence*. Novato: New World Library, 2014.

Bekoff, Marc and Jessica Pierce. *Wild Justice: The Moral Lives of Animals*. Chicago: University of Chicago Press, 2009.

Blakeslee, Nate. *American Wolf: A True Story of Survival and Obsession in the West*. New York: Crown, 2017.

Bradshaw, John. *The Animals Among Us: How Pets Make Us Human*. New York: Basic Books, 2017.

Burger, Joanna. *The Parrot Who Owns Me: The Story of a Relationship*. London: Pan Macmillan, 2001.

Castricano, Jonedy, ed. *Animal Subjects: An Ethical Reader in a Posthuman World*. Waterloo: Wilfred Laurier University Press, 2008.

Darwin, Charles. *On the Origin of Species By Means of Natural Selection or The Preservation of Favoured Races in the Struggle for Life*. Ed. and intr. William Bynum. Harmondsworth: Penguin, 2009 [1859].

Darwin, Charles. *The Descent of Man, and Selection in Relation to Sex*. Harmondsworth: Penguin, 2004 [1879].

Foster, Charles. *Being a Beast: An Intimate and Radical Look at Nature*. London: Profile, 2016.

Godfrey-Smith, Peter. *Other Minds: The Octopus and the Evolution of Intelligent Life*. London: William Collins, 2017.

Griffiths, Niall. *Sheepshagger*. London: Vintage, 2002.

Griffiths, Niall. "Birds of Prey I have Known and Loved." *Planet*, May 2011, pp. 36–45.

Haraway, Donna. *When Species Meet*. Minneapolis: University of Minnesota Press, 2008.

Lockhart, James Macdonald. *Raptor: A Journey Through Birds*. London: 4th Estate, 2017.

Lorenz, Konrad. *On Aggression*. Abingdon: Routledge, 2002 [1963, in translation 1966].

Morris, Jan. *Wales: Epic Views of a Small Country*. Rev. ed. Harmondsworth: Penguin, 2000.

Peddie, Ian. "Warmth and Light and Sky: Niall Griffiths in Conversation." *Critical Survey*, Vol. 20, No. 3, 2008, pp. 116–138.

Pinker, Steven. *The Better Angels of Our Nature*. Harmondsworth: Penguin, 2012.

Radinger, Elli H. *Die Weisheit der Wölfe: Wie sie denken, planen, füreinander sorgen – Erstaunliches über das Tier, das dem Menschen am ähnlichsten ist*. München: Ludwig, 2017.

Richter, Virginia. *Literature after Darwin: Human Beasts in Western Fiction, 1859–1939*. Houndmills: Palgrave Macmillan, 2011.

Safina, Carl. *Beyond Words: What Animals Think and Feel*. New York: Henry Holt, 2015.

Sapolsky, Robert. "The Evolution of Behavior." Lecture 10. *Biology and Human Behavior: The Neurological Origins of Individuality*. Set of audio lectures, 2013. https://www.thegreatcourses.com/courses/biology-and-human-behavior-the-neurological-origins-of-individuality-2nd-edition.html (12 May 2018).

Scientific American. “How did the ‘Smile’ become a friendly gesture in humans?” *Scientific American*. 21 October, 1999. https://www.scientificamerican.com/article/how-did-the-smile-become-a-friendly-gesture-in-humans/ (16 Nov. 2017).

Spencer, Herbert. *The Principles of Biology*. Vol. I. London: Williams and Norgate, 1864.

Uexküll, Jakob von. *Umwelt und Innenwelt der Tiere*. London: Forgotten Books, 2015 [1909].

de Waal, Frans. *Are We Smart Enough to Know How Smart Animals Are?* London: Granta, 2016.

Williams, Florence. *The Nature Fix: Why Nature Makes Us Happier, Healthier and more Creative*. New York: Norton, 2017.

Wilson, Edward O. *The Diversity of Life*. New York: Norton, 1992.

Wohlleben, Peter. *Der Wald: Eine Entdeckungsreise*. München: Heyne, 2013.

Gdańsk Transatlantic Studies in British and North American Culture

Edited by Marek Wilczyński

The interdisciplinary series "GdańskTransatlantic Studies in British and North American Culture" brings together literary and cultural studies concerning literatures and cultures of the English-speaking world, particularly those of Great Britain, Ireland, the United States, and Canada. The range of topics to be addressed includes literature, theater, film, and art, considered in various twenty-first-century theoretical perspectives, such as, for example (but not exclusively), New Historicism and canon formation, cognitive narratology, gender and queer studies, performance studies, memory and trauma studies, and New Art History. The editors are leaving a broad margin for the innovative and the unpredictable, hoping to attract authors whose approaches will point to new directions of research as regards both thematic areas and methods. Comparative Polish-Anglo-American proposals will be considered, too.

Vol. 1 Mirosława Modrzewska: Byron and the Baroque. 2013.

Vol. 2 Andrzej Ceynowa / Marek Wilczyński (eds.): American Experience – The Experience of America. 2013.

Vol. 3 Marta Koval: "We search the Past…for Our Own Lost Selves." Representations of Historical Experience in Recent American Fiction. 2013.

Vol. 4 Tomasz Basiuk: Exposures. American Gay Men´s Life Writing since Stonewall. 2013.

Vol. 5 Klara Naszkowska: The Living Mirror. The Representation of Doubling Identities in the British and Polish Women's Literature (1846–1938). 2014.

Vol. 6 Urszula Elias / Agnieszka Sienkiewicz-Charlish (eds.): Crime Scenes. Modern Crime Fiction in an International Context. 2014.

Vol. 7 Justyna Kociatkiewicz / Laura Suchostawska/Dominika Ferens (eds.): Eating America. Crisis, Sustenance, Sustainability. 2014.

Vol. 8 Agnieszka Pantuchowicz / Sławomir Masłoń (eds.): Affinities. Essays in Honour of Professor Tadeusz Rachwał. 2014.

Vol. 9 Janusz Semrau / Marek Wilczyński (eds.): Image in Modern(ist) Verse. 2015.

Transatlantic Studies in British and North American Culture

Edited by Marek Wilczyński

Vol. 10 Małgorzata Grzegorzewska / Jean Ward / Mark Burrows (eds.): Breaking the Silence. Poetry and the Kenotic Word. 2015.

Vol. 11 Dominika Oramus: Charles Darwin's Looking Glass. The Theory of Evolution and the Life of its Author in Contemporary British Fiction and Non-Fiction. 2015.

Vol. 12 Miłosz Wojtyna: The Ordinary and the Short Story. Short Fiction of T.F. Powys and V.S. Pritchett. 2015.

Vol. 13 Bartosz Wójcik: Afro-Caribbean Poetry in English. Cultural Traditions (1970s-2000s). 2015.

Vol. 14 Izabela Morska: Glorious Outlaws: Debt as a Tool in Contemporary Postcolonial Fiction. 2016.

Vol. 15 Edyta Frelik: Painter's Word. Thomas Hart Benton, Marsden Hartley and Ad Reinhardt as Writers. 2016.

Vol. 16 Małgorzata Grzegorzewska: George Herbert and Post-phenomenology. A Gift for Our Times. 2016.

Vol. 17 Anna Cholewa-Purgał: Therapy Through Faërie. Therapeutic Properties of Fantasy Literature by the Inklings and by U. K. Le Guin. 2016.

Vol. 18 Agata Handley: Constructing Identity. Continuity, Otherness and Revolt in the Poetry of Tony Harrison. 2016.

Vol. 19 Dominika Oramus: Ways of Pleasure. Angela Carter's 'Discourse of Delight' in her Fiction and Non-Fiction. 2016.

Vol. 20 Aneta Dybska: Regeneration, Citizenship, and Justice in the American City since the 1970s. 2016.

Vol. 21 Maciej Reda: The Apology for Catholicism in Selected Writings by G. K. Chesterton. 2016.

Vol. 22 Przemysław Uściński: Parody, Scriblerian Wit and the Rise of the Novel. Parodic Textuality from Pope to Sterne. 2016.

Vol. 23 Jadwiga Węgrodzka: Popular Genres and Their Uses in Fiction. 2018.

Vol. 24 Stephen Butler / Agnieszka Sienkiewicz-Charlish (eds.): Crime Fiction. 2018.

Vol. 25 Susana Nicolás Román / Marek Wilczyński / Łukasz Gałecki (eds.): Women in Edward Bond. 2018.

Vol. 26 Aleksander Bednarski / Robert Looby (eds): Redefining the Fringes in Celtic Studies. Essays in Literature and Culture. 2019.

www.peterlang.com

www.ingramcontent.com/pod-product-compliance
Lightning Source LLC
Chambersburg PA
CBHW060756310726
48980CB00002B/116

9783631775301